Tide to Atonement

Pawleys Island Paradise, Book 2

Laurie Larsen,

EPIC Award-winning author of *Preacher Man*

Random Moon Books
A Phase for Every Fancy

All Content by author Laurie Larsen
Cover Art by Steven Novak
Formatting by Polgarus Studio
Published by Random Moon Books
Published in the United States of America

A Letter from Laurie …

Dear Reader,

I hope that you will thoroughly enjoy reading about Jeremy and his love story with Emma Jean. For an author, her books are like her children. We try to love them all equally. But this particular book was a special one for me. I loved writing it and I think it's one of the best books I've written. I hope you agree.

The pace with which I wrote this book was unusual for me. Generally it takes me between six and eight months to write a book of this length, producing about 3000 words a week consistently. That's how I started out on this one. I had about 22,000 words done at my normal pace, when the holidays and other projects stalled me. I hadn't worked on it at all in three months, when my local Romance Writers of America chapter offered a 30-day writer's challenge. We would write all month to hit an aggressive page count goal, and post our results every day. Everyone would post messages of encouragement. We'd all be in it together.

It was a productive month for me. I committed to — and achieved — 30,000 words in 30 days! A huge increase to my normal pace.

But then again, other projects took priority. It's the reality of an independently published author. I'm responsible for everything! Writing is just a fraction of all the other stuff I do to get books published. So, *Tide to Atonement* had to sit at about 52,000 words for two more months, untouched.

Then, the chance of a lifetime! A group of writers invited me to join them in Hilton Head, South Carolina for a writers' retreat. All we'd do is write. Well, and eat. And drink wine. And walk the beach. But our main priority was writing. It was just what I needed. It was only four days, but boy, I made the most of them. My very ambitious goal was to finish the book, which meant writing 20,000 words in four days. I'd *never* written that much before in so little time.

So, I broke it down into smaller chunks. In order to write 20,000 words during the retreat, I'd have to write 5000 words a day. That sounded better. I gave it my best shot. But the first day I only hit 2400. And the second I only hit 4600. I was getting there, but at that rate, there's no way I'd hit 20,000 in two more days.

But, then the magic happened. The ocean atmosphere inspired me, and I brainstormed plot with my generous writing partners. I really knew these characters, and I'd figured out the nuances of the story. And I wrote.

By mid-afternoon on the final day, tears in my eyes from the emotion of the story, I'd reached THE END. As a reward, I spent a couple hours soaking in the pool, soaking in the sun, and letting my tired mind vegetate.

Next in the series, I'll take on a love renewal story of Jeremy's sister, Marianne and her husband, Tom. They go through the wringer in *Tide to Atonement*, and they come out the other side a little worse for the wear. Their story will explore how married couples deal with tragedy and the deterioration of their relationship as life goes on. Look for the story (and a title) in early 2015, but meanwhile, enjoy an excerpt at the end of the book.

Happy reading, and remember, life is a beach!

Laurie

Chapter One

Jeremy Harrison was in the zone. He laid one last swipe of his brush across the top surface, then took a step back to study his latest creation. A homey shade of blonde maple, the dresser reached slightly over waist-high — at least, to a six-foot-two body like himself. It was his latest design, the "his and her" model, a column of five drawers on each side, separated by an open armoire-style cabinet. The stain was complete. Now, to soak in for a day or possibly two, to allow the high sheen to be brushed with fingertips without danger of leaving prints. After that, he'd check the drawers and make sure they rolled in and out smoothly with no sticks. Then he'd choose handles — brass? No, something more burnished.

He absentmindedly rubbed a hand over his lips, then spit out the taste of polyurethane. Searching for a clean cloth, he lifted his feet high, careful not to knock over any cans of thick liquid, the finishing tools of his trade.

A distant sound wormed into his consciousness. Buzzing, sort of like a mosquito or an angry pack of them. Infuriating in its persistence. Sounded like an alarm. Had he set …?

"Well, dang it!" He ran off the canvas tarp laid in his backyard that he called his work space and into the house through the backdoor. The timer on the microwave was buzzing away and after a quick study, Jeremy realized it had been sounding for at least four, five minutes. He turned it off. He'd set it this morning, knowing he'd get wrapped up in furniture-making and lose track of time — he always did. And normally, that was good. But not today.

Today he had an important appointment in town he couldn't miss. Miss? Heck, no, he couldn't even be late. He hustled to the bathroom at the back of the tiny house and shucked off his sweatshirt, boots and jeans. Jumping into the shower, he emerged two minutes later, dried with a towel, and raced into his bedroom. A quick study of his closet had him pulling out a pair of khaki pants and a button-down light blue shirt. Didn't take much study. There weren't that many choices in there anyway.

Who needed a Wall Street wardrobe when you lived in a beach town in rural South Carolina?

Dressed now, he swung back to the bathroom and made a quick swipe of his hand over his jaw. Shave? His eyes lighted on the digital alarm clock on the counter. Nah, no time. He'd shaved sometime in the last, what, three days? Neil wouldn't mind.

Passing through the kitchen, he peered out the window for a glance at the dresser in the backyard. He shifted his gaze to the sky. No rain in the forecast, nothing but sun expected today. The dresser would be fine.

He raced out the front door and jumped into his truck. These monthly meetings were part of his life now, and he best learn to accept them. At least he'd moved to monthly from weekly. That was one thing to be thankful for.

And one meeting a month with Neil was a heck of lot better than where he came from.

* * *

He didn't mean for his truck tires to squeal as he maneuvered into a parking space. But tardiness was frowned upon and he was cutting it close. He jumped out of the old pickup and took a cleansing breath, lowered his shoulders and walked intentionally.

The County Courthouse in Georgetown was a mere eleven miles from his home on Pawleys Island, but tourist traffic being so erratic, he'd settled into the habit of allowing at least forty minutes for the drive. Now that tourist season was over and autumn had made residence, he didn't need the full timeframe, but as Neil had taught him, it was better to be prepared. Early was always better than late.

Screvens Street sparkled today with the sun glittering off the scrubbed sidewalks and immaculate brick buildings. At the center of them all stood the courthouse, a Pawleys Island historic landmark. It was a pastel yellow and white wooden building with six impressive pillars adorning the second floor balcony. In order to reach that level, Jeremy had the choice of identical closed stairways on the right or left of the building that circled up and met at the front door.

His visits to this landmark had become so routine that he barely noticed the grandeur today. He trotted up the stairs, entered the building, walked to the Probation Office at the back of the third floor, gave his name to the receptionist and sat in a folding chair in the waiting room, amidst about a dozen other offenders. He was twelve minutes early.

He lowered his head to examine his shoes. No eye contact with those seated around him, that was something he learned during his decade in prison. Mind your own business. Keep to yourself. There was no telling when you might see something or hear something you would be asked about, just because you had your head up, curiously looking around. Not worth it.

"Hey, man." The voice came from the chair beside him. He swiveled his head and recognized a guy who'd spent a few of his last months with him in Columbia at the pre-release center. He scanned his brain for a name but couldn't come up with one.

"Hey." He nodded at the man, dressed in a similar outfit as his — neat-looking khakis and a button-down shirt. This man had sneakers and white athletic socks on though, instead of dress shoes like Jeremy's. Heck, it didn't matter. The ex-con was making an effort. Scraping up extra money for luxuries like leather shoes when the only time you wore them was to your probation appointments, took time. "How you doin'?"

"Good, good." He was nervous, Jeremy could tell. He sat hunched, his shoulders rounded, and rubbed his palms briskly together, creating an uncomfortable slipping sound. "Trying to find a job. Ain't easy."

"No. No, it's not." One of the court's requirements, hold gainful employment. You had to report on your job-hunt attempts at every appointment. Among other things. Drug testing, community service.

The man sighed, his manic tension cutting through Jeremy's calm façade, making him feel nervous, too. Jeremy turned his head and tried to create an invisible wall between them. He didn't mind helping, but he needed to stay calm, serene. That was the name of the game with this process.

"I'll do anything, man. I've tried getting the most menial jobs. Fry cook, bus boy, bag boy at the grocery store. They just don't want me. I'm dying here."

Jeremy squeezed his eyes to the desperation in the guy's voice. There were consequences to not meeting the court's probation requirements. He himself hadn't had to serve them, thank God. But you had to keep your nose clean. Don't stand out. Follow the rules, as best you can.

"Sorry, man. Keep looking. Ask your officer for a hand. Maybe he could make some calls for you."

The man wiggled in his chair. "What about you? You working? What're you doin'?"

Jeremy exhaled. "I'm trying to start up my own business."

"Oh yeah?" The man looked over at him with interest and in Jeremy's opinion, leaned a little too close. "Doin' what? You wanna hire me?"

Jeremy let out an uncomfortable chuckle. "Nobody on the payroll. I'm barely making ends meet. But doin' what I love. Wood working. I make furniture."

"Oh." The man turned away, to Jeremy's relief. "I don't do nothing like that. I wonder if I could start my own business. Might be the only choice I have left."

"Harrison."

Jeremy looked up, glad to be called. "Good luck, man." The man nodded as Jeremy checked in with the receptionist. Jeremy said a quick silent prayer, not even fully formed thoughts and words – just a sincere sentiment to God: *help this man, help get him on his feet*.

"You can go on back to Neil's office."

Jeremy nodded and headed back.

The word "office" was a stretch, but hey, who was he to judge? He edged into Neil's closet-sized room stuffed full with a desk, Neil's chair, two facing chairs and a filing cabinet. A few framed certificates scattered across the walls, but Neil didn't seem to be much into decorating. Stacks of files littered his desktop and the man himself was so big, he dwarfed everything around him.

Neil had been Jeremy's parole officer since he'd been released towards the end of the summer. He'd quickly recognized Neil as an advocate to help him adjust to life in the free world. Neil had high expectations and held him accountable for his behavior, but he made the rules clear and praised Jeremy when he saw results. That was fine with Jeremy. He never should've made the mistakes that had landed him in prison anyway and after serving his sentence, all he wanted now was to get his life back on track. He understood the odds stacked against him — he'd earned every single one. But by following the rules, he'd get there.

One step at a time.

Neil was bent at the waist, his powerful lineman's body folded in half in his chair as he tried to get a closer look at something under his desk. They had talked once or twice about his college career at Clemson. Football had never been Jeremy's sport, but he could certainly see how Neil would intimidate the defenders lined up across from him before the whistle blew. But inside that monstrous body and competitive scowl was the heart of a saint.

Jeremy waited in the doorway. Neil mumbled, sounding frustrated. "Can I help you find something?" Jeremy ventured.

Neil straightened at the sound and banged his head on the partially-opened desk drawer. "Dang!" the big African-American man eked out in pain.

Jeremy scooted around a chair and over a box of papers sitting on the floor, trying to get closer. "I'm sorry. Did I surprise you?" He reached out a hand toward the big man.

Neil was rubbed his aching head, distracted, a smile playing on his face. "When do I move out of this cubicle into a space befitting my size and accomplishments? That's what I want to know."

Jeremy smiled, thankful that he was cracking jokes.

"Can you reach that business card on the floor there?" Neil asked, pointing.

Jeremy leaned, reached, picked it up, handed it to Neil.

"No, it's for you. Keep it."

Jeremy frowned at the card. "Seminal Magazine?"

"Yeah. Have a seat."

Jeremy made his way back to his chair and did as he was told. He waited for explanation, knowing it was coming.

"Do you know what the word seminal means, Jeremy?" Neil slid into his own chair, folded his hands on top of his desk and focused on Jeremy.

Jeremy took a breath. He was never good at English, had a horrible vocabulary. Books were never really his thing, he was always good with his hands. "Ummm ..."

Neil shook his head. "No matter." He reached under a stack of files and pulled out a thick book — a dictionary. He handed it to Jeremy.

Jeremy flipped pages till he located the word. "Influential, formative, pivotal, inspiring."

"Good." Neil held a palm up and Jeremy handed the dictionary back. "Nice name for a magazine, huh?"

Jeremy nodded cautiously, wondering what this had to do with him.

Neil continued, "I got a call from them last week. They like to do stories about people who display some of those words you read. Pivotal, inspiring. Ground-breaking. Me and the editor talked over some story ideas. Turns out they want to do a feature on some of our success stories."

Jeremy fidgeted, not liking where this was going.

"I told the lady some of our Values Statements. You know all those. You memorized them a few months ago."

Jeremy nodded, hoping to God Neil wasn't going to call on him to recite them.

"Promoting and maintaining a safe community. Treating people with dignity and respect." Neil leaned back in his chair, let his eyes roll thoughtfully to the ceiling. "What are some others?"

Jeremy sighed, the small card now digging into his palm. "Uh, the ability of offenders to change."

"Yes! That's a good one." Neil's smile formed, white teeth amidst dark complexion. "What else?"

Jeremy could come up with one more, so he hoped that was the last one Neil was after. "The relationship between staff and client can have a profound impact on successful outcomes."

"You got it. I knew you would."

That was one of the things Jeremy liked about Neil. He was genuinely happy when one of his caseload succeeded. The man could scare the crap out of him, and had on several occasions, but he was not without his virtues.

"So, I shared those values with her, and all the rest …," he pointed to the framed paper hanging on the wall behind him. Jeremy swore to himself. They were right there, behind Neil's head! "…and she asked me if I had any success stories she could interview and feature in an article about Georgetown County."

Jeremy went motionless and felt his eyes widening as he stared at Neil.

"I had a few. And you're one of them. Jeremy, you're one of my best success stories."

Jeremy shook his head. "No, no. Thanks for recommending me, Neil, but no, I'm not interested."

Neil's forehead creased, his lower lip protruded a little bit. "You don't want to be seminal? You don't want to help influence others to overcome challenges and be successful? I have to tell you, I'm surprised at that, Jeremy."

His palms were starting to sweat and his breathing was a little labored. "I'll help however I can. But not to be featured. I don't want to tell my story and I don't want to be made public. You understand. But I'll help organize the other offenders and drive the reporter around. Uh, what else …?" He was grasping at straws now.

Neil's mammoth face twisted into a pained expression and it about killed Jeremy to know that his refusal had caused it. Everything about the man was big. He had big emotions, big disappointments, big pride and big hope. So far, Jeremy had worked hard to fulfill all the goals Neil had set out for him. But this … he really didn't want to do it.

"I have to say that's very disappointing, Jeremy. You are a role-model, whether you know it or not. You have a story to tell, and I want you to have the chance to tell it. I can't force you, of course, but my job is to rehab you. To get you out of your comfort zone, to try new things. I know you can help others. And isn't that one of our values? To help the community and make things better? I really thought you bought into all those values. You said you did, back when you first got released."

A sinking feeling hit Jeremy's stomach. Neil was using the ole guilt trip on him. Of course he believed in the county's probation values. Of course he'd memorized them and recited them when Neil ordered him to. He was trying his very best every day of his life and he'd never allow himself to fail again. He looked up at the big man before him and realized that he couldn't tell him no. He admired him too much and Neil had been too good to Jeremy to disappoint him.

"I don't want to talk about my crime. I've tried hard to work through that and ..."

"No, no. The focus is on your transformation, your new story, how you're making yourself a success. Very little about why you were in jail."

"I'm not what I'd call a success ..."

"Not yet, but you're working hard, aren't you? And look at it this way, it might generate some interest in your work. You might get some orders out of this. That would be nice, wouldn't it? Call it free advertising."

Jeremy took a deep breath and let it out.

"Well, if you're gonna be stubborn, give me the card back." Neil held his huge hand out across the desk.

Jeremy looked down at the card. "I'll do it."

The transformation was instantaneous and real. An immense smile jumped onto Neil's face. He got up and came around, pounding Jeremy on the back in his excitement. Jeremy choked and concentrated on keeping himself from flying across the room.

"That's the man! Good job. I knew I could count on you. You're going to be very seminal, I just know it. Great."

They spent the next ten minutes discussing Jeremy's progress. Then, Neil advised, "I'll include your name on the list to the magazine. The reporter ..." he waggled his finger at the card Jeremy was still holding in his hand.

"Emma Jean Slotky," Jeremy read.

"Yes, she'll call you at your cell number. Make sure you pick it up, now."

"Yes, sir." Jeremy got to his feet and they shook hands again, their standard good-bye.

Neil checked Jeremy's folder a last time. "Oh, it's your turn to drug test today. You know the drill."

Jeremy nodded and ducked out the door. A few steps down the hall, he heard Neil's call, "Oh uh, Jeremy?" He headed back, stopped in the doorway, eyebrows raised.

Neil rubbed his own chin and pointed at Jeremy's. "The article includes some pictures. How about you make some time to shave, huh?"

Jeremy groaned and nodded. As he made his way to the receptionist's desk for his little white cup, he seriously considered accidentally/purposely losing his cell phone.

* * *

Emma Jean Slotky gathered her laptop, notebook, pen, purse and 20-ounce water cup and pushed back from her desk. It was time for an assignments meeting. Working for a magazine was her dream job, but she had to admit next time, she needed to dream a little bigger. Like a full-color glossy in a big city that could afford a huge staff, expense accounts and elaborate travel. Working for Seminal Magazine was fun, but it was right here in Myrtle Beach where she was born and raised and counting her, the entire staff was only seven people. Two writers, two editors, the art director, the distribution manager and the secretary. Money was always tight. Budget cuts were a way of life, as were the fear of bankruptcy. But the job made good use of her English degree and her love of writing. It was a kick to see her byline every week. And it was better than working at the Piggly Wiggly.

Peggy, the associate editor kicked off the meeting, discussing the specifics of the next issue. Emma jotted down a few notes while Peggy covered each article planned. Then, Peggy got to Emma's main assignment for the issue and Emma perked up.

"Emma, you're going to be the primary writer on the feature piece this issue. The article will run 1000 words, eight photos and span five full pages over the centerfold."

Emma smiled. It sounded prestigious and she chuckled at Peggy's attempt to make it seem like a big deal. But the reality of it was, there were two writers on staff and they had a weekly mag to fill. One or the other of them had to take the feature piece every week and Peggy usually split it evenly with Brad. Emma would write the article and take the pictures, then Peggy and her assistant editor would do the layout and proofing. Shortly after, it'd go to print. Then, on to the next issue.

Peggy went on, "I reached out to the county Adult Probation office. I got three ex-offenders who are turning their lives around and making a successful re-entry to society."

Emma looked up from her notes and blinked. "Wait. Ex-offenders? You mean prisoners? Ex-cons?"

Peggy nodded.

Emma cleared her throat. "You mean you want me to interview three prisoners? Are they violent?" She glanced around the room to see if anyone shared her discomfort.

Peggy flipped through her spiral notebook. "Two are men, one woman. And none of them were convicted of violent crime. If you want, you can meet them with the probation officer present. I'm sure he wouldn't mind that. Of course, time's of the essence, and it'll be slower to schedule if you need to rely on him being free. That man sounded busy."

Peggy slowed down to stare at Emma for a moment. "Are you uncomfortable with the assignment? We can't drag our feet on this, you know that."

Emma hesitated. How could she ever expect to move up the reporting ladder to a more prestigious magazine if she was afraid to take on the challenging, potentially dangerous stories? If she turned this one down, she'd be stuck reporting on fashion shows and poetry readings her whole career and Brad would get anything that pushed the envelope. "Of course not. It sounds interesting."

Peggy bobbed her head, that problem avoided. "Good." She handed Emma a folder. "Here's the info from the probation officer with the three subjects' names and limited info. Feel free to do some internet research on them. Then, move forward with the interviews and photos."

When the meeting was over, Emma went back to her desk and fired up her internet browser. There wasn't much on the first two. The woman subject had started a non-profit community theater project for children. One of the men was spending all his volunteer hours helping at prisons, sharing his experiences of incarcerated life and traveling all over the country to make a difference in the lives of current prisoners.

The third subject built handcrafted wooden furniture and was offering his finished pieces for sale at craft fairs across the state, as well as taking custom orders. She glanced at images from his sparse website. The man had talent. She'd take some pictures of his finished creations to include in the article.

She Googled his name, Jeremy Harrison. Weeding out the numerous stories that didn't apply to this particular Jeremy Harrison, she zoomed in on a local newspaper article detailing his arrest and trial. She studied the details and a tremble slithered down her forearms to her hands.

"Harrison and Son?" she murmured to her monitor. "Wait," she used her finger to scan the article for details. "Ten years ago ..."

She snatched her laptop and purse and left.

* * *

A few minutes later, she pulled into the driveway of her parents' house. Knowing it would be unlocked, she stormed through the front door. "Dad?" she yelled, figuring he was home. He was always home; he was unemployed.

His voice rose above the din of the TV in the basement. She headed for the stairs.

"Hi, baby girl." He waved to her from his recliner, his feet up and the table beside the chair littered with cans and snack wrappers.

"Dad," she said urgently. She kneeled beside him, balancing the laptop on her knees. She reached over, grabbed the remote from the arm of his chair and muted it. He frowned at her. "Dad, Harrison and Son, where you worked, was based out of Pawleys Island, right?"

Her dad stared at her, creases of concentration in his forehead. He shook his head, but she interpreted it not as a negative response to her question, but as his general confusion.

"Dad, I'm sorry for buzzing in here like this, but this is important. Was Harrison and Son based out of Pawleys?"

"Yeah."

"What was the Harrison boss's name?"

"Hank."

"Oh." Hank. She sank onto the carpet on her rear end, her legs stretched in front of her. Hank Harrison was her dad's boss who underbid their construction estimates, embezzled money, evaded taxes and ran the whole company into the ground. Hank Harrison had caused her dad to lose his job and hit the unemployment line. He hadn't earned a decent salary from a decent company since. Hank Harrison was the one who was a good employer before he suddenly went crazy and started breaking the law.

It was still the most painful topic in the Slotky family annals. The start of her dad's drinking, depression, counseling.

"I'm sorry to bring it up, Dad. I know it still hurts. Just forget it. I had it wrong. I was just given an assignment to interview someone about making a fresh start out of prison and his last name is Harrison and he's from Pawleys Island. I thought it was the same guy."

Dad grabbed for the remote. "Hank Harrison never went to prison."

Emma got to her feet. "Okay. I had the wrong guy."

As he turned the sound back on, he said, "Although his son did. His son was the mastermind behind all the problems. Jeremy Harrison."

Chapter Two

The infernal buzz of the microwave alarm reached Jeremy as he worked in the backyard. With a curse, he shoved his goggles to his forehead and carefully lowered his power saw to the ground. Time to stop. Horrible time to stop on this particular project, he'd barely begun. But he had to anyway.

He was working on a long country kitchen table that seated ten comfortably. He actually had an order for it, so he wasn't just building it for inventory to sell later. He had a paying customer and they didn't come around that often. Last thing he wanted to do was keep him waiting.

But he had an appointment. With a reporter.

He sighed and tidied up his work area. The reporter — what was her name again? — had mentioned the possibility of taking pictures of his work in progress, along with a few of his finished pieces. So he better make sure this stuff was camera-ready.

He quickly completed his task and jogged inside to turn off the timer. He glanced at the notes he'd taken when she called. Emma, that was her name. Best to remember that when she was here.

He showered, shaved (as per Neil's instruction) and dressed in work clothes — jeans, t-shirt, cowboy boots. No point dressing up, but he made sure they were clean.

He didn't linger, but returned to the kitchen. He opened the fridge and glanced inside. He could offer her a drink. He had a few choices, Pepsi and a pitcher of iced tea he'd made yesterday. What about snacks? Would she want a snack? He pulled open his pantry and it was practically bare. He shut it. He wouldn't offer a snack, and hope she wasn't hungry. So much for southern hospitality.

Out of tasks, he took a moment for a silent prayer. He closed his eyes. *Father, please be with me today. I don't feel good about this interview, so I need Your help to get me through it. Keep me focused, keep me calm. Help me know what to say. Amen.*

He walked into the front room and sat, fidgeting. At least he had a straight view out the front window. A few minutes passed and a small gray car pulled up on the street outside his house. A young woman stepped out and flipped her hair over her shoulder. He stared, captivated. The hair was so long and full, it must constantly get in her face. Looked like she'd perfected the move of tilting her head to the side and then back to make her glorious mane tumble behind her without lifting a finger. It was a gorgeous light brunette shade, not real dark, but not quite blond. The color of a sorrel horse's coat.

He clamped his mouth shut and snorted. Nice job, Romeo, comparing a beautiful girl to a horse. No wonder he had no practical experience with women.

He watched as she opened the back door of the car, pulled out a canvas bag, and hoisted it over one shoulder. She wore sunglasses to shield her vision from the beach town sun. Although it was November, the sun was present to some degree. She made her way toward his house and he took the chance to observe her appearance. She was medium height, probably five-five or so; medium build, not too thin, not too heavy, but her actual figure was disguised under office clothes and a jacket.

His heart rate increased and his fingers and toes tingled a little. Not only did he have to do this interview under duress, but now he had to keep his cool around a gorgeous woman. Women were a phenomenon he'd had no exposure to in the … well, in the last ten years. He could count on one hand the number of females he'd actually made conversation with since he'd been released, other than his sister Marianne, his dad's new wife Leslie, and during a quick wedding visit, Leslie's college-age daughter Jasmine and a few other wedding guests. And family didn't count.

It's not that he didn't like women. He *did*, at least, he'd done his share of admiring women. Mostly from afar. It was just a simple fact that he'd never been comfortable around them. And whatever practice he had with women, wasn't really with grown women — it was with girls. During his high school and college days.

Keep his head on. This wasn't a date. It was business. A chance to help with something Neil felt strongly about and potentially advertise his business.

He stepped over to the front door before she rang it, then counted to five after. Taking a deep breath, he fixed a pleasant smile on his face and opened the door. "Hello!" he said heartily. A flicker of surprise crossed her face and he advised himself to tone it down. "Welcome, Emma. Please, come in."

"Jeremy?" she asked.

"Yes. Jeremy Harrison. Pleased to meet you." He held his hand out for a shake.

She was in the midst of crossing the threshold of the doorway. She came into the living room and took his hand.

"Nice to meet you." Her words were mumbled, but her voice sent a shiver down his spine, or maybe it was the contact with her hand. But she was having trouble making eye contact with him. He wondered why.

She removed her glasses, stuck them in her purse and shook her head again, making her hair shimmer and bounce. He waited for her to tell him what she wanted to do — it was her interview, after all. But a moment of silence stretched into a few and it became awkward as she glanced around the room with a slight frown on her face.

"So," he started, "tell me what you want to do. We could sit at the table if you like, or go out to my work space. Or the shed in the back where my finished pieces are."

"Is this your house?" she asked abruptly.

The question threw him off. "I live here …"

"Do you own it?" Now she looked him full-on for the first time and he was drawn to her eyes, a brown like the color of cocoa. She seemed intent on an answer and he stumbled on one.

"N-no, I … don't own anything. It's my father's house, actually, but he got married and …"

"Hank?" She looked back at him. "Hank Harrison is your father?"

"Yes." It was a little unsettling, yet expected, that she knew everything about him and he knew virtually nothing about her. Of course, she had been briefed on his background and his record was public knowledge.

She dipped her head and her hair took a plunge, hiding her face for a moment before she lifted her chin and it bounced back in place.

"Could I offer you a drink?"

"No." Her answer stung and she must've noticed his reaction because she added, "Thank you."

Jeremy scratched his head. They were off to a heck of a start. And he had no idea where to go next. Fortunately, Emma finally gave him some direction.

"Could we sit together and do the interview?"

"Yes." He walked a few steps across the tiny front room to the doorway of the kitchen, then hung back and motioned, allowing her to walk in front of him. She settled in at the kitchen table, put her big bag on the floor, unzipped it and pulled out a laptop. She turned it on. He settled in across from her, working on keeping his breathing steady.

Her preparations done, she began the interview. "So, I'm here with Seminal Magazine and I'm writing a feature article regarding second chances and success stories in the community following incarceration. Your name was provided by your probation officer. Do you mind if I record this conversation so I can refer back to it later? I have a recording app on my laptop."

He looked at it warily. His discomfort increased knowing he was being recorded and she could listen to it over and over. But he'd look like an idiot if he refused. "That's fine."

"Okay." She made some clicks on her computer. "Please state your name and town of residence."

He did, although he had an uneasy memory of doing something similar when he was arrested. The woman had a gorgeous face, but she sure wasn't doing anything to make him feel at ease with this interview process. Wouldn't a warm demeanor aid a reporter in coaxing more out of a person for a better story?

"Tell me about your criminal record and why you were incarcerated."

He jerked a little at the question and wondered if she noticed. Way to get right at the tough stuff. "Uh, I was arrested for tax evasion, predatory lending and loan sharking."

She stared at him.

"I served ten years and was released in August."

"You owned a construction company."

"No, not exactly. My dad owned the company. I worked for him."

"But the company, Harrison and Son, no longer exists. I looked for it on the internet."

He drew a shaky breath. "Right. The company went bankrupt."

"When you were in charge."

Her words couldn't have injured him more if she'd picked up a carving knife and plunged it into his chest. A tidal wave of pain and sting opened in his brain. Everything she'd said was accurate and there was so much more to the story. His big ambitions to take his dad's little handyman business and move into the big stuff — constructing new homes, big beach homes for high-dollar price tags — mansions for rich clients on the shoreline. He'd gone to college, gotten his business degree; he was equipped to improve his dad's company into something to be proud of.

But it had gone terribly wrong. He'd gotten a few clients, but underbid the projects, much lower than his competitors. He'd won the jobs, but now had to operate on a shoestring budget. He still thought taking a loss on the first few houses would be a smart business strategy, then after their name and reputation were well known in Pawleys Island, he could raise prices. But it all went ugly, all went bad. Because of him. He had to lay off workers, he couldn't finish the jobs, clients sued him. He had no choice at the time but to get loans, no matter the source.

He'd destroyed his dad's business and in the process, his family's security and future.

He rose to his feet, walked a few steps to the counter and leaned against it. He had to put a little distance between them. "Could we move on, please? Talk about the present? My new business?"

"So you have a new business now."

He made an effort to shove the heavy stuff back where it belonged, in the background of his mind. "I'm just starting up. But I'm determined to do it right this time. Start small with appropriate pricing. My reputation will be all about high quality and innovation."

"Houses?"

"No, no. Much smaller. Furniture. I build custom-made wooden furniture."

"Do you plan to get back into home construction someday?"

"No. I don't." He was feeling a little better now that the subject was one he was more comfortable with.

"Because you failed at home construction?"

He blinked, then squeezed his eyes shut. "If you don't mind, I'd like to focus on the present and the future. I'm done talking about my past. You understand?"

"Can you hide from your mistakes that easily?"

"Easy!" he spit out. "I spent a decade of my life serving my punishment for those mistakes. Not a moment of it was easy."

He paced to the other side of the kitchen, his fists clenched. Why was she being so hostile toward him?

"And what about the victims of your crime? The people who worked for Harrison and Son who lost their jobs, through no fault of their own?"

He took a deep breath and turned back to her with a calmer voice. "You're right. I'm not the only one to pay the consequences for my bad decisions. I have to live with that every moment of every day, for the rest of my life."

She nodded but didn't continue.

A few moments passed. His heart rate had about returned to normal. "Look, I apologize for my outburst and for my defensiveness. I'm sure you didn't mean to do it, but you're really pushing my buttons here. My probation officer told me I wouldn't have to go into detail about my crime. Did he understand that wrong?"

She was staring down at her laptop. She pushed it shut and slid it back into her bag. "This interview isn't going to happen today." She stood and walked out of the kitchen.

A part of him was relieved, but a part was apprehensive. This obviously hadn't gone well. What would he tell Neil? What would *she* tell Neil? He followed and caught up with her just as she was opening his front door.

"Emma, please, wait."

She stopped, but didn't look up. Now that he held her captive what would he say to her? He'd already apologized for the disaster this interview had become.

"Do you still plan to use me for the article? Or move on to someone else? I honestly am fine either way." He studied her as she thought it over. "I just want to do what's right and if you want my help, I'd be happy to cooperate. But I don't want a repeat of the way it went today." He didn't mean to be harsh, but he wouldn't allow her to insult him either.

She turned to face him. "I'm afraid I've been unprofessional with you. I let my personal feelings get in the way of my job. I shouldn't have done that."

"Personal feelings?" Now he was confused. They'd never met, as far as he knew.

She dug in her bag, pulled out a business card and handed it to him. "Give me two days to cool down and please call me. I'll let you know our next steps."

She slipped through the door and out of his house before he could say another word. He watched her stride across his yard, get into her car and drive away. He slid his gaze to the business card, a duplicate of the one Neil had given him. He looked at the name with new eyes: "Emma Jean Slotky, Feature Reporter."

Slotky. Slotky. The name sounded familiar. Why?

Maybe it was time for a visit with his dad.

* * *

Emma flew off the little side street, drove a few blocks down, then pulled the car over. She needed to breathe and clear her head. She shoved the car in park and rested her head in her hands. What was she thinking? She'd never been so rude during an article interview before. She knew the ropes. Put them at ease, make them comfortable, engage them in a chat about common interests. That's how she got the most out of the interview subjects.

Not insult the man, alienate him and aggressively question his answers.

Not that he didn't deserve it. He'd caused her family all kinds of trouble when her dad got laid off. She would've loved to get eye to eye with Jeremy Harrison ten years ago and given him a piece of her mind, right up in his face. Yell and yell till it was all out and he'd never forget it.

But not now, a decade later, when he was done with his prison sentence. He seemed to be trying to make a new start. Was that authentic, or just an act for the article? Darn, he seemed to be honestly rehabilitated, with a positive can-do attitude and the desire to do the right thing. Or, had he just manipulated her and his probation officer into believing he was? The evil Jeremy Harrison who lived in the Slotky family annals was capable of that deception, and so much more.

She shook out the tension in her shoulders. She had a problem. She was assigned to write a compelling story, the feature article. That wasn't going to happen if she'd just as soon bite his head off. And what if Jeremy or his officer called Peggy and reported Emma's unprofessional behavior? That definitely wouldn't do her career aspirations any good.

She sighed and checked her reflection in the car's inside mirror. She dabbed at her face and fluffed up her hair. She'd have to cool down and consider her next move. She could very easily ask Brad to meet with him. She could still do the other two subjects, ask Brad to meet with Jeremy, then consolidate his story into hers. But Peggy had assigned this to her. She could assume Brad was equally loaded up with assignments. She didn't want to be the weak link, and besides, with the budget troubles the magazine was having, they wouldn't hesitate to fire her if she gave them a valid reason. And she couldn't afford to be fired due to poor performance.

She needed to face this thing straight on.

She leaned back in her seat and frowned. It really was an opportunity, if she looked at it the right way. Dad's lay-off had been a family tragedy for a long time. Now she was face to face with the guy who'd caused it.

Maybe she'd been placed on this assignment for a reason. Maybe she was supposed to learn something from this. But what?

She sat in her seat and tried the deep breathing exercises she'd learned in college when life handed her a little more than she could take. Stress was unavoidable, but it was nice to have a technique to deal with it. Some of her friends had a faith in God and prayed for help. Some did yoga. She breathed.

In, out. In slowly, wait for ten seconds, out. Soon, her pulse was back to normal, her limbs no longer tingled and she felt marginally better. She pulled out her cell phone to see if she could reschedule the other two interviews to sooner and worry about Jeremy Harrison later.

* * *

Jeremy locked up his bungalow and shoved the key in his pocket. He smirked at his word choice. Bungalow was one of those words realtors used to make a place attractive. Sounded so much better than, *a four walled square house smaller than a tin can.* But he was grateful to his dad for letting him live there rent-free after Hank had moved into a big beach house with his new wife, Leslie.

As he walked by his old pickup truck, he patted it, making a solid thud sound. One of the perks of not paying rent was his ability to save up and buy this old truck. It was older than dirt and had over 150K on it, but the price was right. To give it a break tonight and to get a little exercise himself, he'd walk over to his dad's. Nothing on Pawleys Island was that far.

Growing up in a tourist beach town had mostly perks and few disadvantages. He and his sisters had been raised in the sand, surf and sun. Barefoot, swimsuit-clad, suntanned kids out on the beach from dawn till dusk, then back in only long enough to eat dinner and grab a jacket, then back out with a flashlight to look for crabs digging holes in the sand. By bedtime they were so exhausted, they plunged into sleep to rest up for more magic the next day. It was an idyllic, enchanted and captivating childhood.

He knew the town like the back of his hand, so after twenty minutes of walking and a few turns, he started down the gravel beach road that boasted, among other large rental homes, The Old Gray Barn. His new stepmom had a long history with the house, having stayed there every summer of her childhood and formed so many fond memories there. At the beginning of this summer, she'd taken a pilgrimage to Pawleys and re-discovered the meaningful house. She became part of the Harrison family, both figuratively and literally, when she married Jeremy's dad and they bought the Barn together. Dad knew it had been lovingly cared for over the years because he'd done the lions' share of the repairs and maintenance himself, through his handyman business. The house had survived Hurricane Hugo in 1989 completely intact, despite the neighboring houses on either side being destroyed. It was a solid old girl, and now, had the perfect owners who appreciated her rustic beauty.

Reaching the house, he trotted up the front steps onto a wooden deck that boasted half a dozen rocking chairs. The house rested on stilts to allow the high tide to flow underneath it nightly. He rapped on the front door, then, remembering his dad's repeated invitation, opened the door and shouted, "Dad? Leslie?" Inner turmoil warred. Sure, Hank was his dad, however, he and Leslie were still newlyweds after all, and by letting himself in, Jeremy could be walking into an unwelcome surprise.

"Jeremy? Out on the porch. Come on back."

Jeremy walked through the combination great room/dining room, across plain scuffed wooden floors, swept clean and scattered with throw rugs. On the opposite wall he opened the sliding glass door and stepped out onto the screened porch, which featured an ocean front view and more wooden rocking chairs where family and friends could rock, watch the ocean and listen to the waves.

"What a nice surprise," Leslie said as she rose and gave him a quick embrace and kiss on the cheek.

His dad waved from his chair, not bothering to get up. "Want an iced tea, son?"

"No, that's okay." It was an automatic response, but truth was, after the longish walk he was sort of thirsty.

Leslie gestured toward a chair. "Make yourself comfortable. We have the pitcher here. Let me just get another glass in case you change your mind."

She patted his shoulder on her way by and his heart swelled. Leslie was a breath of fresh air, and just what this sad, practically destroyed family needed. He'd ruined so much that was good about the Harrisons and although he'd paid his debt to society, his imprisonment would never come close to restoring the family to how it was, or how it would be flourishing now without his errors.

He sank into the chair next to his dad. He couldn't be happier that his dad had found happiness, finally.

"Hey Dad, how's it going today?"

Hank nodded. "Can't complain. Working over in Litchfield this week and next. Bunch of condos that need kitchen renovations. Countertops, cabinets."

"Sounds like a lot of heavy lifting. Do you have help?"

"Yeah, I do. I hired a helper for this job. Young guy with a much better back than I got."

Jeremy smiled. "Gotta keep yourself fresh in the evenings for your new bride, huh?"

Hank swatted his son's arm and they both chuckled, just in time for Leslie to return. She handed Jeremy the glass. He helped himself to the tea and had gulped almost a full glass before he looked up and saw both Hank and Leslie staring at him, amused. "Sorry. Guess I was thirsty after all."

Hank settled back into comfortable silence, the sound of the early evening waves surrounding them all.

"So," Jeremy said, "I had an appointment with Neil this week."

"Things going well?" Leslie asked.

"Sure, yeah. In fact, Neil asked me to take part in a project about success stories, people who make a good transition to society after incarceration."

"That sounds like an honor, to me."

Jeremy shrugged. "Let's not go that far. But yeah, he picked three of his offenders to be interviewed for a magazine article and one was me. In fact, Dad, I wanted to run a name by you. The reporter came by to interview me and her name sounded familiar. Does Slotky ring any bells to you?"

Hank studied him for a moment, then said, "Sure. Gary Slotky? He was one of my seasonal help for the handyman business before we expanded. Had him at least eight, nine years. Once you started building up the home construction piece, you hired him on full-time." Hank rubbed his chin. "Seems to me he had some kind of specialty skill you needed for homes. Dry wall? Or roofing? Something like that."

Jeremy took a long breath. "Did he have a family, do you remember, Dad?"

Hank squinted. "Yeah, couple a kids, if I remember right. Daughters. Or maybe just one."

"Teenagers?"

"Could be."

"You don't remember any names, do you?"

Hank shook his head. "Why?"

Jeremy dug in his pocket for the business card and handed it to him. "The reporter seemed to have a chip on her shoulder from the moment she stepped in the house. An attitude, you know? Pressing on a bruise type of questions, never let anything drop, and asking pointed questions about the victims of my crime. It surprised the heck out of me, considering the article's about rehabilitation and making a success."

Hank read the card. "Emma Slotky." He shrugged and handed the card back. "Could be Gary's daughter. Slotky's not that common a name. Want to do a search for her on Leslie's laptop?"

He was tempted, but decided not to. He was most likely going to see her again and he could just ask her. Apologize to her personally, take responsibility for his actions. Again and again in his freedom, he faced discrimination against ex-cons. This was no different. Best to deal with it with understanding and patience, knowing that if he was in her spot, he'd be angry too.

"So Jeremy, why don't you stay for dinner? We've got plenty."

It didn't take much convincing. Between Leslie's invitation, his own empty cupboard at home and the smell of beef stew on the stove and biscuits in the oven, his stomach's growling left him little room to argue.

Chapter Three

Emma pulled off Route 17 onto two-lane Milltown Road. Traveling just twelve miles away from the neon lights and tourism of her hometown, Myrtle Beach, made a world of difference. More peaceful, secluded, quiet. More in her element, away from the hustle bustle and the omnipresent traffic.

She'd been coming here since she was eight. That was the age she'd fallen so head over heels horse-crazy that her parents agreed to let her take riding lessons. Probably just to shut her up. Grieders' Stables, halfway between Garden City and Murrell's Inlet became her home away from home. The moment she emerged from the car on that first day, she knew she belonged. A mid-sized mongrel dog ran out to greet her. A prissy, scaredy-cat girl would've screamed and run but Emma knew the dog was welcoming her. On the walk from the small gravel parking lot to the arena and barn, she spied a peacock. The first time she'd ever seen one in person, it displayed his tail for her and she was mesmerized forever.

But the horses. Chica the Palomino, Maggie the black half-thoroughbred and Junior, the huge gray gelding. They didn't belong to her, but they might as well have because she gave over her heart and commitment to them on Day One. It was Mom and Dad's expectation that to help pay for lessons, she'd work in the stalls. She gained a 360-degree education in the care and maintenance of her new favorite animals. She fed them proper measurements of oats, hay and water. She measured their vitamin supplements and made sure they swallowed them down. She learned every aspect of grooming, from bathing to brushing to picking the hooves and braiding the manes. And of course, the mucking. Horse stalls got rank pretty fast and there were always stalls that needed mucking out. She'd been nine when she took over that job. It wasn't her favorite, but hey, it was part of the package and she never really minded it. She even got to tolerate the smell.

Several of her friends at school gave up riding when they were teens. Too many other things to do — sports teams, cheerleading and boys, boys, boys. Not Emma. She thrilled when her legs grew longer because she knew it would aid her in riding, give her better balance. She started with English equitation and proceeded into stadium jumping, then foxhunting and steeplechase. She was fearless. Although occasionally the horses changed, her passion for them never did.

When Dad lost his job, Emma was terrified that the family wouldn't be able to pay for her lessons. But she was determined. After getting the news and spending an afternoon in her room sulking, she straightened her shoulders, marched straight up to Mr. Grieder and told him she'd double her work chores, triple them if needed, if she could continue to ride and take lessons at his stables. Mr. Grieder agreed and a partnership evolved. Mr. Grieder added to her chores and used her to exercise the boarded horses whose owners paid for that service. Of course, it wasn't work to Emma. It was what she lived for.

Now, she was a grown woman with a career and an apartment of her own. She'd been riding for over fifteen years now. Although her time commitment had to decrease because of her work schedule and other commitments, her love and passion for the horses never had. She made it a priority to come out here at least once a week. Although money never exchanged hands in either direction, she'd check in with either Mr. or Mrs. Grieder to find out how she could help that day. It was therapeutic.

Today, she pulled her car into the same gravel parking lot she remembered from her first visit. Another mongrel, this one named Rex, came running over, barking. She got down on her knees to make it easier for him to jump up and lick her face.

He got his fill of her and wandered off. She straightened and walked to the barn.

"Hello?" she called when she entered. Quiet peacefulness swept through the large building. Dust from the enclosed riding arena hung in the air, tiny sparkles glittered when intersected by sunbeams. The arena was abandoned of riders. "Anyone?"

Horse snorts and hoof pounds gave her a feeling of home.

"Hey, little lady."

She turned at the beloved voice. Mr. Grieder stepped up behind her, leading a compact white horse on a line, its neck arched and tail carried high. The animal was exotic-looking with blue eyes, an unusual color for a horse.

"Hi Mr. G. Who do we have here?"

He turned to consider the equine beauty. "This here's Aladdin, a new boarder."

She stepped carefully to him and offered her outstretched palm. The horse sniffed her hand and then puffed air out. An acceptance of her, if she ever saw one. She dug in her pocket for a stub of the carrot she'd brought, cut into three pieces.

She put the treat on her palm and held it out to him again. He nuzzled her palm with his velvety muzzle and swiped the treat away, munching contentedly while twitching his tail.

"Hello, Aladdin. Nice to meet you. He's a beauty."

"He's a full bred Arabian. Good stock."

"I don't think I've ever seen an Arabian in person."

"You got some time?"

Emma smiled. That was his customary way to broach her chore assignment. "You bet."

"Would you give this one a bath? Use the hose over there and the sponges, and because he's so white, you use the bluing like they use in the laundry. Helps his coat sparkle. Then, walk him around outside till he's pretty dry. Doesn't have to be perfect, but the drier the better. Then put his blanket on him and put him back in the stall."

She gave a single head bob. "Sounds good, Mr. G."

"Then feel free to take Apple for a spin. Either indoors or out, your choice. He could stand to stretch his legs, the ole boy."

She gave him a grin. He knew she loved riding, and loved Apple. Her reward for working hard on Aladdin's coat.

The hours passed happily as she completed her work with Aladdin, then took Apple for a leisurely trail ride in the woods surrounding the stables. They both enjoyed the full-out gallop she coaxed him to, returning home across the open field once the barn was in sight. Nothing caused her heart to pound like the exhilaration of horse racing.

As she walked Apple to cool him down, then groomed him, then fed him and said her farewells, her mind slipped back to the one person she had needed a mental distraction from. Jeremy Harrison. Since she left his house yesterday in an angry huff, a moment barely passed when she wasn't thinking of him. She'd tortured herself several times, replaying her angry interview questions on tape, cringing at her unprofessionalism. She heard his responses and his diligent attempt to answer honestly and calmly until she'd pushed so hard, he couldn't help but explode in frustration. Yes, he'd broken the law. Yes, he'd screwed up his father's company, and along with it, her father's job and livelihood.

But instead of hating him, she now felt something ... different. Sorry for him? No, absolutely not. He deserved his sentence and he'd paid the consequence without asking for any special favors. Now he was released from prison and determined to make his own way in the world. He wasn't asking for sympathy.

Intrigued by him? Yes, maybe. Did it have only a little to do with his rugged good looks? His dark hair, flung back from his face, just a bit too long, with a subtle trace of curl at the ends. His jaw line, noticeably pronounced, covered with the faint stubble of whiskers. His bright blue eyes — definitely the most captivating thing about his face, the color of a Carolina summer sky. And his lips. No. She wouldn't think about the man's lips. Definitely not. Because then she'd have no choice but to rate the kissability of those lips — and since they were full and sensual, housing the bright white, straight teeth underneath that he'd graced her with on the rare appearance of his smile — she'd have to give his lips high marks.

She began her walk to the car, waving over her head at Mr. G. Stop it. His face was simply his face. Everyone had one. So, his happened to be handsome. So what? It had absolutely nothing to do with her involvement with him. From this day forward, her interest in him was purely professional. He was an interview subject, he had an unpleasant connection to her family and he was trying to make his way in the world. She'd do her job, get her interview, and then leave him the hell alone.

She drove north back to Myrtle with her plan made, her work cut out for her. Research his story so she could make good use of their limited time together. Keep her anger in check and her head on straight. And ignore the completely inappropriate budding of attraction that she felt for him. No problem.

She sighed. Now, she just needed to wait for his call.

* * *

The doorbell rang and as many times as he'd lectured himself about staying calm and steady, his pulse started to race. Along with it, his breath got a little shaky. Dang! What was wrong with him? He'd faced plenty of conflict and adversity in his life. Facing a beautiful female reporter with a connection to someone he'd wronged ten years ago, and answering her justifiably angry questions about his actions, didn't even hit his Top 10 Most Difficult Life Situations.

Did he say beautiful?

He made his way to the door, willing his mind to ignore the fact that yes, the fair Ms. Slotky *was* beautiful with her long brown hair, fit body and a face that could grace the cover of beauty magazines.

He came to a stop with his hand on the knob and gave his head a stern shake. But her appearance had nothing to do with him, or why she was here, or what he needed to do today. He would try to neutralize the situation, and give her the information she needed to write a decent story about him. A story that would satisfy Neil and allow him to move forward and focus on his business.

He took a breath, pushed it out and opened the door. "Ms. Slotky. Nice to see you again. Please, come in." He gestured with a broad arm of welcome.

"Thank you." She came in and looked up at him. "Please, no need to be so formal. Call me Emma and I'll call you Jeremy. Is that all right with you?"

"Of course. Could I interest you in a cold drink?"

This time, she accepted so he strode to the kitchen and got her a class of iced water. She had followed him into the kitchen so when he turned, she was sitting at the table, readying her laptop. He got himself a glass too.

"Do you mind if I record our conversation?"

"No." He wondered if she'd listened to the recording of their last conversation.

When it appeared she was ready to begin, he said, "Emma, I ..." just as she began with, "Jeremy, there's something ..."

They both came to a stop and Emma chuckled. Jeremy said, "Go ahead."

She nodded. "I just wanted to apologize for my unprofessionalism last time I was here."

He shook his head. "No, please. That's not necessary."

"No, really. My job is to ask you appropriate questions so you can open up and tell me your story. I was angry when I came in here and I let that anger affect the interview. So, I'm sorry."

He held his tongue. He wasn't used to people apologizing to him and no matter what she'd done, it wasn't nearly as bad as what he'd done — to her family, if he'd gotten his intel right.

"Well, I was going to apologize to you, so you beat me to it."

She furrowed her brow. "Why would you apologize to me? I was the one who was rude."

He sighed and moved his glass in a small circle on the table, widening the wetness on the wood. "You gave me your business card, and your last name sounded familiar. So I asked my dad for help and he reminded me that we'd hired your father. Gary Slotky?"

Her face blushed a sudden red, and she turned away.

"Is that your dad?" he asked quietly, not wanting to hurt her, but needing to bring the truth out in the light.

"Yes." She brought her hands up to her hair and pushed it off her shoulders, flung it behind her so her face was unencumbered.

He put his head down and wondered what to say next. "Then your anger was warranted. I had it coming."

A slight glimmer of a smile passed her lips. "Regardless. I pride myself on my professionalism. Our last meeting wasn't my finest hour."

He turned his head so he could see her. "Would you like to talk about our ... connection?"

Her response was swift. "No."

That was fine with him. He didn't really want to talk about it either. He just wanted to do a conflict-free interview so she could move on and write her article.

"How long ago were you released from prison?"

"Three months ago. This past August."

"How has your assimilation into society been?"

"Just fine."

She looked up at him. "You want to expand on that?"

He cleared his throat. "It's good to be out." He smiled.

She grinned. "King of the understatement, I see. So, what is your routine like now?"

"Right now, I'm working out of my home here, in my backyard, so I just get started. No commute." He took a look at her face to see if she'd acknowledge his lame attempt at levity. She had been making some notes on paper. She stopped and looked at him again.

"Then what?"

"On a really good day, I have hours on end to work on my furniture. Once I'm in the zone, I could go all day and night. Sometimes I have several pieces going at the same time, in different stages of development. Sometimes just one and I focus all my energy on that. I build wooden furniture, tables, dressers, chairs, whatever the customer wants, really."

"Where did you learn to do it?"

"In prison. They had a woodshop and I signed up for classes twice a week. Once my work was done for the day I was allowed to work on my wood pieces for an hour or so a night. I ended up finishing a few and sold them online. They let me deposit the money in my account and I'd use it to buy more supplies. I gained some good skills."

"So your hope is to build up this furniture building business into a livelihood?"

"Yes."

"Have you thought about getting a day job, then doing your furniture at night?"

He hesitated and wondered how honest he should be with her. He shrugged. "It's difficult for someone in my position to get a full-time job."

"Your position?"

"Yes, someone with a record, an ex-offender. Employers aren't usually willing to give a chance to someone with a past.

Not that I blame them, don't get me wrong. There's so many people looking for work in this economy, why not take the best choice you got? And that's rarely someone who's spent time in jail."

"Do you think someone like yourself couldn't work successfully for an employer?"

"Oh no, no that's not what I meant at all. If given a chance, I would work hard and be very loyal to an employer. And maybe someday I'll find one. But for the most part, for every job opening there's a line out the door applying for it. Employers have the luxury of weeding out the candidates and picking the best. In most cases, an employer wouldn't allow someone with a record to rise to the top."

"Do you feel discriminated against?"

Jeremy was starting to wish he'd never gone down this line of conversation. Verbal communication was never particularly his strength; he was best with his hands. How would he get his meaning across without sounding like he was a) complaining or b) feeling sorry for himself?

"Do I feel discriminated against, because I broke the law and went to prison? Yes, I'd have to say I do. But do I deserve every bit of that discrimination? Yes, I do. If I were in the employer's place, making decisions about who to bring into my business and I had a choice between a solid citizen with a good work record, and some guy who'd just been let out of the joint, I'd pick the non-offender too. I can't blame them. But I still have to support myself somehow."

"Have you considered going on social services like welfare?"

"No. I'm healthy, educated and I have skills. I just need to work hard and produce and stay clean and honest, and I'll make it. I've never been afraid of hard work and I don't mind putting the hours in. I just made some really stupid mistakes when I was younger and I'll do whatever I have to, to get over those."

They wrapped up the interview and Emma asked to see the furniture. She grabbed her bag, unzipped it and pulled out a big camera with a long lens. He opened the back door and let her pass in front of him, trying not to take a subtle sniff of her hair as she walked by.

Coconut scent.

He had pulled a few in-progress pieces from his shed and they sat on a tarp in the backyard. A twin dresser and the long kitchen table, then the start of a bookshelf. The dresser was virtually done, just awaiting one more coat of stain. The table was solid and sturdy, but required more sanding. The bookshelf was just a shell right now, a frame and four shelves. Emma stalked around them, snapping photos from different angles.

"Tell me about these pieces," she said, squatting to get a better angle of the dresser's intricate wood design.

"These are all commissioned pieces. I'm being paid to custom-build them for clients."

"How does that work?" She moved to the kitchen table and leaned in close to its surface, making him wonder how the final shot would look.

"I have a catalogue on my website to give clients ideas of what I could make them, but I'm also able to customize whatever piece they have in mind. Usually I sit down with a client and get an idea of what they're looking for — dimensions, color, style — before I get started on it."

She moved on to the bookshelf and took a few shots before turning back to him. "Do you have more?"

He nodded. "Yes. I don't have the space here to store my completed inventory. My sister has a storage shed and she's been nice enough to give me some space at her place."

"How much do you have stored over there?"

Jeremy thought. "A couple desks, a few more bookshelves, a full bedroom set."

Emma dropped her arms holding the camera. Without thinking, he moved closer and took it from her. She gave him an odd look.

"Oh, I'm sorry. It looked heavy. I didn't mean to grab it from you." He handed it back to her.

She chuckled. "It does get heavy. I only use it for article photos. The magazine prefers the type of shots it takes." She took it back from him. "I'd love to see the rest of your pieces but I don't have time today. How about I write the article and take a look at the photos I already have, then I'll decide if I have room for more in the layout?"

"Sure."

"I'll be in touch." She walked toward the door. Jeremy hustled to keep up with her. Guess they were done. Good. Ever since Neil had told him about the article, he couldn't wait for it to be over. This was what he wanted.

He followed her through his house to the front door. As if as a second thought, she stopped suddenly and turned back to him, almost causing him to collide into her. He caught himself and stepped back.

"See? We were able to be professional."

He nodded and soaked in the sight of her happy grin, her striking lips spreading to expose straight white teeth, transforming her eyes into sparkling beacons of happiness. "Yep, you're right, we were."

She ducked her head, staring at her feet for a second, then back up at him. "I'm glad I gave you a chance. You're not exactly the monster I'd made you out to be in my mind."

With that, she took off down the front porch steps, across his tiny yard and into her car. Good thing she hadn't hung around because he had no idea how to respond to that sentiment.

* * *

Emma started her car and drove away from there as quickly as she safely could. She'd done her professional duty. She'd gone back to her interview subject, apologized for her previous rude behavior (as much as it had killed her to do it) and she'd conducted a successful interview. She now had the information and photos she needed to complete her assignment; write her article and layout the format for the magazine pages.

She didn't need to ever see him again. This whole crazy interaction was almost over. She'd write the article, turn it in and be done.

As she drove, her mind wandered. Why had life put the two of them together at this particular time? For years, she'd hated him, as had her father and her mother. Well, hated him without knowing him personally. She'd never met him back then. But his actions had sent her small family into a downward spiral that to this day, they'd never recovered from.

Her dad, never particularly ambitious, was now discouraged and beaten down. He'd lost his job at a time when jobs were hard to come by, and after a taste of unemployment benefits from the government and the accompanying abundance of free time … he'd accepted this new lifestyle as the best he could do. Hours to sit around, watch TV, putter around the yard and drink beer. Always the beer.

Mom's job as a customer service associate at a local insurance agency became the small family's primary income. Thank God Mom had a job when Dad got laid off. It kept the mortgage paid and food on the table. But no money for luxuries.

As she drove, her mind went back to Jeremy taking the heavy camera from her. He'd recognized her discomfort from holding it, shifting it to different angles to get the right shots. Her arm muscles had ached, but how had he known that? She hadn't said a word, nor did she think her facial expression had given anything away.

She sighed. So, he was a southern gentleman. Thousands of boys in this region were raised that way. So what? There was nothing special about him or his politeness. And it certainly wasn't a reflection of his character.

Her little car headed home, to her parents' house. Twenty minutes later, she pulled into the driveway of a small but homey little ranch house, red with white trim. Well, a color that used to be red, now sort of a sun bleached sienna. The house could use a new paint job, and if she were honest with herself and really opened her eyes, she could make a long list of improvements the house could tolerate, to pull it out of its shabby, worn condition. She wasn't thinking of that now. Someday, when she'd saved some money, maybe she could go shopping at the home improvement store and help her folks out with some much-needed supplies. But now she needed to talk to them both about her meeting with Jeremy and get their thoughts on his past sins and present challenges.

"Mom? Dad?" She walked in through the front door. The drone of the television floated up the stairs from the basement.

"Emma!" Her mom rushed into the living room from the hallway. Her bedroom was at the back of the house and if Emma had her guess, she'd say Mom was putting folded laundry away or something equally industrious. Emma closed the distance between them and pulled her mom into a hug.

"Wow, nice greeting!"

Emma smiled into her neck. If she ever had the chance to be half as good a mom as hers was, she'd consider herself a success. She pulled back. "How's it going?"

"Good, good. I was just straightening up a little bit. This house collects clutter, I swear."

Emma looked around. There were, indeed, little stacks of things sitting in corners, along the walls. With a house as small as theirs, it was important to keep everything in its place. "Maybe you could ask Dad to do some clean up while you're working. Then you wouldn't have to work all day, only to come home and clean at night."

Mom gave her a closed-mouthed smile, more like a grimace actually, and shrugged. "I don't know about that."

"Mom, he needs to have some sense of accomplishment. Look around this place, inside and out. He could break all the chores down and you could come up with a schedule. Do the cheaper stuff first while we save up for the more expensive jobs. It might make him feel better. What do you think?"

"It's an idea ...," Mom said tentatively.

"And I want to help you buy some supplies. You know, paint, stain, whatever. It would make a big difference around here."

Mom looked at her for a moment, silent, then reached out and squeezed her hands. "You're a sweetie." She led her to the kitchen table. "Here, sit. Can I get you something? Are you hungry?"

Emma shook her head. "No, I …"

"I made fried chicken last night and have several pieces left over." Mom bustled around the kitchen, reaching into the fridge, pulling things out, rustling through the cabinets, finding disposable dishware. "Some salad. Why don't you take it home and eat it tonight for dinner? Or stay tonight. I have stuffed peppers on the stove. You like those, don't you?"

Emma laughed. Cooking was one thing Mom loved to do and bestow on her only child. Who was she to refuse?

"I wanted to talk to you and Dad together, if that's okay."

Mom stopped bustling and looked over. "Big news? Good news?"

Her mom had a transparent face, never could keep a secret, and she knew exactly what she was thinking. "Mom, nothing like that. Just want to talk, that's all."

Mom went to the head of the basement steps and called for Dad. When he emerged, he was walking pretty steadily, leaning on the railing for support on the way up the stairs, but once he got to the kitchen he walked without stumbling. He gripped his beer can in his hand.

"Hey, sweetie pie," he said, leaning in and placing a kiss on Emma's cheek. She was sure he meant it to be a light one but he misjudged the distance and ended up stabbing her cheekbone with his nose. Unexpected pain brought a stab of tears to her eyes and she guessed he'd hurt himself too, but he pulled away without a trace of discomfort.

"Hey, Dad." She sighed, running her hand over the sore spot. "I can't remember, did I tell you about the article I'm working on? It's about people who have broken the law, served their time in prison, and are now assimilating successfully back into society. I was given three subjects to interview."

Dad rubbed a hand over his mouth. "Yeah, you mentioned this story the last time you h came by."

Emma frowned. So she had, she'd almost forgotten her brief mention. The man had a steel trap for a mind, despite numbing it consistently with alcohol. It pained her that he was wasting his life in a beer fog every day, sitting in a recliner in his basement. He could accomplish something, it wasn't too late. But she'd pushed him before and it had only ended it an argument, and her mom, God bless her, hated conflict and would rather ignore it than address it.

"Oh, that's right, I forgot. So, I've done all three interviews and I just need to write the article now. But the last one, the one I just finished, was with Jeremy Harrison." She glanced first at her mother, then her father. Their faces froze, eyes open wide, interested expressions seared on their faces, like a movie frame that lost connection and stayed past natural time and distance.

Then, both of them started talking at the same time — loudly, angrily. Their words interwove and rose, and she was unable to understand what either were saying. Slowly, the din subsided, leaving Mom with the beginning of tears in her eyes and Dad frowning and pacing the small room.

"Why did they give you that assignment? You shouldn't have to interview that ass. Conflict of interest, I'd say." Dad now leaned on the counter, his back to her.

"They had no idea I was even connected with Jeremy Harrison."

He spun around. "Why didn't you tell them? Or at least tell them you have a confidential reason you shouldn't do the article?"

"I thought briefly about it, but decided against it. I ran off to do the interview with him. Unfortunately, I was angry, and was very rude and unprofessional so I cut the interview short."

Dad's lips turned up on the side. "Gave him hell, did you? That's my girl."

"I did, Dad, but later I thought better of it. It was beneath me the way I talked to him. I'm a professional journalist. I want to work in a bigger market someday. I don't want this being a black mark on my record."

Dad clenched his fist and pounded it into his other palm. But Mom saw the reason in her statement. "That's good, Emma. The man already ruined your father's career, leaving him with no options. You don't want him to do the same thing to your career. I'm proud of you."

Dad ran a hand through his thinning hair. "So what are you going to write about him?"

The way he asked it, Emma knew exactly what he had in mind. Write an explosive story to seek the family's revenge on the Harrisons.

"I'll just write about his furniture-building and some of the challenges he's facing getting his business started up."

Dad stared at her, redness moving up his neck and into his face. He grabbed his beer can off the table, took a wet slurp and squeezed the can, slamming it in the general direction of the trash can. It bounced off the side and onto the linoleum. Emma jerked.

"No. Not a tame little 'ain't he swell' type story, Emma. What's wrong with you? Don't you have any family loyalty?"

Her mom reached over and rubbed her dad's arm but didn't speak.

"Dad, I'm going to do the story I was assigned to do. I'm going to try to go into it without any preconceived notions. He strikes me as being very sorry for his actions. He's not looking for any handouts and he wants to work hard to get back on his feet."

Her dad froze, his eyes wide, his mouth dropped, staring at her. Emma calmly met his gaze, but inside she was churning. Then he broke his stare and turned to her mom. "I don't believe what I'm hearing, Edna. I really don't. Our little girl, showing loyalty to the Harrisons. The enemy. What is this family coming to?"

With that, he turned on his heel, no doubt to head back to the basement. Emma jumped to her feet and reached for his arm. "Dad! Daddy, come on. Stay and talk." But he slithered from her grasp and clumped down the stairs. Emma turned to her mother, tears breaking through and rolling down her cheeks. "He doesn't understand. I didn't do anything wrong. Did I?"

Her mother reached around her neck and pulled her in close. "Shhh, shhh. Now's not the time, honey. You let him settle and stew. He'll be back. He can't listen to reason now."

She whispered against her mom, "Do you think I'm wrong to do the story?"

Mom stayed silent long enough that Emma pulled back and looked at her face, reading her expression.

"We'll talk more about it, honey. I want to hear your reasons. The Harrisons did some horrible things to our family and your father's never really recovered from that.

Things would be very different now, if Jeremy Harrison hadn't run the company into the ground."

Thoughts swirled in Emma's head. She'd heard that her whole life, a family legend. But now, other thoughts intermingled, traitorous thoughts, that she wasn't ready to share with her mother yet.

Why? Why had Dad never recovered? The company he worked for laid him off ten years ago. How many others could claim the same thing all over the country? All over the world? Why hadn't he bounced back? Why did he just roll up and agree to fail?

Chapter Four

J eremy pulled his truck into the sandy parking lot across from the Seaside Inn, the beach hotel owned by his sister Marianne and her husband Tom. It had served as his first home when he was released from prison in August and Marianne was extremely generous, letting him stay for several months and feeding him in their delicious dining room, to boot. Someday he would pay her and Tom back, somehow.

His family's over-the-top generosity and acceptance had been the most surprising element of his life after serving his time. He didn't deserve it. And it had been hard to accept at first. He didn't understand it. He was sure he wouldn't show the same forgiveness if the positions were reversed.

He'd done some horrible things. He'd destroyed the family business, he'd blown through his dad's life savings, he'd let the insurance lapse so that when his mom got sick, she was uninsured.

By the time she died, he was locked away facing a decade of imprisonment. How could his family possibly forgive him for all that? Serving his time to society was one thing. But actually being accepted back into the family with loving arms? It was unbelievable.

He opened the truck door and hopped to the ground. He tried not to think about it because of course, it upset him. It made his hands shake, his breath catch. They treated him much better than he deserved, but that didn't mean he wanted them to change anything. He was just at a loss as to where their generosity and forgiveness came from.

So, he stilled for a moment, closed his eyes and repeated a favorite phrase in his head, *"Thank You, God. Thank You for Your mercy and Your grace."*

Feeling steadier, he trotted across the thin road, across the lawn of the Seaside Inn and up the front steps. A wide wooden building painted gray and white, it opened into a huge great room that guests were welcome to treat as their home away from home, with its couches and easy chairs and a fireplace. In one corner stood a counter where either Marianne or Tom, or sometimes their little daughter Stella, stood sentinel, ready to greet guests and respond to their needs. To the left of the big room was the doorway to a large dining room that served two meals a day to guests and fortunately for him, the occasional member of the family who hadn't had a home-cooked meal in a while. Across the back of the building was a screened-in porch that covered the entire length of the inn, where Marianne served coffee, tea, juices and baked goods every morning. And outside of that, past the wooden exterior decks and about a football field length of clean white sand in low tide, was the Atlantic Ocean. Jeremy's most favorite spot in the world.

Nobody was in the great room so he walked into the dining area. It wasn't meal time but Marianne was setting tables in prep for later tonight. "Hey sis," he said as he approached her, laying a kiss on her hair as he leaned in.

"Jeremy! Good to see you." The big smile on her face proved that she meant it.

"Busy?"

She glanced around the dining room. "Not bad. We only have a half dozen rooms full and only four couples put dinner reservations in. Mel's making shrimp scampi tonight. Want to come by?"

He automatically shook his head. "No, thanks."

"You got plans?"

"Well, I …" He refused to lie to her. Honesty was one of the big tenets that Neil preached. No reason to lie. A man's character is built on telling the truth. "No, not really, but I …"

She let her lips slip into a small smile. "But you what? Don't like Mel's scampi? I know that's not true."

"No, that's not it."

"Let me ask you this then. If you didn't come over for a steaming hot plate of shrimp scampi — with fresh shrimp, by the way, over white rice, homemade biscuits on the side with melted butter, a fresh vegetable salad with my very own ranch dressing, and oh did I mention, peach cobbler for dessert? Ala mode? If you weren't over here eating all that with us, what would you be having?"

Her description had rendered him motionless. His mind wandered back to his own tiny kitchen and he mentally opened the fridge … nothing there except half a carton of milk, some wrinkled apples and a half pound of coffee beans. How about the pantry? Some canned goods — tuna, several kinds of soup and a few cans of green beans. He was sure he would've put together a simple meal made of those ingredients. And been perfectly satisfied with it.

Until he'd heard in detail what was on the Seaside Inn menu tonight. "Dang it, Marianne." He ducked his head at her laughter at his expense, but the final straw was when his traitorous stomach let loose a loud, long growl.

"It's a date then. Be here at six. And bring your appetite."

It slipped out before he could stop it. "I will pay you back, you know. Every meal, every night in the room you gave up for me when you could've rented it to guests."

She rumpled his hair. "I'm not worried about it, big bro. All in good time."

He shook his head. He couldn't describe why her boundless generosity made him uncomfortable. Knowing Marianne, she knew exactly how he felt, but didn't care. She would continue to shower him with meals and help whenever she could. He pulled her into an embrace, patting her on the back. "I love you, sis."

They broke apart and he turned just a moment to make sure his emotions were under control. Turning back to her, he said, "I need to load up a few of my inventory pieces and take them over to the high school."

"Oh yes! The holiday craft fair. You got a booth?"

He nodded. "So you've heard of it? That's good."

"Definitely. It's a very popular event around here to kick off the pre-holiday season. Thousands of folks will go through."

He let out a cheek full of air. "It was pricy to rent an artisan's booth, but if I just sell one piece I'll break even. Two pieces, I'll make a profit. It's a gamble but I figured I'd give it a try."

Marianne tapped her chin with her index finger. "How big's your spot?"

Jeremy shrugged. "I've seen it. Not huge. I figure I could fit a few dressers, a few bookshelves, a media shelf. Nothing big like a table."

"Unless you stack items. Put a shelf up on top of a table?"

Jeremy considered. "That's a possibility."

"Here." Marianne led him to the front counter and handed him a stack of the inn's business cards. "Tell people you have more inventory here and they can stop by anytime and see it."

He accepted the cards and pocketed them.

"In fact…," Marianne spun in a circle and went to her computer. She clicked on an icon on the desktop and before he knew it, she was showing him the rough draft of a flyer she'd created. She pulled a small digital camera from her desk drawer and handed it to him. "Go take some shots of the pieces. We'll include them in this flyer and print out a big stack. It'll have contact info, with the address and phone number of the inn. We don't want you to lose any potential customers just because your booth is too small to display all your pieces."

Jeremy stood still, the camera in one hand, the other hand rubbing his forehead. There she went again. It was a brilliant idea — that just put him more in her debt.

Although … if he sold more pieces, he could begin to pay her back sooner. He smiled at her and went out back to the wooden storage shed where his sister generously allowed him to store his stock. He spent a half hour moving furniture around so he could get decent shots and came back with close to twenty digital photos.

When he returned, Marianne had designed, created, printed and hung mini-posters of his furniture sale at the high school tomorrow and the following day. He looked at her, eyebrows up.

"Hey, my customers have good taste. They'd want to know about the chance to buy hand-crafted custom wooden furniture."

* * *

Saturday morning, Emma slept in and awoke in her little apartment in Myrtle Beach proper, inland from the coast about six miles. She'd been in her own place a few years now, and loved the independence. However, she couldn't get over a niggling guilty feeling for no longer living at home with her parents. Of course, it was normal for a woman her age to live on her own, but in light of her family situation, it would be helpful to her parents to combine her income with theirs and pay the bills all together.

She sighed. That's why she still put aside a little cash every month and either gave it to her mom to help out, or just bought groceries for them and dropped them off. It was part of her reality.

She hopped out of bed and arranged the bedding neatly, then moved to her galley kitchen to make cereal and coffee. While waiting for the brew, she opened her door, picked up the newspaper delivered there and opened it, absorbed in the print while she walked back to her couch. She flipped through the sections, then to the community calendar. An ad caught her eye – the annual Craft Fair at Myrtle Beach High School.

She'd been there before and it was generally well attended by artisans of all kinds and shoppers wanting to get a jump on holiday shopping. She liked to buy a new tree ornament or two every year, and an addition to her Santa or snowman collections. Handmade was better than mass-produced.

She scanned the ad for participants: knit and crocheted goods, cut wood decorations, jewelry, basket weaving, custom wood furniture.

She wondered if Jeremy Harrison would be there. He hadn't mentioned it, but it seemed like a good market for him. If he were, she could get some shots of him interacting with customers. It would be good for the article.

Right?

She smiled and headed for the shower.

* * *

Jeremy arrived at the high school ninety minutes before the show opened. He'd loaded everything he could on his truck, but he'd have to make at least one, maybe two more trips to the Inn and back. He left the merchandise in the truck and wandered into the front door. Not many people had shown up yet. He made his way to the check-in desk and gave his name to a harried-looking woman.

She ran her finger down a list of names on a clipboard, made a notation and handed him a big 12 printed on a square card. "Here you go. You're in the cafeteria in front of the vending machines. Pretty good spot. Everyone will pass through there at one point."

"Thank you," he said. "I have several trips to make. Could I unload what I have now and leave? Are the items secure?"

She nodded. "The only folks in and out of here now are other artisans. Doors don't open to the public until nine. Do you need help carrying stuff in?" She motioned and several teenage boys leaning against the wall looked over.

He chuckled. "That'd be real nice. Thank you."

"Boys! Here's your chance to work. Look alive, now."

Jeremy headed over to the three boys. "Look at it this way. Lifting heavy furniture builds biceps, and girls love buff muscles." The boys grinned at each other and rolled their eyes.

They made quick work of unloading two dressers, two bookshelves and a coffee table, and carrying them to the booth. Jeremy convinced one of the boys to drive back to the Inn with him by promising a donation for the marching band, which was benefiting from the craft fair. With the kid's help, he loaded the remaining pieces into the truck and was about to head back to the fair when Marianne called to him.

"Jeremy. Wait!" She jogged to him, clutching a big book. He watched her curiously.

"Whatcha got there, sis?"

She panted as she finished the last few steps. "I made this for you to display at the show."

It was a photo album with a rich brown leather cover. He opened it and saw that it held plastic-covered pages containing 8x10 photos of his furniture, the ones he'd taken last night. It was striking, full of class.

He moved his eyes to meet hers. He was debating what to say when a sting hit his eyes. "Sis. This is unbelievable."

"You like it?" she said with an enthusiastic smile. "I think it'll look real nice at your booth. Just set it on one of the pieces. Or prop it open so people can see what's in there."

He took a step closer and pulled her into a hug. "Marianne, what would I do without you?" he murmured into her ear.

She squeezed him. "Anything I can do to help, you know that."

He pulled back and flipped through the book. It really was impressive. "When did you do this?" He was stunned.

"It didn't take long. I uploaded the images you took to the drug store website, and the prints were developed in less than an hour. I picked them up and bought the album while I was there. Slipped them in and … done. Easy peasy."

Jeremy flipped the book closed. "Thank you, sis. How much do I owe you?" He knew she wouldn't take any money but he wasn't about to take her generosity for granted.

As expected, she punched him on the shoulder, dismissing his question. "Go on back. I'll stop by later this afternoon to check out your booth and do some shopping for the Inn."

She waved to the teenage helper as Jeremy hopped up into the truck. They were back to the fair about forty minutes after they'd left.

The doors opened and masses of people came in. The organizer was right – he was in a very central location that drew traffic. He sold four or five of his smaller pieces before noon. He talked and talked till he was hoarse, describing his custom furniture, his process, his prices. At least a dozen customers took flyers and business cards with them and promised to call for a quote. The leather-bound photo album was a hit. He couldn't count how many times he looked up and saw someone flipping through it. Several customers left their phone numbers with a request for Jeremy to follow up with them next week.

At one point he was gulping from his bottle of water during a break in the action and he caught a glimpse of a woman in the distance who looked a lot like Emma Slotky, the reporter. He swallowed and took a closer look. She was gone. He moved and took a few steps but either it hadn't been her, or she had moved on.

"Excuse me, do you make the furniture?" a voice interrupted him.

"Yes, ma'am," he replied, put his bottle down and went back to work.

Around two o'clock, Jeremy had just wrapped up a sale when he heard a female voice, "Smile!" He looked up and saw Emma with a camera to her eye. He held a hand up to block his face.

"I thought I saw you earlier."

"Really?" She looked somewhat pleased with that statement. "You're the most awful photography subject in the world. Move your hand so I can get a decent shot."

He reluctantly dropped his hand. "I hate having my picture taken."

"Why?"

He shrugged.

She snapped a few shots of him despite his refusal to pose, turned the camera around and looked in the small viewfinder. She said with a delighted tone, "Well, look at that; you're very photogenic! The camera loves you, baby." She turned the screen towards him but he rolled his eyes.

"Why are you taking my picture?"

"For the article. It dawned on me that I don't have any of you, just your furniture. This is a great setting to take shots of you surrounded by adoring fans."

He scoffed. "Yeah, right. Adoring fans."

She raised an eyebrow. "I don't know what you're laughing about. You've had more traffic than any other booth. Do you know how long I've had to wait to get a chance to talk to you? In fact, I have several shots of you talking to customers, with a long line waiting."

"Really?"

"Yeah, man. You mop up at these fairs? How many of these have you done?"

"I've done a few."

"If I were you I'd find a bunch more and sign up."

He had to admit it had been a successful day, and there were still four more hours left today, and a whole day tomorrow. Emma put her camera down and started scanning the remaining furniture pieces. "Your work is lovely, and it's very reasonably priced. You could probably raise your prices and still sell them."

"Something to consider for later, but for now, I want to keep my prices low. My business expenses are low so I can pass that savings on to my customers."

She nodded. She studied his face for a long moment which caused his skin to go warm. She pointed at a bag sitting on a table. "Are you hungry?"

He was, but he said, "No, I'm fine."

She chuckled. "I bought a couple hamburgers. I'm hungry, but I don't think I could eat both of them. Will you share one with me?"

He sighed. "You bought me lunch?"

"No. I bought myself some lunch and I have more than I need." She turned her back and pulled two wrapped burgers out of the bag, then unwrapped one and turned to him again. After a second's hesitation, she took a big bite. The delicious scent of the beef wafted to him.

"Mmmm," she moaned.

Without another thought, he grabbed the second hamburger, unwrapped it and took a bite. She choked out a laugh with her mouth full. Struggling to get control, she quickly chewed, swallowed, then punched him on the arm.

"Sorry," he mumbled while eating. "This thing is good."

They finished their hamburgers before more customers came. When he got busy again, Emma picked up her camera, took a few shots and slid away into the crowd with a wave. All he could think as she walked away was how he liked the way her hair bounced, then he forced his attention back to his customer.

Chapter Five

The sanding machine sputtered to a stop, and Jeremy ran one hand along the freshly worked surface. Soft and smooth. Perfect. It had been over a week since the fair and the orders kept coming in. Lots of orders. Lucrative orders. Maybe the fair was his big break? He worked day and night now, but he was in his element, at his happiest when he was creating, alone and in the zone.

A long, rolling growl emerged from his stomach. So long that it was impossible to ignore, it literally shook his mid-section with its urgency. He put down the sanding machine. He chuckled and headed across the yard to the backdoor of his house. Inside the kitchen, he glanced at the clock. Two in the afternoon. He'd worked till one am last night, slept about 5 hours, then got up and continued this morning. He'd forgotten to eat. Again.

He made a quick sandwich, grabbed a half-empty bag of chips and sat at the table. He devoured the sandwich and stepped back to the counter to make another one. Needing something to read while he ate, he strode through the bungalow, opened the front door and reached into the mailbox hanging next to the door. He grabbed a small handful of mail and returned. A big manila envelope cradled the smaller envelopes. He pulled it out. The return address said "Seminal Magazine."

He ripped it open and pulled out three copies of the magazine, along with a handwritten note from Emma.

"Jeremy, your comp copies. Feel free to use them for advertising your business. If you need ideas, let me know, I have a few. It was nice working with you and I wish you the best in your … everything. Emma."

He considered the note for a moment, then set it aside. He flipped the first magazine open, paging through. It wasn't a particularly impressive magazine compared to the ones he saw on the rack in the grocery store, but it was a local business that had been serving the Myrtle community for decades. His flipping slowed when he encountered the feature article — his. The article spanned five pages or so, but the huge picture on the first page was him. Not a posed shot, he was standing in his booth at the craft fair talking to a customer. He hated pictures, but even more so since his release from prison. There was just something about putting himself out there, publicizing his image and his story that was completely opposite of what he'd learned inside.

Lie low under the radar, don't bring attention to yourself — that was how he'd survived. Never stand out. The price could be fierce if you did.

He put the mag down for a second to calm his racing breath. He wanted to read the dang article, and no way could he with his hands shaking like this.

A minute later, he picked it up again and read. Although the article featured three ex-cons, it began with him:

"Light white ash, perfect for a nursery ensemble. Aromatic cedar, formed into chests to store your linens — lay your head against the sheets and breathe in the smell while you drift off to sleep. Formal cherry wood, reminiscent of Victorian living rooms.

"Have you ever wanted to pick and choose your furniture, made to your specifications? To fill a particular nook or corner, or furnish an entire room? But the price stopped you. You're not made of money, after all.

"Now, you can. Pick and choose to your heart's desire: a new wood craftsman is in town, and he's making gorgeous wood furniture, all of which will hold its cherished place in your family's future generations. And ... the prices are reasonable. In fact, they're a downright steal."

Jeremy flinched. Heat flooded his face and he blinked rapidly.

"Jeremy Harrison is no stranger to stealing. In fact, he just finished a decade of imprisonment due to some stealing he's done in the past. But he's done with that now. He's served his time and now just wants a chance to earn a living doing what he loves — a craft he learned while imprisoned."

Jeremy let out a roar, threw the magazine on the floor and stomped out the door.

* * *

In a few days, it was time for his monthly check-in with Neil. As he made his way over to Georgetown, his cell phone rang. He had no intention of answering it (a state law was being debated in the Senate as to whether or not it would become illegal to talk on the phone while driving, and he wasn't about to push his luck) but he pulled it out of his shirt pocket to see who it was. The reporter ... again. She'd left two messages in as many days to find out if he'd gotten the magazines and what he thought of them. He wondered if she truly cared, or if she was trying to rub it in. What had her intentions been? To help him or destroy him?

He cursed under his breath and jabbed the phone in his pocket. When he'd discovered her past connection to him, he should've called Neil right then and put his foot down. Find another ground breaking role model. Not him. His instincts had been on prickly alert and he'd ignored them. Now, he had to deal with the bashing she'd inflicted on him in the article.

His best bet now was to put the article behind him. Hope the small circulation worked in his favor, and no one read it. He certainly hadn't shared his comp copies with his family. Let it slip into oblivion.

He ducked his head and ran up the stairs to the waiting room, gave his name and sat down.

"You again."

The words came from his left and he rotated his head in that direction. The face looked familiar and he remembered why. He'd served time with him in Columbia, but he'd also run into him last month, right here in this very spot.

"Oh, hey man. How are you doin'?"

"Not good at all." The man was stick-thin, even skinnier than he remembered him. He had an itchiness to him, his eyes wide, like any little sound would startle him. He maneuvered around the outstretched legs of the few men sitting between his seat and Jeremy's, squatting down in front of him. He lowered his voice and Jeremy had to strain to hear him.

"This ain't goin' well at all. I was in prison for eight years and couldn't wait to get released. Now I've been out a few months and they're out to get me. I swear they want to send me back there, I swear they do."

Don't get involved, don't get involved. "When you say 'they,' who do you mean, exactly?"

"My probation officer. I'm here today on a disciplinary call. They claim I broke into a gas station but it wasn't me, I swear it wasn't. They don't want people like me outside, they want to send me back."

"Wait. Were you arrested? For a break-in?"

"Yeah, but they let me go. They got nothin' on me. I didn't do it, man!"

"But why were you a suspect?"

"They're treating us like babies. Can't do anything, they start to get suspicious."

This conversation was getting too far into territory Jeremy had no interest in finding himself. He didn't owe this guy anything, and obviously this ex-con was not adjusting well to life on the outside. Best to shut down connections with him ASAP. "Sorry, man. The best you can do is the best you can do. Keep trying. It's not easy but it's worth it."

He planted a look on Jeremy, a combination of irritation and detest. "What are you, an inspirational speaker? What the hell. I got real problems, man. Can't find a job. When I got one, I got fired. They suspect me of a crime just because of who I was hanging out with. Now I'm in trouble with my officer. He's goin' ta be pissed today, man." The man brought his fingers up to his mouth and nibbled on his nail beds, skittering his gaze around like a paranoid soul. "In fact, you better watch yourself, too. Remember Leroy? Leroy White from the big house?"

The name came roaring into Jeremy's head from a long-recessed memory. Leroy, yeah, he remembered him. The decade Jeremy had spent behind bars had brought up several encounters with the big, mean low country man with a nasty streak of violence. Jeremy had just been moved from his first facility to his second, and he was going through the ritualization most men had to go through as a new inmate – establishing where he was going to fit in among the other prisoners.

The meanest and the strongest were in charge. The weakest and the most scared were their servants. Jeremy made sure he was somewhere in the middle, and several times over the course of his imprisonment, he'd had to prove that he wasn't someone to mess with.

Forcing himself to face his apprehensions, to push himself way out of his comfort zone, to fight with his fists, as viciously as possible – to establish where he belonged in the hierarchy. He could remember having to do it at least four times in ten years. He never spoke about it to anyone. But it was critical for survival. Once he proved himself to the new leaders as a fighter, not a wimp, they usually left him alone.

Leroy White was the king of the hill at McCormick Correctional Institution. By the time Jeremy got transferred there about three years into his sentence, Leroy had already fought everyone, sliced anyone he could. He had his servants but was happy to find more. He was a huge, muscular man, accustomed to working his muscles instead of his brain. He'd established his dominance by not only destroying his opponents, but by his opponents coming to the conclusion that bowing to him was preferable to actually fighting him.

Not Jeremy. Although his crime wasn't a violent one, and he had no history of violence in his past, he knew the game and he'd already decided he'd play it. He had a long time to serve and he wanted to emerge as unscathed as possible. The encounter was predictable and he fully expected to be beat to a bloody pulp by Leroy or one of his lieutenants, but he'd give it his best shot and only go down when he was no longer able to stand.

Jeremy ripped his thoughts away from his memory to tune into the words of the ex-con in front of him. "Leroy's out, can you believe it? And he's settled in Myrtle Beach. He can't find work neither, and we ran into each other. He's getting bored trying to keep it clean. He was just telling me he needed a lot more excitement than he's getting, keeping his nose clean. Man, I sure wouldn't put it past him to break into the gas station, steal some cash, get away. Not just for the money, but for the excitement."

Jeremy's pulse increased, his heart pumping wildly. "What was Leroy in for anyway? What was his original crime that put him in?"

The skinny man rubbed a hand over his whiskered chin and adjusted his squat. "Oh wow, I don't know. He was in before me, so we never talked about it. But rumor, from some in his group, he did a little bit of everything. Theft, arson, assault. Never killed no one, as far as I know."

"Wilson." The name floated out over the people in the waiting room and the skinny man's head jerked to the woman at the door calling.

"That's me, man. I gotta go. Wish me luck. Eddie, by the way." He jabbed his hand at Jeremy as he stood. "Eddie Wilson."

Jeremy took it and nodded. "Jeremy Harrison. Good luck. Stay clean."

As the little man sauntered toward the door, Jeremy fought a sick feeling in his gut. The advice was pointless. Eddie wouldn't stay clean and it was just a matter of time until he screwed up and was arrested again.

But Leroy White was worth the nausea all on his own. That nightmare of a man, just eight miles down the road from him?

"Harrison." He got up and went back to Neil's office. Right into Neil's beaming face.

"My man!" Neil presented a huge palm to him to shake. When Jeremy reached his own hand out, Neil pumped it up and down and pounded his shoulder enthusiastically. Painfully. Jeremy coughed, the breath almost knocked out of him.

"Good job, man! Nice article. Doesn't it feel good?"

Jeremy paused, confused. When Neil released him, he made his subtle escape to the chair facing Neil's desk. "What feels good?"

"The article!" Neil picked up an open copy of the magazine from his desk and held it up, Jeremy's picture mocking him. Neil pointed to it. "Don't tell me you didn't read it!"

"I read enough," Jeremy mumbled and looked away.

"Ahhh, now." The disappointment in Neil's voice was evident despite the fact that Jeremy was stubbornly focused on his own lap. "You didn't like it?"

Jeremy looked up first at the article, then Neil's big face, lined with concern. Unable to think of words, Jeremy shook his head.

Neil quietly folded the magazine shut and placed it on his desk. "I can't imagine why."

A surge of anger soared through him again. "She bashed me! She talked about my history of stealing and even made a crack about how I price my pieces as a steal — and I know a *lot* about stealing!" He emphasized in all the appropriate parts.

"Well now, Jeremy. I never knew you to be such a hot head." He picked up the magazine again, flipped through to the article. He scanned it silently. "Okay, here it is. But that was just her hook. The story's about ex-prisoners, so obviously all of you had committed a crime in the past. Yours involved stealing. But did you read on? What came next?"

Neil stared at Jeremy and he felt a little twitchy under the examination. He shrugged, trying to waylay the attention, but Neil wouldn't let it slip.

"Tell me, now. What did the article say after the stealing part?"

"I don't know," he admitted.

"Well, you tell me." Neil leaned forward over his crowded desk, handing him the magazine. Jeremy let out a breath. He knew Neil enough that he'd follow this through to the bitter end. Neil saw it one way, Jeremy saw it another and in a battle of wills, Neil would always win.

Jeremy took the magazine, his eyes on Neil's. Angry thoughts swirled through his head but he wasn't stupid enough to reveal them on his face or in his words.

"Okay, pick up where you left off. Go on." Neil waved his hand at Jeremy.

Jeremy looked down at the print, but the words were not in focus. "You want me to —?"

"Read it." Neil raised his eyebrows at Jeremy. "You know how to read, right?"

Jeremy nodded. He stared at the words until they were clear and began to read. "Jeremy Harrison is a hard-working individual with a ton of talent. The Myrtle Beach area is fortunate to host a furniture craftsman with his skills and potential." Jeremy let the magazine dip and rolled his eyes.

"Go on."

Jeremy sighed and looked into the resolute eyes of his probation officer. He rubbed a hand over his chin and looked at the magazine again. "Harrison is a great example of a rehabilitated offender. He doesn't expect forgiveness, he doesn't want anyone to forget his past sins. He just wants a chance. He'll do what he has to do to work and survive in society. Buying his furniture accomplishes two things. First and foremost, it provides the customer with a solid piece of high quality furniture that will grace any room and last for lifetimes. Secondarily, it helps Jeremy achieve his goal. For purchasing information, see the inlay at the end of this article. You won't be sorry."

Reading the article took a lot out of him, although he wouldn't admit that to Neil. He laid it nonchalantly on the desk, then looked down at his lap, concentrating on calming his shaking hands. Neil knew how to use silence to draw out conversation and he did it often. Like now.

Finally, after Jeremy was breathing normally again, he drew his attention to Neil.

"What do you think now?"

Jeremy shrugged. But he knew that wouldn't be a sufficient response. Neil waited. "It's better than I originally thought. I just don't like the attention, that's all."

Neil frowned. "Do you realize you won't be able to sell furniture if no one knows about you?" He snatched up the mag and pointed out the pictures of him, flipping the pages. "Those are darn fine photos, son. Look at you!" He smiled fondly as he gazed at them. "But beyond the sales approach, that reporter paid you a fine compliment! She said you are rehabilitated. You know what that says to me? That you're a success. You did a crime, you paid your price, and now, you're doing exactly what we asked you to do. You're making yourself a fine citizen. She paid not only you a compliment, but me too!" He jabbed a thumb into his chest. "That's my job, now. I'd say she praised both you and me."

Jeremy sat quietly and mulled over Neil's words. This was a pattern with the both of them. Neil often saw things differently than Jeremy, but when Jeremy thought about it, Neil generally had a point.

Maybe he had a point about this, too. Maybe Emma hadn't been attacking him. Maybe in her own way, she was helping him.

"Thank you, Neil," Jeremy said softly and was gratified to see his officer's face transform into a big, happy smile.

"Atta man. Now, I think the polite thing to do is to call her and thank her very much for the story."

A little dig grabbed Jeremy's stomach, but he wouldn't argue. What point was there to that? Neil was right. "Yeah, okay. I'll call her."

When his appointment ended, Jeremy returned to his truck and pulled the cell phone out of his pocket. He located Emma's number and hit the Call button.

"Hello?" Her voice in his ear caused a shiver, a shortness of breath.

"Hi, Emma?"

"Yes."

"Jeremy Harrison."

"Jeremy! I was wondering if you got the copies."

"Yes, yes I did. Thank you for sending those. And uh, thank you for the article. Really."

"Oh, you read it."

"Yeah, I did."

"What'd you think?"

He paused. "Very nice. Thank you."

He thought he heard her chuckle. "Really?"

"Yes." An awkward conversation, by most standards, but he'd probably never speak to her again, and there was no reason to tell her why he'd been avoiding her for the last few days. He'd gotten here eventually, thanks to Neil. That was good enough.

"Well, I uh," he started.

"Did you read my note? I have a few ideas to help with your advertising. Want to hear them?"

"Sure." He paused, thinking she'd launch into them, he'd jot them down, done.

"I'm off at five. Where will you be after that?"

"I'll be at my sister's inn this evening, the Seaside Inn."

"Working?"

"Yeah."

"Perfect. I'll drop by."

She hung up before he could say good-bye, leaving him with an unsettled feeling.

* * *

The drive back to Pawleys Island went quickly due to very little traffic in the late afternoon. Instead of going straight home, he made a quick turn onto Ocean View Road and headed toward the huge beachfront house on stilts that his dad and new bride Leslie had bought together, beginning their life together just a few months ago. Theirs was a love story filled with long-term devotion to their first spouses, loss of that stable love and depending on prayer to lead them together. He couldn't be happier for his father for finding his second love after a lifetime with Jeremy's mom.

His tires crackled on the seashell mulch covering the driveway to The Old Gray Barn. He pulled up behind Leslie's car, noticing his dad's truck was absent. He jogged up the wooden stairway to the front porch, knocked loudly and pushed the door open, yelling, "Leslie? You here?"

"Sure am!" he heard from the kitchen and he pushed through to head there. She was stirring something in a big pot on the stovetop and she took a moment to pull him into a hug and pat his back before turning back to it. "So nice of you to stop by for a visit. Would you like to stay for dinner?"

Jeremy was well aware that his reputation as a food mooch preceded him, at least among the women in his family. He couldn't help leaning toward the pot and taking a long sniff. A mixed aroma of shellfish, vegetables and broth put a smile on his face. "Wow, Leslie, wow, is all I can say."

"Shrimp gumbo with some whitefish, carrots, celery and potatoes."

Instead of rejecting the invitation immediately like he normally would, he studied the pot for a while. "Is there enough for three?"

She patted his arm. "You could invite a few friends over and we'd still have enough. Your dad set the traps this morning and harvested the shrimp before he left for the day."

It was a deal. Leslie hoisted three plates and silverware settings onto the rustic kitchen table and Jeremy laid them out.

"Where is Dad, by the way?"

"Still working. He should be back within a half hour."

"Business good these days?"

"Sure seems to be. He's got more than he can handle, I know that."

"Really?" The table-setting done, Jeremy took a seat while Leslie laid out half a loaf of homemade bread and a saucer of butter.

"Well, Beach Management calls him every time one of these old houses needs work, often between rental weeks. That could be full-time, but then he's built up some loyal customers he's worked for before, who ask him back. He doesn't like to say no. But he doesn't like to schedule them too far out either, keep the folks waiting."

A bead of sweat popped onto Jeremy's forehead and he wiped it away. This conversation was making him distinctly uncomfortable. This subject was getting dangerously close to . . .

"Yeah," he stammered. He was well aware that his dad had a thriving handyman business, and probably had too much work to handle on his own. Erase fifteen years, and this is exactly the position his father was in then. He'd made his living as a small business person – and raised his family on what he brought in as a single-person business doing whatever handyman work he could get his hands on. He was talented at the work – then and now – but he wasn't that great at the business side of it. Advertising, organizing, estimates, deadlines.

That's why Jeremy had come up with the brilliant idea to go into business with him – Harrison and Son. Expand beyond handyman work and move into contracting, new home construction.

Jeremy came suddenly to his feet, causing Leslie to startle. "Jeremy? You okay?" Her worried eyes followed him as he stood, then paced on the kitchen floor, back and forth.

Harrison and Son – the beginning of the end. The end of his life as he knew it, the end of his freedom, the end of his mother's insurance, and ultimately, the end of her life.

"I gotta go," he threw out, and stumbled out of the kitchen, heading for the front door.

"Wait! Jeremy!" Leslie's voice followed him but he couldn't help it, he had to get out of there. Anxiety attacks were less frequent now than when he was in prison, but this was the start of a doozie. His best plan was to get home, sit in his quiet house and take deep breaths till it passed.

Leslie caught up to him, reached out and wrapped a hand around his bicep. "It's okay, Jeremy. Don't go, please."

He thrashed his arms, catching her hand and throwing it off him. He hoped he hadn't hurt her, but his vision had narrowed to a tunnel and only one object: the door. He had to get there. Everything else in the room went blurry.

He was almost there when the door opened of its own accord. He hadn't pulled it open. He froze, unsure of this turn of events. Then, his dad's face appeared. "Jeremy," it said, friendly and warm.

He plowed past Hank. He heard Leslie's voice and although he couldn't make out her words, he recognized the concerned tone, and then Dad's reaction: he tightened his strong worker-man hands around both Jeremy's arms and brought them tightly down to Jeremy's sides, pinning them there. He guided him over to the couch and into a seated position. Jeremy didn't object, didn't fight it. He knew what Dad was doing, and why, and it was the only choice.

"Take a breath, son. It's all right. Breathe in, that's good. Now hold. Now out. You got it."

Jeremy squeezed his eyes shut and focused on his dad's words and he did as he was told. Breath in, breath out. Soon the overwhelming anxiety started to lift and the breathing was less labored. Finally, he opened his eyes and looked directly into his dad's.

"Sorry," he murmured and turned away.

But his dad pulled him in close and gave him one of those awkward father/son hugs that both parties liked, but neither liked to particularly admit. So much history and meaning was absorbed into that hug and neither of them were talkers, but they knew exactly what was behind it, what came before it, and what the other man would say if he had the inclination to talk.

One more hardy pat on the back, and his dad pulled back and studied his face. "You okay?"

Jeremy sighed. He didn't have to explain. His dad knew. "Yeah."

"Good to see you, son." His dad's smile formed on his sunburnt face and he knew from the way it spread to his blue eyes that he spoke the truth.

"Good to see you too, Dad."

Leslie chose that moment to make her entrance. She had kindly disappeared during the remnants of the attack, but now that he was recovered she came out and greeted her new husband with a kiss, pressing against him.

"Jeremy's staying for dinner with us. I made gumbo out of that delicious shrimp you pulled out this morning."

Jeremy thought of arguing, but it was important to get back to as normal a life as possible, despite the occasional relapse. "Yes, thank you. And Leslie ... I'm sorry. Did I hurt you?"

She waved her hand, eliminating the incident just as easily as that. They busied themselves getting the food on the table, sitting down and praying. Before he knew it, the anxiety attack was ancient history.

* * *

After dinner, Jeremy drove to Marianne's inn. Along the right side of the long building, in the back facing the ocean, he walked to the storage shed. He flipped out a tarp, then pulled out a baby's changing table and dragged it into the center. He examined the half-finished piece, remembering the pregnant woman and her husband who had hired him at the craft fair. Their joy and enthusiasm about their new family had beamed on their faces. He was doing an entire set – crib, dresser and changing table – eventually painted white and he'd promised them in three weeks' time. From the looks of the mom, the aggressive date would still be pushing it.

"Hi."

He was so absorbed in thoughts of the young couple, he hadn't even been looking for her. "Hello there."

For some reason, his words made her giggle. Which caused a twinge of ... something ... in his belly.

"What's this?" she asked and came close. He took a deep breath when she neared and the scent of coconut and skin lotion made him grin despite himself. He couldn't help staring, her brown hair pulled into a tight ponytail that bobbed each time she turned her head, and her face beaming with natural joy and beauty.

She was waiting for a response to her question and instead he was staring at her like a gawking teenager. She looked up at him, her eyebrows popping up in curiosity.

Focus, focus, he told himself. "Nursery set. Did you see the pregnant woman at the craft fair?"

She shook her head.

"She was big – probably due any week now. Anyway, they wanted a custom-made furniture set with a crib, a dresser and a changing table. This is their first baby and they plan to have more so they'll be able to pass it down."

"Oh," she whispered, and then he was flustered to see tears in her eyes. "Jeremy, do you know what this means?"

He shrugged, at a loss over her emotional reaction.

"You will be a part of this young family. You'll build this beautiful furniture for their first little baby and it'll be passed on to more children, and more generations. You're not just filling a furniture order. You're helping build their legacy to their family." She reached up and rested her hands on his arms, cupping his elbows. "This is so special, don't you see that?"

A smile leapt onto his face, pleased at her revelation. And the feel of her hands on him.

"You're an artisan, Jeremy, building special items for families to share."

Where her hands rested on his arms, a warmth blossomed, and his heart raced in response. In her excitement, she dropped her hands and dug in her purse that was strapped over her shoulder. She grabbed a tiny notebook from it and jotted something down. Concentration on the task made her tongue poke out the corner of her mouth and for just a moment he imagined tasting it with his own.

Until he forced himself to look away. Holy moly, what was he thinking?

"Okay," she announced. She started to turn the notebook toward him, then guarded it back into her chest. "This is just an idea, but see what you think of this as a way to brand your work."

She revealed the scribbling. In the corner was a small seascape – ocean waves with a sun overhead, crashing onto the sand. A message read, "Made for your family by Jeremy Harrison. It is my hope that this piece of custom-made furniture, built especially for you and yours, holds a place of honor in your family for generations to come."

He knew she was watching for his reaction as he read it. "Uhhh,…"

"Do you like it?" she asked with a smile. "We could have them made in mass, laminated, maybe a photograph of the beach in the background, and then place them inside the furniture somewhere – in a drawer or taped underneath a table. A little treasure your customers will find." She studied the scrap of paper, then looked back at him. "What do you think?"

He had very little thought about the idea. In truth, he wouldn't bother with it if it were up to him. He was still very new to the furniture building business, and who was he to presume that his furniture would be sturdy enough and special enough to be passed down for generations? He had never been one to toot his own horn, and now, less than ever.

But what he did think about was her reaction to her idea, and the fact that she was doing this for him. She was enthused and moved to tears about a way to help him in his business. And that was something he could never forget.

"I think it's great."

She beamed her smile. "Really? Do you mind if I move forward with designing and producing these cards? I'll keep you posted along the way and I'll let you know of budget."

"You'd do that for me?"

"Well, I don't think you'd have time to do it. With all the jobs you have in progress here, you're busy building. I like the idea and I think it sets you apart, so I'll go ahead and work on it and see if I can't take care of that for you."

Standing close to her, breathing in her scent and listening to her rave about his business, his heart felt fuller than he'd ever remembered it. He lifted the control he generally kept over his emotions and his actions, and lost himself for a moment.

He leaned in, put his lips on hers and closed his eyes. For a second, there was no movement, no sound, no sight. Then, she reciprocated. Her lips moved and she tilted her head. He rested his hands behind her neck, then feathered his fingers through her hair. Their lips danced, in tune with each other. He couldn't remember the last time he'd shared such an intimate kiss with a woman.

He broke their contact and watched her, his breath coming in little pants. He didn't have a clue what to do next. She hadn't fought him, of course. But he was way out of practice in the forays of fledgling relationships between men and women.

"That was nice," she whispered.

"Yeah. Really nice."

In the twilight, their bare feet dipping into cool, moist sand and the light disappearing, she looked so good that all he wanted was to do it again. But he stopped himself. This wasn't just about his wants – he'd have to move through this carefully so as not to blow it with her.

"I like you, Jeremy." She said it softly, shyly.

"Good. Because I'm thinking I like you, too."

She giggled again. Why did everything he say make her giggle? Well, it was probably better than some other reactions.

"Let's not make this weird, okay?" she said.

"Okay."

So they discussed more advertising ideas she'd brought as the sun set over the ocean and the gulls chirped overhead. And he couldn't keep his eyes off of her.

Chapter Six

J eremy pulled into the parking lot of the local hardware store. Finishing the baby set would require some supplies — knobs and pulls — and although this place on the island didn't have as much selection as the mega-store in Myrtle Beach, he usually found what he was looking for and it saved time. The sun hit his eyes as he slid out of the truck. It was going to be a hot day for this time of year. He reached back into the truck, grabbed his sunglasses from the visor and slammed the door.

He made his way to the section displaying the handles and knobs and selected a few. Gathering them up, he headed toward the paint section, decided he needed a basket, located one, and loaded it. When he reached the check-out lane, he was the only one in it. He unloaded all his purchases while the clerk rang him up.

He wrote his check for the final amount and handed it over.

"I'll need your license, please." The clerk took it and looked between the license and the check. Then up at Jeremy. Then back to the license. Then back to Jeremy.

Spending a decade in prison had given him instincts that trouble was close, and they weren't failing him now. His hair prickled on the back of his neck and his breathing started to speed up. He tuned in on the man working check-out. He was in his mid-forties and showed signs of having worked hard. His hair was receding, lines etched in his face from wiping sweat off his brow in the sun, and his hands carried the calluses of manual labor.

"Jeremy Harrison?" His words were tense, as if spit out of the man's mouth.

Jeremy stayed alert, but inside, he was rolling his eyes and sighing. It happened occasionally that his name caused a negative reaction. He sure hoped this one wouldn't result in an altercation, but it had happened before and he was ready.

"Yes sir?" He looked the man straight in the eye. A glimmer of recognition swept over him but not to the point of knowing the man's name or even how they knew each other.

"From Harrison and Son Construction?" The man squinted his eyes now, studying Jeremy as if trying to find similarities between the man standing before him and the one he last remembered who answered to that name.

"Used to be. That company hasn't existed for a while now. As I bet you know."

The man handed him his license back and Jeremy slid it into his wallet, replaced it in his pocket. The man's mouth was clamped shut while he finished the transaction and handed Jeremy his bags. When he was done, the squint had become a full-fledged scowl.

"Do we know each other?" Jeremy ventured.

"Oh, I know you all right. Or I should say, I knew you. You took my money to build a house. And you not only left it half done, but the half that was there was shoddy. I had to end up knocking the dang thing down. Set me back a long way. Took me five years before I could afford to build again."

A fireball of nausea flew down Jeremy's esophagus and landed in his stomach. Only by pure will did he avoid running to the bathroom at the back of the store to relieve himself of his breakfast, scant though it was.

"I'm sorry. I'm sure sorry. I know my actions set a lot of people back, caused a lot of pain."

"You're damn right they did. I can't believe you walked right in my store. Years I spent cursing your name up one side and down the other. Now I get the chance to tell you face to face just what a chicken shit loser I think you are."

Jeremy nodded. "Yep. Go ahead." He steeled himself for a barrage of words, studying his work boots. No sound. Nothing. He looked back up at the man who was examining him with a curious look on his face. "Give me all you got," Jeremy encouraged.

"I just did."

Jeremy lifted one side of his mouth. "Hey, whatever you got to give me can't be any worse than I told myself, sir. Ten years I sat in prison. Gives a man a long, long time to consider his mistakes. I was young, I was stupid. I was immature, I was greedy. I took a perfectly stable and honest business my dad had worked for years and destroyed it. I became a dishonest man and I never stopped, until the law stopped me. Believe it or not, half of me is glad that I got arrested and charged. Because it finally forced me to stop the runaway train."

Both men were silent for a few moments. "You're not gonna get sympathy from me, if that's what you're after."

"No, I'm not after that at all. I deserve every nasty word, every nasty look, every time my name's been run through the mud. I earned that, fair and square."

The man's face had calmed, the lines less pronounced, his mouth looser.

Jeremy held out his right hand. "I'd like to say I'm sorry. I'm sorry for all my actions and how they impacted you. I'm sorry for the hurt I caused you. I mean it, sincerely. I know it doesn't erase what I did, but I want you to know, I did serve my time. I did a lot of thinking and I've reformed. Now that I'm out, I do my very best every day to never go down that road again. I'm under probation and I never miss a meeting with my officer. I'm going to do it right this time."

The man listened, keeping eye contact through Jeremy's apology. But he hadn't reached out and taken Jeremy's handshake. That was okay. Jeremy dropped his hand quietly, grabbed his purchases and made for the door. "Have a nice day, sir."

When he was safely outside, Jeremy let out a breath, and took a moment to calm his racing heart. He bent at the waist, resting his hands on his knees. Eyes squeezed shut, he let his prayer fill his mind, *You're with me, Lord. Stay by my side. Help me every day.* Then, he straightened, stretched out his tight shoulders and went on with his day.

* * *

Emma finished her work day and on her way to the car, decided it was time to make a visit to Grieders' Stables. It had been a week or more since she'd gotten her horse fix. She rarely let that much time pass between stops.

Buckling her seat belt, she pulled out of the parking lot but curiously, instead of turning in the direction of her little apartment in Myrtle to change into her stable clothes, the car turned in the opposite direction, almost like it was its own decision. She smirked and went with it. The car was heading toward Pawleys Island.

She savored the bright sun shining through her windshield, and when the road dipped close enough for a glimpse of the ocean, she took notice. Even though she was born and raised here, she wasn't the type to not appreciate the beauty and her luck at being native. By the time the little car was crossing the bridge to the island, her radio was blaring and she was singing along: "Lay down, Sally! No need to leave so soon!"

When she was only a few blocks from Jeremy's house, she reminisced on last night's kiss. Again. Afterward, she'd laid in bed, absentmindedly running her fingers over her lips, grinning. It was a good kiss. It was a good start.

Of course, the smart side of her brain cautioned her. *Not a good match. Not a good fit. He could hurt you. With his history … and what he did to your family.*

She shoved those thoughts out of her head. He'd made mistakes and served his time. He was a different man now.

And she liked him.

She couldn't help the attraction she felt for him. She'd fought it, hadn't she? And her heart wanted what it wanted. Just then, she made herself a promise. She wouldn't over-analyze this one. She'd take it day by day and just let it be.

She pulled in front of his house, ran to the door and knocked. The fact that there was no answer even after waiting a little while, coupled with the sight of his big monstrous pickup truck sitting right there in the driveway, led her to walk around the back. And she was rewarded with the sight of Jeremy, his tee shirt soaked in sweat and clinging to his chest, leaning over the top of a long, squat dresser about waist-high, working the electric sander. He gripped the power tool in his hand, pushing long, even strokes across the smooth wooden surface, back and forth, back and forth. Protective goggles covered his eyes along with the upper half of his face. His biceps bulged and the muscles in his lean back strained against the wet cotton. He took her breath away.

She just stood, enjoying the view.

When he seemed satisfied with his progress, he turned the sander off and pushed his goggles back on his forehead. She did nothing to attract his attention and yet he turned. When he saw her, a big grin popped onto his face. "Emma."

She made her way over to him and forced herself to admire the piece of furniture, not the handsome piece of man who stood in front of it. "Magnificent."

"Thanks. I've been working on it all day. Well, started late last night, actually. I'll be ready to paint it and finish it soon."

"Part of the baby set?" She let her fingers run over the dusty surface.

"Yes. I'm on target to meet the deadline they asked for."

"Cool." She pulled her eyes from the wooden piece to meet his gaze. "Feel like a break? Can I pull you away for a few hours?"

He only hesitated a second and a half. "Okay." He looked up at the sky, probably judging the likelihood of a rain. He lifted a large tarp from the ground and covered the dresser. "I'll need a shower."

She almost objected — she was taking him to a horse stable after all — but bit her tongue.

"I'll be quick."

She smiled and nodded. He led her inside and fixed her iced water, then disappeared. He was right — ten minutes later he emerged with fresh clothes, smelling like men's soap. He stopped in front of her.

"You don't really need to be clean, where we're going."

"Oh?"

She laughed. "One of my favorite spots in the world." He was giving her a curious look like he was trying to solve a mystery. "Do you want a hint? Give me a second."

She walked out the front door to her car, opened the trunk and pulled out a gym bag. Carrying it back in, she set it on the floor and pointed to it. "All the hints you need are in there. Be my guest."

He leaned over to unzip the gym bag. One by one he pulled out items. "Blue jeans, tee shirt, cowboy boots. Hard hat. Are we going to a construction zone?"

She grabbed the hat from him. "Really? Hard hat?" She took his hand and rubbed it over the velvet covering the hardness. "Ring any bells?

He smiled at the black velvet helmet with a little knob on top. "It's a riding helmet. What, are we going to ride horses?"

"That's right! Have you ever ridden before?"

He looked up to the ceiling. "Oh, once? Maybe twice. Long time ago."

She stepped in close. "Don't worry. I'll take care of you." As she looked up at him, he leaned in for a kiss. It wasn't as heart-stopping as last night's, but it was warm and nice and it made her pulse race. When he was once again the one to pull away, she caught the neck of his shirt and pulled him back for one more.

Now they were done.

"Guess we're getting used to the kisses, huh?" She hated to point out the obvious but she felt obliged to acknowledge this new part of the relationship between them.

"Guess we are. You having any issues with that?"

She smiled. "No, I'm not. How about you?"

He shook his head and ran a gentle hand over her hair, like if he pressed too hard he feared she'd break. Although she wasn't fragile, and she had no qualms about showing him that, he was tender with her. And she liked that.

She changed clothes in his bathroom, and they walked out to her car hand in hand. After driving thirty minutes or so, they pulled into Grieders' Stables. During the drive she'd regaled him with childhood stories about the place, and how much the people meant to her, so when Mr. G came striding up to her, she was happy to see that Jeremy treated him with the respect befitting the man she owed so much to.

After a quick introduction, Mr. G said, "You up for some riding today?"

"We sure are!" Emma said with enthusiasm, swinging her gaze over at Jeremy, who didn't look quite as happy as she was.

"Chores are about caught up, this time of day. But poor Apple hasn't had a trail ride in a week or more. Want to take her?"

"Of course. How about a mount for Jeremy?"

He ran a hand over his chin. "Everybody else is either out, or was out this afternoon." He took in Jeremy, his size and approximate weight. "I bet Apple could carry you both."

She nodded. "Thanks, Mr. G. We'll let her stretch her legs, then groom her when we get back."

The old man waved and ambled away. Emma grabbed Jeremy's arm and led him to the barn. "Apple's a sweetheart. She'll give us a nice, trouble-free ride today."

He glanced at her with a dubious expression. "Whatever you say."

She led the way to Apple's stall, released the latch and slipped inside. The horse neighed softly in recognition and nuzzled Emma when she got close. She lifted her arms, wrapping the big animal in a hug. She looked over at Jeremy, who was studying her actions. "Don't be scared."

"Oh, I'm not. I've been through worse."

She froze for a second. Yes, she imagined he had been through worse. In the ten years he'd spent in prison, she was positive he'd encountered his share of trouble and danger. Lots of situations he'd have to fight his way out of, or else he'd be injured or worse. But that part of his past was the last thing she wanted to talk about today. And from the tense look on his face, it appeared he didn't want to talk about it either.

"You want to come in here and meet Apple?"

He moved immediately, pushed himself off from his lean against the wall, and followed her through the door and into the stall. He must've come to terms with his uncertainty around the horse because he held his flattened palm out like a pro, let Apple smell and nuzzle it, then lifted his hand, laid it on the horse's neck and ran it down to her haunch.

"Good. You're a natural."

He smiled. "Can she tell how fast my heart is beating?"

"Nope. But if your hands are shaking, she can detect it through the reins."

He shook out his arms and clapped once, causing Apple to bob her head in surprise. "Oops, sorry, girl. No jitters here. I'm ready for ya."

Emma took a lead rope that hung inside the stall and snapped it onto Apple's halter. She led the horse out, onto the cement floor hallway outside the stall door. She tied the rope securely to a metal ring attached to the wall. "She'll be safe here while we go get her grooming supplies and tack. You know, her saddle and bridle."

Jeremy nodded and followed Emma about two doors down. A stall, same size as Apple's, had been transformed into a tack room with at least ten saddles resting on stands sticking out from the wall. Emma grabbed one and handed it to him, along with a bridle and a bucket of grooming tools. They returned to Apple and quickly brushed her down to get the dust and straw off, then Emma saddled her up. Jeremy stood back and observed.

"Talk about being a natural."

She smiled. "I've spent most of my life around these creatures. I'm lucky." She stepped back from Apple, now ready for their ride. "I'm thinking the best way for us to ride tandem is for you to sit behind the saddle...," she patted the spot on Apple's back, "and me to sit in the saddle itself. I don't think there's room for both of us in the seat."

"Whatever you say, boss."

"It's an English hunt seat saddle, which means there's not a lot of room."

"Yeah, okay. I'm fine with it."

Emma put her left foot in the stirrup and swung herself up on the horse. Then she kicked the same foot free from the stirrup and said, "Okay, you do the same thing I just did, but land behind me."

Jeremy swung up and landed behind the saddle. The only question was, what did he grip to help him stay on? She suggested several options for him — nothing to hold on behind him, maybe hold onto the back of the saddle in front of him.

"I'm starting to reconsider this," Emma said. "You have no stirrups, no reins and no saddle. You'd have to rely entirely on your balance and you're not experienced enough to have it yet. Plan B."

And with that, she slid off the horse, landing on both feet on the ground. "Here, scoot forward, into the saddle." He did, lifting his legs and rear end over the back of the saddle, and rested in the seat.

"Now, me." Emma put her foot in the stirrup and swung up behind him. She leaned forward and wrapped her arms around him, holding tight. She settled her hands casually over his stomach, the firm abs apparent through the thin tee shirt fabric. "Fringe benefit. I'll be fine."

He turned his head. "You sure?"

"Yeah. But you'll have to steer. Go ahead and grab the reins and I'll give you a quick lesson."

A few minutes later, they took off. Emma loved the trails that surrounded the stables. Whether she was on a short ride or a long one, there were many paths to choose from. This time, for Jeremy's sake, she kept Apple to a trail that was a fairly direct shot from home. A well-worn dirt pathway cut through a big, open pasture with grass about two feet deep. Birds chirped as they flew overhead and the grass blowing in the faint breeze sounded a little like applause. Apple knew the trek well and moved forward with little guidance from her riders.

Although she'd ridden her share of bareback and could've balanced without help, she wrapped her arms around Jeremy from behind and leaned in against his back. His scent of bath soap and wood chips filled her nostrils. Her close proximity to him allowed her to hear his whisper.

"What?"

"I said, 'Amen,'" he said with a chuckle.

She chuckled. "You were praying?"

"Can't hurt, right? Praying for no injuries, for you or for me." He rubbed a hand over Apple's neck and gave it a little pat. "Although mostly for me."

She swatted his back.

"Let's face it. I need the prayers more than you do. You have skill and know-how."

They settled into the pace and gait of the horse underneath them. "So do you pray a lot?" she ventured.

"Oh, yeah. Habit I picked up, you know, while I was incarcerated. I mean, I prayed before that, I was a Christian and was raised to go to church. But it became a way of life in prison."

A moment passed while she pondered that. "Because ...?"

His chest expanded as he took a big breath, let it out. "Life wasn't easy in there. You had to keep your wits about you to survive. I figured out early on, I didn't want to be alone. I needed to rely on God to watch over me and get me through."

She had no idea what life in prison was like. Other than movies and TV shows, and those probably weren't authentic. "What was it like in there?"

As Apple strolled away the distance under her feet, the question hung in the air. She knew he'd heard her, but the longer it went unanswered, she wondered if she should repeat herself.

"I don't want to talk about it. No offense, but I haven't really talked to anyone about it. Other than God. He was there with me so I wouldn't have to explain anything." He smiled and she saw his cheeks move from behind him. "I spent a decade of my life paying for my mistakes. I learned how to live in there, but that doesn't mean I liked it. Now,

I'm all about the future and making sure that I'm a good man and a productive citizen. No sense looking behind me."

She nodded, although he couldn't see her. His approach made sense. They sank into a comfortable silence, their bodies moving in time to Apple's stride. "Church was one of those things my parents quit doing when my dad started having his problems."

She regretted saying it when his shoulders tensed. She hadn't brought it up to make him feel bad. But it was unavoidable — Jeremy was at the heart of the worst event that had happened in her family. The fact that he had paid his debt and was sorry about it, didn't change that.

Deciding to forge ahead with her point, she said, "I remember enjoying church and youth group. I loved the church building itself. The sanctuary, the rows of pews, the red cushions and carpet. And the pipe organ. I not only loved to hear it — huge mountains of sound filling the big room — but I was fascinated by the pipes themselves. The thought that all those pipes of different lengths actually carried music and blasted it out their ends. Amazing."

She was happy that he seemed to relax. She placed her hands squarely on his back, massaging him across its expanse. She smiled when he moaned.

"I could get used to that. That feels wonderful."

She kept it up. It not only made him happy, it gave her a great excuse to put her hands on him and feel his muscles with nothing but a thin layer of cotton between them. Eventually her fingers fatigued and she had to stop. He turned his head toward her with a smile. "Thank you for doing that."

"Sure."

She did a quick calculation in her head. They'd probably covered at least three miles by now, and Jeremy was doing great. He seemed to have a natural seat and wasn't having any trouble at all. Why not venture into more challenging terrain? "Let's take this left here. It's a little more up, down, rocky, woodsy path."

He snorted. "I graduated from slow walking on the flat grass? You may be giving me more credit than I'm due."

He followed her instruction and steered the horse. Apple chose her footing a little more carefully, balancing her riders on her back as she maneuvered down a rocky path. Jeremy and Emma had to be more cautious as well, ducking when a tree branch crowded them. After a few minutes, Emma was able to continue with the topic she didn't want to let drop. "So do you go to church now, Jeremy?"

"Yeah. Not the one I grew up in. I still know way too many people there, families who know my story. Not that I'm trying to deceive anyone or hide anything. It's just that I want a fresh start. So I found a nice church about ten miles away. Very welcoming, good services. I enjoy it. Gives me a little break from work in the week, too."

She waited to see if he'd say anything else. When it was clear he wouldn't, she debated either thumping him across the head, or just coming out with what was on her mind. "I wouldn't mind going with you sometime."

Again he turned his head so she could see his smile. "Really?"

"Yes, really. Would you take me?"

"Absolutely."

"Okay then." She squeezed his mid-section with both her arms for good measure.

Apple stumbled, then righted herself. Jeremy jerked forward and Emma did too.

"Whoa, baby girl," Emma said softly. Apple continued walking, but then stumbled again, this time coming to a halt on her own. This was so unlike her, Emma felt a creeping anxiety in her heart. "Apple …"

As they stood motionless, Apple raised her left front hoof off the ground and held it there. "Jeremy, something's wrong. We need to get down and check her out." She slid off Apple's back in a whoosh and Jeremy followed suit. Emma raced to the horse's head and rubbed her face, murmuring soft sounds of comfort. She took hold of the lifted hoof and examined it, using her finger to touch it gently. Apple bobbed her head and responded with a neigh and a firm push of air out her nostrils.

"I don't see anything in this hoof. No rocks wedged in, no cuts or abrasions. But she's obviously favoring this foot." Emma ran her hand down the leg and noted that it was more swollen and puffy than usual. That symptom, combined with the tenderness of the foot, gave her a quick diagnosis: Apple had gone lame.

She quickly examined the other three legs, running her hands down from thigh to hoof, tapping the hoof itself to determine if any were tender. They weren't. Just the front left. She turned and met eyes with Jeremy. She brushed a tear out of her eye. This animal was like a family member. She hated seeing her in pain.

"Looks like Apple's one leg is lame. It's swollen around the knee, and the hoof is so tender she can't put any weight on it. She's in pain, Jeremy. We have to get her home, but we can't ride her back."

His eyes went wide. "Can she walk?"

Emma thought of the distance they'd covered, an estimated four miles, maybe more. "No way. We need to call Mr. Grieder and ask him to bring the trailer to transport her."

Jeremy nodded his head and reached for the phone in his pocket. Pulling it out, he tapped at the screen with his finger. His eyebrows took a dive. "I don't have any bars at all out here. How about you?"

Emma shook her head. "I didn't bring my phone. It's in my purse locked in my trunk."

Jeremy stepped closer to the horse, patting her haunch, murmuring soft words to her and running his hand down her swollen leg. He glanced up at Emma, concern carving lines in his forehead. "Did I do this, Emma? Was I too heavy for her and caused injury to her leg?"

A little hand gripped her heart. A man that had concern for animals, in her book, was a man worth keeping. "Oh Jeremy, I don't know. It could be, or maybe not. We have no idea why she went lame. Maybe she's got a broken bone and Mr. Grieder didn't realize it. Maybe this rocky path was too much for her with both of us onboard. But please," she ran her hand over his arm to emphasize her point, "don't blame yourself for this. You did nothing wrong."

His tension eased slightly as he gave her a reassuring smile and looked back at the horse. "I hate to see her in pain." He gave his head a slight nod as if he'd come to a decision. "You stay here with her. I'll hike back to the barn and get Mr. Grieder."

"Are you sure? Or I could do the walking."

"You're better with Apple. Keep our patient as comfortable as possible. I'll keep an eye on my phone during the trek and see if I can make a call eventually. Regardless, I'll get back to the stable in less than an hour and we'll bring the trailer as soon as we can."

She studied his face, trying to deal with the overwhelming emotion in her heart. "Thank you," she whispered.

He gave her an anxious smile and a quick peck. Then, looking around, he said, "You might want to see if you can get her back to the open pasture. Not sure the truck and trailer could come down this far."

"Good point. We'll take it slow."

Chapter Seven

Jeremy made his way cautiously, his boots stumbling over the rocky terrain of the advanced path. Last thing he needed was a twisted ankle when Emma needed his help and he alone could provide it. After a half mile, the path spilled out into the open pasture they had ridden through. The sun baked him as he walked on the thin dirt path through the high grass. A bead of sweat popped out on his brow.

The rest of the trip would be manageable at a faster pace. He launched into a jog, kept that pace about ten minutes, then slowed, disheartened by his panting. Although he was never what you'd call an athlete, he had always been in decent shape, without spending hours in the gym ensuring that it was so. As a kid, he could run all over the island, from friend's house to friend's house, without increasing his breathing rate at all. Of course, he wasn't a kid anymore. He'd probably spent more time and effort working out when he was in prison, than any other time in his life. It was an approved activity, a way to get out of the cell. As one day blended endlessly into another, exercise offered a way to break the drudgery.

Sweaty men lifting weights, running the track, initiating altercations just because they were bored. Jeremy kept to himself, stayed in the corner, keeping a careful eye on the action-makers.

He shook the unwelcome memory out of his head and kept walking. He figured he'd swallowed at least a mile of the trip, three left. His thoughts circled back to Emma, wondered how she was doing with Apple, helping her past the tricky ground to the open pasture where she could rest. If anyone could persuade Apple to walk with the injured leg, it would be Emma. That girl was great with horses. You could see it just by watching the two of them together.

As his walk stretched out, his mind wandered to a topic he hadn't let himself think too much of: he and Emma. Warmth ran through his chest at the thought of being part of a couple. Was it too soon to think of Emma and himself as a couple? What was she thinking?

He truly was in a different world here, with no idea what to do, or in all honesty, how he'd gotten here. Emma seemed to be pursuing him, and he had absolutely no idea why she would. With the history of pain he'd inflicted on her family, why would she want anything to do with him? He couldn't get his mind around that. However, he couldn't deny that she showed signs of liking him. The kisses. The visits. The offers of help. And, the kisses.

He smirked as he walked. If anyone could hear his thoughts, they'd accuse him of an extremely juvenile mindset. And they were probably right. What did he know about women?

One thing was sure, he decided, keeping his steps moving forward. He was open to this unexpected addition to his life. He'd never dreamed he'd have the good fortune of meeting a good woman — a beautiful, talented woman like Emma — and forming a relationship with her. He would consider it a gift from God, to a sinner who didn't deserve it, and treat it that way — with care and tenderness. There were so many ways he could screw this up, either unintentionally due to inexperience, or by slipping into bad habits. But the mere presence of a woman like Emma in his life showed God's promise to him that he could earn a normal life back.

Someday.

Soon, Grieders' Stables rose on the horizon and he jogged the remaining distance. He entered the barn but wasn't sure how to locate Mr. Grieder. Yelling his name out like a maniac probably wasn't the approach he wanted to take. Fortunately, as he stalked through the building he ran across a door marked "Office." He knocked and waited till a man's voice told him to enter.

"Mr. Grieder, there's been an incident."

The old man stood right away, his forehead creased with lines of worry. "Is it Emma? Did she take a fall?"

"No, sir," Jeremy replied, his heart just a little warmer that the man's first concern was for Emma. "It's Apple. She began limping and Emma examined her. Her left front leg is swollen. Emma thinks Apple is lame."

The man limped out from behind his desk. It was probably unnecessary but Jeremy finished as he followed Mr. Grieder through the door, "Emma wants you to bring the trailer to pick her up."

The horseman waved a hand over his head and they went to the big pickup truck outside already attached to a horse trailer. Mr. G hoisted into the driver's seat. Jeremy raced around to the passenger side and barely got in and had the door closed when the truck took off.

"Where are they?"

"We'd gone through the big pasture and just onto a rocky path."

Mr. G nodded as if that made perfect sense. "I can use the road for a couple miles, then pick up the pasture on the north gate and drive through that way."

Jeremy nodded. As they drove, tension filling the air, Mr. G said, eyes straight ahead, "You and Emma?"

Jeremy hesitated. How would Emma want him to answer that vague question? "Friends."

Mr. Grieder nodded. It seemed to be enough but Jeremy felt compelled to continue, "We haven't known each other long but she is a really nice woman."

Mr. G puckered his lips. "Love her like she was one of my own. Known her long enough for her to be my own. Great girl."

Jeremy mulled that over. Although he glanced over, the old man stayed fixed on the road. Was there a warning issued in those words? Or was he just being paranoid? "I'm looking forward to getting to know her better."

A moment of silence passed and he hoped he'd satisfied the man's unspoken questions. Jeremy was ready to let the uncomfortable subject drop.

Then, "You take good care of her, and behave yourself, now."

A smile popped onto Jeremy's face. "Yes, sir. I sure will."

They arrived at the north gate. Jeremy jumped out and opened it, then closed it again after Mr. G drove the rig through. He half-expected the old guy to take off without him in his haste to locate his favorite girl. But he didn't. Jeremy hopped into the truck again and off they went, bouncing so heartily that he wondered if he'd need a trip to the chiropractor after all was said and done.

Emma and Apple waited right at the spot Jeremy thought they'd be. Apple stood with her injured leg bent, in no apparent distress. Mr. G went right to the horse and bent, gently running fingers over the leg. Emma waited expectantly for a verdict. He straightened slowly, patted the horse's chest and said, "Yep, she's lame."

"Poor baby. I shouldn't have taken her out today," Emma said in a rush. "I shouldn't have put two people on her and I shouldn't have taken her down there." She pointed to the entrance in the trees to the rocky path.

Mr. Grieder came closer and pulled her into a hug. "Hush, now. There were no signs. She's been fine. It's sort of like starting your car. Every day it starts fine. One day, it won't start. The battery's dead. It happens. We'll call Doc Weaver and he'll take care of her. Don't you worry."

Emma squeezed him and nodded. They worked together to coax Apple into the trailer. Once back to the barn, Mr. G called the vet, who came out on an emergency call. He treated her the best he could, with wraps and medication. Apple was getting a vacation. Rest and relaxation till she felt better.

It was 2 AM by the time Emma dropped Jeremy off at his house. She started to open her car door.

"No, I don't want you walking out there in the dark."

She smiled and sat back in the seat. Jeremy leaned in and ran his fingers under her hair at the base of her neck. Her soft strands felt like silk cascading over his hand. He watched for invitation in her eyes and seeing it, he placed his lips on hers, slowly brushing them, side to side. She gasped and he deepened the contact, extending it to a long, passionate exercise that caused his heart to explode. The kiss lasted forever, and yet, not nearly long enough. He broke contact and pulled back slightly to look at her. Her eyes were closed, her skin was flushed and her hands waited restlessly in her lap. But not for long. She reached for his face and without opening her eyes, she pulled him back. This time, she ran her tongue over his lips. He opened his mouth and they began a whole new adventure.

He wanted to lose himself in the moment, and yet he was afraid that if he did, his hands would betray him and he would take a step that would destroy their budding relationship. He needed to take this slow. He couldn't be greedy. He needed to put her needs in front of his own.

So, he forced his hands to stay in the vicinity of her face, her hair, her neck. It was enough, he told himself. More than he deserved, but he would willingly accept. When their passion slowed, he ended their intimacy by placing one more kiss squarely on her lips. "You are so beautiful, Emma."

Her happy beam rewarded him. "And you're a great kisser," she replied.

He smiled in wonderment. "You must bring out the best in me."

That pleased her. "Look, I'm sorry for such a late night. Hopefully you won't be yawning all day tomorrow."

"I'll be okay. But what about you? Don't call your interview subject by the wrong name."

"Don't slice off a finger with one of those power tools."

"Ouch."

She laughed, then quieted, looking at him intently. "Good night, Jeremy."

"Good night, Emma." On his way to the front door, she drove off and it occurred to him he hadn't asked her for another date. Dang, he had to get up to speed on this dating stuff.

* * *

Jeremy managed to wait a few days before calling Emma. He didn't want to seem over-eager, even though the amount of time he spent thinking about her proved he clearly was. "I'd like to take you out to dinner."

She giggled. "Oh, like a date? A real date where you scrub up, put on a nice outfit, pick me up and take me to a restaurant?"

Her joke struck him speechless for a moment. If she put that much pressure on him, he was going to feel nervous. "Well, I can't promise too much scrubbing or the niceness of the clothes. But I will pick you up and take you to an actual restaurant. How's that?"

"Hmmm, will you pay the check?"

"Of course."

Deal." They settled on a time, and when it came, Jeremy pulled his truck into a parking spot at her complex. He slid down from his seat and located the right apartment. Emma opened the door immediately when he knocked and it gave him the idea she'd been standing just inside the door, waiting for him. Whether it was true or not, he kind of liked that.

"Hi," she said. She grabbed his hand and pulled him inside.

"Hi." He looked around the place. It was the first time he'd seen Emma's place. It was cozy and colorful. The walls were painted an ambitious shade of royal blue, with white trim. Her couch, setting in the middle of the main room, was red; cushions strewn across it were yellow, lime green and purple. "You like color."

"You think?" she asked playfully. "Come here." Still holding his hand, she pulled him closer. As their lips joined, she laid her free palm on his chest.

This woman released emotions in him that were either long buried, or he'd never known before. By simply placing her hand on his chest as they kissed, fireworks exploded inside him. He placed his hand on top of hers and squeezed it.

"Want a tour?"

He nodded, unable to speak momentarily while his breathing evened and he concentrated on reducing one particular body part back to normal size.

She led him to the kitchen, a breakfast nook, down the hall to a closet containing a washer and dryer, poked his head into the bathroom, then into the bedroom at the end of the hall. That's it, just a one-bedroom apartment, but it was all adorable like her, clean and neat and reflected her love for books, horses, the beach and … volleyball?

"Did you play volleyball?" He picked up a pair of trophies, one in each hand, while studying several more like them that he left on her dresser.

"Yeah, star center at Myrtle Beach High."

He nodded, impressed. "Nice job. Did you play in college?"

She shook her head. "My height betrayed me. You can play pretty decent volleyball in high school when you're only five seven. But college is a whole 'nother story. Those chicks are all six foot two or taller." She shrugged. "I didn't mind. I enjoyed it, and I had a lot of great experiences on the team. Met a lot of great friends. Traveled some. But I was ready to leave it behind me. College was for studying and learning and preparing for my future."

He set the trophies back. "Wow. You sound like you were one mature college girl."

"I'm the first in my family to ever go to college. I was determined to do it right and not blow the opportunity."

He nodded. "I was the first in my family, too." Then he dropped his head, let out a breath. "But I guess we both know how that turned out." He turned to the door.

She patted his back. "You're doing the best you can now, aren't you?"

He turned back and met her eyes. He nodded. He refused to feel sorry for himself for how his life turned out. Why would he? He had no one to blame but himself. No one did this to him. It was his decisions, his mistakes. But he wasn't about to let his past ruin his future. Or for that matter, tonight.

"Would you like to go?"

She burst out in a grin. "Yep." She headed for the door, then turned around and gave him an exaggerated examination, down, then up. "You scrub up well, by the way."

He laughed and followed her out.

He'd chosen a place called Quigley's Pint and Plate. It was casual, moderately priced, but didn't scream chain restaurant. It was the only place in town with its own brewery. The menu offered a wide variety of entrees, seafood and otherwise, as well as sandwiches, burgers and salads.

On the drive there, Emma turned and looked out the back window. "Aren't you turning there?"

He shook his head. "No, why?"

She shrugged. "I just figured you'd want to go to the Seaside Inn. Their food is terrific, and you have an in with the owner."

"Nope, not tonight. I want you all to myself, and I don't want to share you with my sister and my niece, both of whom would be torturing us all night long." He smiled.

They arrived at Quigley's. Inside, they sat at a table by the window that offered them a gorgeous view of the ocean. They had just ordered drinks when Jeremy heard, "Fancy meeting you here."

He looked up and saw his stepmother, Leslie, and his dad standing a few steps away, looking sheepish. "Oh, hi, Leslie."

She turned and motioned to his dad, who stepped up and nodded.

"Leslie, Dad, this is Emma Slotky. Emma, my dad, Hank Harrison and his new bride, Leslie."

Emma went into high gear, smiling, greeting, shaking hands and making them feel welcome. Her genuine pleasure at greeting them made him want to eat his previous careless comments about family. Not for the first time, he just sat back and observed her and thanked God that she was in his life.

"Well, son, we don't want to bother you, but we also didn't want to sit in the corner and not let you know we were here. We'll get our own table now." His dad was backing away.

"Nice to meet you, Emma," said Leslie warmly and turned to follow her husband.

Then Emma said, "Why don't you join us? We haven't ordered yet and the table's plenty big enough for four."

His dad politely declined, just as Leslie was agreeing with enthusiasm. Jeremy sighed and discretely rolled his eyes at his dad.

Of course, the four dined together. His parents got to know Emma, and she got to know them too, and Jeremy had to admit that he hadn't had quite that nice a dinner in a very long time.

* * *

A few days later, Jeremy was beginning work on a large dining room table. His trio of baby furniture was finalized and delivered and the parents couldn't be happier. Well, with the furniture. The mom was now overdue and dreadfully uncomfortable, so they weren't happy about that. Hopefully that baby was on its way soon.

He worked, set up on the tarp in his backyard. His wood stock was measured, double measured and cut. He cut his notches in the right place, and he was now gluing the various pieces of the table legs together, clamping them in place to his big metal work table, to aid in proper drying. He was so engaged in his work that when his dad circled around the house and entered the backyard, he didn't even notice till his dad said his name.

His head jerked up. "Hey, Dad."

Hank walked over to study the pieces of wood, long and short, notched and straight. "What's this gonna be?"

"I call it a Farm House table. It's a big long dining table, probably hold ten comfortably."

Hank nodded, looked around at a few other projects in various stages of completion. "Business good, son?"

"Yeah, it's getting there. It feels like I'm busy all the time. Which is good. Not making a mint, but I'm making ends meet." He patted his dad on the back. "Life is good, Dad." He smiled, knowing his dad worried about him. Dads do that, but their circumstances were so far from normal. The fact that his dad even spoke to him was a miracle, considering everything Jeremy had put him through. Their relationship was another gift from God, a gift wrought from patience, forgiveness and grace. "I'm about ready for a break. Feel like a glass of lemonade? I've got some inside."

Hank nodded and followed Jeremy into the house. "I finished a job today and found myself with a few free hours."

"Great. So business is good for you, too." Jeremy pulled two tall glasses out from the cupboard and filled them with ice. Then he reached into the refrigerator and poured them full of lemonade.

"Son, things just couldn't be better."

They took their drinks into the living room and sat, facing each other in the small room. "I can't tell you how glad I am to hear that, Dad. I suppose Leslie has something to do with that, eh?"

His old man ducked his head, found a spot on his jeans leg and scrubbed at it a little. "That woman is a blessing, that's for sure. She's just what I needed, at exactly the time I needed it. God was watching out for me, I know that."

Jeremy nodded as he drank. He agreed with his dad's thoughts. Their story was nothing short of miraculous, and the transformation that Leslie helped forge in his dad's then-lonely, sad existence was impressive.

"You enjoy living at the beach?" The Old Gray Barn had a large part in their story — it was where they first met, it was the one piece of real estate that spoke to Leslie and helped convince her to stay here on the island instead of returning to Pittsburgh, and it was where the two of them committed their love to God and each other at a surprise wedding (surprise for Leslie). He never could quite believe his dad had the guts to pull that one off.

"Oh yeah. That old place is special and the view can't be beat. Leslie loves it. She'll wake up early before school and walk the beach every morning. Sometimes I'll join her, sometimes not. But she never misses a day. It's like her fuel to start her engine." He chuckled. He leaned forward and patted Jeremy on the knee. "Say, we really enjoyed meeting Emma the other night. Nice girl, son, really nice girl."

A feeling of embarrassment swept over him and he didn't know why. He was a grown man, and most grown men had relationships with women. But he'd been taken out of commission for so long, he didn't know how to deal with it. "Yeah, she sure is."

"Pretty, too."

Jeremy nodded. "And a good writer."

"Yep."

Both men sat in silence. It seemed their discussion of the new woman in Jeremy's life had ground to a halt and neither of them had the emotional depth to dig any deeper. And neither really wanted to. The acknowledgement was enough.

Hank finished his lemonade and got to his feet. "Well, good to see you, son. Glad things are going well." He put his hands on Jeremy's arms and pulled him in for a hug. "Don't be a stranger. Why don't you bring that little girl over to the house one night for dinner? Leslie loves to cook."

"Will do, Dad. Thanks. And thanks for stopping by."

Jeremy watched Hank drive away, then went back to work.

* * *

A few days had passed and his conversation with his dad still weighed on his mind. His dad was a wise man, a fact sometimes forgotten because his words were few. Jeremy took after him in that way. Neither of them spoke that much, but that didn't mean they weren't thinking. Or feeling.

As he leaned over his latest project, getting into a rhythm, sanding back and forth, his mind focused on his dad. When his mom had died, Hank was lost. Understandably so. They'd been a team for so long, and she'd died such a painful death with leukemia. He'd watched the love of his life dwindle away, the life seeping out of her, till he was left alone. His new life left him with all the same problems — unpaid medical bills, disappointment in the mistakes of his only son, a failed business, inability to make ends meet — but now, without the woman who knew him better than anyone and provided that support system that all people need.

Ten quiet, lonely years went by. While Jeremy spent his time behind bars, trying to repent for his crimes, Hank spent those same years in this tiny, shabby bungalow, alone. Sure, Marianne did her best to include him in her family activities, let him know how important he was to her, Tom and Stella. But life had pretty much been sucked dry of happiness and love for his dad.

Until one day he met Leslie. She caught his eye, his interest, his trust. She wasn't looking for love, and neither was he. But somehow, love grew between the two of them, despite bad timing and broken hearts. And now, look at them. In love, enjoying their life together, sharing their families with each other.

Jeremy stood and wiped a hand over his brow. The sun was particularly bright today for a late November day at the beach. Putting down his sander, he realized what he had to do. Not all important tasks in life were pleasant, and he was sure this one wouldn't be. Didn't mean it wasn't the right thing to do.

He went inside and showered, dressed in fresh clothes and jumped in his truck. The drive to Myrtle Beach passed quickly as he ran through his mind what he wanted, needed to say. He checked the address he'd written on a yellow post-it until he made his way to a quaint reddish ranch house with a carport on the side. He parked on the street and as he walked up the driveway to the front door he couldn't help noticing the shabbiness of the exterior.

The door opened after three doorbell rings. He'd just about given up. Mr. Slotky stood inside, staring at him through the screen door, his eyebrows furrowed.

"Yeah? Who are you? What are you selling?" The man's words slurred and he reached a hand up to rub his forehead.

"Mr. Slotky, could I talk to you for a moment, sir?"

"Who? Who is it?"

Jeremy was well aware that if he came out with his name now, he'd never get inside the house. Mr. Slotky would slam the door in his face, and rightfully so. He needed to somehow delay the introduction until he could get in and share his message.

"Could I come in, please? I'm not a salesman. I have something important I want to talk to you about."

The man studied him through slightly glazed eyes, then amazingly, opened the door. "Just because you're not a salesman doesn't mean you're not selling anything. You look awful familiar and I have a suspicion of who you are."

Once he was inside, Jeremy held a hand out. "Mr. Slotky, I'm Jeremy Harrison."

The moment of silence was a reprieve before the man exploded. "I thought so! You've got a lot of nerve coming here, Harrison. After what you did to me. I have half a mind to punch you. And don't think I couldn't do it, too." He swayed on his feet and dropped the beer can in his hand. Foamy liquid flowed out onto the carpet.

"You have every right to be mad at me, to hate me. I did some awful things, and I hurt a lot of people. I know that, and I take responsibility for that. I wanted to come here and see you face to face to apologize. That's all."

"What makes you think I want to hear your apology? Why would that mean anything at all to me, you big liar?"

Jeremy steadied himself. "Mr. Slotky, I'm not sure if you're aware of this, but I was sentenced to a decade in prison, and I served my time. I was released this summer. And I'm sure anxious to make things right."

"Yeah, well, I do know that because you somehow pulled my sweet daughter Emma Jean into your messy life with that article. How'd you wrangle that one? Get her to feel sorry for you, betray her father?"

The man turned to step away from the door and got his feet tangled in each other. He stumbled and Jeremy reached out to catch him from falling. Mr. Slotky waved an uncontrolled arm, catching Jeremy painfully on the shoulder.

"No, sir, I didn't have anything to do with that article. In fact, I was against it at first. My probation officer asked me to do it, or else I would've turned down the interview. Last thing I want is publicity. I really just want to focus on living an honest life and working hard."

The man sneered, his hatred evident. "How handy that you get to work hard, after all the lives you ruined. So many people laid off from your company, what they would really like is to work hard, but unfortunately there's no jobs out there to be had."

"That's another reason I'm here today, Mr. Slotky. I want to help you find work. I had a couple ideas about that ..."

"Oh you did, did you? Swoop in like a white knight on a steed and help the pathetic old man? Well, I don't need or want your help. I wouldn't touch it with a ten-foot pole. How about that?"

Jeremy gazed around the room, unsure of where to go next. A few empty beer cans littered the tables and a big basket of unfolded laundry sat next to the couch. The paint on the walls was well worn and the carpet showed signs of wear. "Mr. Slotky, listen to me. You need to get back to work, and I'm sure you could use the extra money. Who couldn't? I'd like to help you make a few connections. You were a roofer, is that right?"

"Yeah, that's right."

"Well, my dad, you remember him, Hank Harrison, he works for a management company for rental beach properties. He does the handyman stuff, but I could talk to him about recommending you for any roofing work that needs to be done. These houses are old, and I would guess there would be roofing work." He eyed the beer cans and Mr. Slotky's uneven stance. "Of course, you'd have to be steady on your feet to do that kind of work," he said cautiously. "You think you could still handle working up there at those heights?"

Mr. Slotky shrugged, looked away.

"It wouldn't be full-time work, but just like any construction gig, they'd contract you for the job they need doing and you'd negotiate a price. If you need any help, you could bring a partner on. How does that sound?" He waited for a response.

Mr. Slotky ambled over to a recliner and threw himself into it. "I'm not crazy about taking help from you, young man."

At least his tone had lowered from yelling to conversational. The man looked exhausted and drained.

"I understand that, I really do. I have a lot to make up for, not just with you, but with others too. I'm sorry for what I did. I want to try to make it up to those that I can who are still hurting from my decisions."

Mr. Slotky pointed a finger at him. "I don't want your charity."

"It's not charity. It's trying to do the right thing, because I did the wrong things ten years ago. Can I talk to my dad? See if he'll talk to his management company on your behalf?"

Mr. Slotky's next words were so quiet Jeremy had to lean closer to hear them. "I don't want your pity."

"No sir, I don't pity you. I just want to help." Jeremy took a few steps over to the couch and sat. They both stayed quiet until about ten minutes later, a snore escaped from Mr. Slotky's lips. The man was napping!

Jeremy struggled with the decision to wake him or just leave him be. He'd obviously been drinking, which he supposed was okay since he wasn't working and wasn't driving. There was no car in the driveway or carport, so he supposed Mrs. Slotky had it at work. However, drinking to excess wasn't a good idea, especially if it was a habit. Which Jeremy had no idea if it was or not.

One thing was certain, though. If he was going to stick his neck out and talk to his dad about putting in a good word for Mr. Slotky, the man better clean himself up and show up for work sober.

He pulled a business card out of his shirt pocket and rose, slipped it into Mr. Slotky's hand. The man had some thinking to do. Was his desire for a job stronger than his grudge against past wrongs? Time would tell.

* * *

A few hours later, the sun was setting and it gave Jeremy an idea. He called Emma. "Hi, sorry for the short notice. You got plans tonight?"

He detected a hint of laughter in her voice. "Actually I do. Editing an article for the magazine. There's something wrong with it and I can't figure out what it is. I've procrastinated over it so much at work that now I have to do it at home."

"Ahh, okay." He hoped his disappointment didn't show up in his voice.

"Why, what's up?"

"Oh no, nothing. You've got important work to do."

"I don't know if I'd call it important. It's a story about a new work out center in Myrtle. I interviewed a few of the instructors and a few clients. I'm just having a tough time putting an inspirational slant on it."

"I'll let you get to it. Don't want to interrupt."

They hung up. Thirty minutes later, his phone rang.

"I think what I really need is a distraction. Were you going to offer me one?"

He chuckled. "Are you sure?"

"Absolutely. We artistic types work on a schedule all our own. You can't push your muse. And it's not often consistent with the deadline."

"I'll come get you."

He drove over and went to her door. She opened it with an excited smile on her face, a pair of snug jeans and a sweatshirt. He loved how she was up for anything, spontaneous. Because he wasn't the type to plan too far ahead.

They jumped in his truck and he drove a short distance away from the craziness of Myrtle Beach and into the country. When he pulled up to the entrance, she shrieked. "A drive-in movie theater?"

He nodded with a smile.

"I haven't done one of these in ages!"

The evening brought a brisk chill to the air, but a clear view of the mammoth screen. Jeremy followed a short line of vehicles and picked a spot halfway through the lot, with empty stalls on either side. He turned to her. "Concession stand?"

She nodded happily. They walked across the lot to the building at the far side. The moon shone in the sky and they had to pick their way carefully in the deep dusk. They stood in line, then ordered hot dogs, popcorn and cotton candy, with sodas. They made their way back to the truck just as the screen lit up and started playing previews.

"I can't believe we got all this junky junk food."

Jeremy smiled and lined all the food up on the dashboard. "Dig in, princess. Dates with me are top class, have you noticed?"

She dug into her hot dog with a vengeance, then slowed her pace with the popcorn, tossing a few handfuls into her mouth before pausing.

"Hey uh, I want to tell you something," he started.

She looked at him. "That sounds ominous."

"No, no. At least, I don't think so. I just didn't want you thinking I've done something behind your back."

She raised her eyebrows.

"I went to see your dad this afternoon."

Shaking her head, she exploded, "What?" Then quieter, "Okay, that's not what I thought you were going to say."

"Are you mad?"

"Depends. Why did you go and what did you say to him?"

"I apologized. And I offered to help him find work."

"Wow. Seriously?"

He nodded. "I have a lot of redemption to seek. I wronged a lot of people. I figure because of us, and our ... friendship ... I should tackle your dad. Ask for forgiveness, try to right the wrongs."

She looked down at her lap and he thought he saw a hint of a smile. She looked at him again. "Friendship?"

"Or, whatever."

"Well, you got guts, I'll give you that. How did he take it?"

"Not that well. But I didn't expect forgiveness with one visit. He's angry. He's got a right to be. This'll take a while. That's okay. I've got time."

She reached over and ran a finger over his cheek. "The more time I spend with you, the more impressed I am."

Warmth flooded his face, and he knew he was blushing. He wasn't particularly used to praise, and had a hard time believing it.

"Did you mention me?"

"Your name came up. He thought I somehow wrangled you into doing that article on me."

She smiled. "Oh, that was your fault too, huh?"

He nodded. "But no, I didn't broach the subject that we're ... seeing each other."

She chuckled again. Then, thankfully, he was off the hook because the previews ended and the feature film started.

"Oh!" she said and pointed out the front windshield. She grabbed her popcorn, slouched down in the passenger seat and leaned her head on his shoulder. He grabbed a fleece throw blanket from the back seat, and flipped it over them. His arm around her while they snuggled felt so right.

* * *

Driving home from work a week later, Emma dreaded the inevitable conversation in her future. It was a nagging thought, never far from her mind. It wouldn't be pleasant, but at least it would be out in the open. The question was, when? Instead of going home, she drove to her parents'.

The time was now. No use procrastinating.

She pulled into the driveway, pleased to see her mother's car at home. Things usually went better when Mom was there along with Dad. Emma let herself in the front door. Standing in the small living room, she noticed three baskets of dried laundry, unfolded. "Mom?"

"Oh, hi!" a muffled voice came from the back of the house. "I'll be right out, I'm changing clothes from work."

Emma wandered into the kitchen. Dirty dishes stuck out of the sink. She sighed and opened the dishwasher. Full and clean. She began to take clean dishes out, putting them where they belonged. Mom came in just as she was starting to load the empty dishwasher.

"Oh, don't work, don't work," said her mom.

"That's okay, I don't mind. You work so hard all day. Was Dad home today?"

Her mom looked at her, brow furrowed. "Well, sure." As if, where else would he be?

"Mom, you need to set expectations for him. Give him a 'Honey-Do' list. He could have done these dishes for you and folded the laundry as well."

Her mom waved a hand, dismissing her suggestion. The woman valued peace in her home, even if it required her to do 99% of the work to keep the house running.

Emma finished loading the dishwasher and her mom said, "So what brings you by? I was going to make some meatloaf. Want to stay?"

Emma thought grimly that after she brought up what she had to, none of them would have an appetite tonight. "We'll see, Mom. Listen, I need to talk to you and Dad about something important."

Mom gave her a worried look. "The last time you came here and said that, it was about that Jeremy Harrison article. That was already published, wasn't it? That's over."

"Um, yes. The article is over. But there's more."

Edna drew in a deep breath and sighed it out. "There's more to tell about the Harrisons? Oh Emma, what?"

Emma ran her hands over her eyes. She'd prefer to protect her parents from what they would consider bad news. But the fact was, she was dating Jeremy. She liked him. A lot. And unless things changed, she could see herself forming a long-term relationship with him. She had to at least make her parents aware of this fact, whether they ever accepted it or not.

She put a hand on your mom's cheek. "It's okay, Mom." She walked to the top of the stairs in the corner of the kitchen and yelled down, "Dad? Hey Dad, it's me. Can you come up, please?"

Some mumbling emerged from the basement. "Wha ... what? Baby girl?"

Emma glanced over at her mother, who grabbed a dishcloth and began busily wiping the counter that didn't really need it. "Yeah, it's me, Dad. Can you come up?"

She went to the table and sat. Gradually, she heard evidence of her father's progression up the stairs through a series of grunts, bumps and footfalls. Soon, he emerged at the top of the stairs in the kitchen. She went to him and placed a kiss on his cheek. He smelled of beer and cigarettes. "How you doing, Dad?"

"Great, sweetheart, now that you're here. Look at our daughter, Edna. Isn't she pretty?"

Mom smiled and nodded. "She sure is, Gary. We raised a heck of a girl, didn't we?"

Emma put her head down, biting her tongue on a smart retort. Whatever success she'd achieved, which was minimal so far, she'd gotten from her own hard work and commitment, not from her upbringing. Although, in a backwards sort of way, maybe her upbringing illustrated for her what she needed to escape by working hard and making her own way in the world.

Regardless, she'd let it pass because she loathed bringing pain on these two people. Flawed though they were, they were her parents. They loved her and there weren't that many people in her life she could say that about. Besides, the subject she was here to talk about would be explosive in itself.

"Okay guys, come sit down. I have something to tell you."

"Good news?" her mom said with a big grin and it pierced Emma's heart. Despite the disappointments in her mom's life, she kept her optimism.

"Yes, I think so. I hope you agree," she said cautiously. When they were all settled at the table, Emma began. "I've been dating someone. A young man. And I think I'd like to see where this relationship goes."

"Oh, that's wonderful, honey! Someone you care about. That's great."

Her dad wasn't quite as happy, but still listening. "What's he do? Does he treat you right? You know you don't have to put up with any man's crap if he don't treat you right. You know that, baby girl, don't ya?"

Emma refused to think about the irony in his words, or look at her mother to see if she'd picked up on it too. "He's very nice, Mom and Dad. He's very respectful and kind."

Her mother grabbed her hands and squeezed them. "Oh that's great, honey. When do we get to meet him?"

She rarely brought boyfriends over, so the fact that she was even talking about this one with them was significant. Of course, they didn't know the half of it.

"So," she stammered, wishing she'd brought a script, then just got to it, "my new boyfriend is someone you know. It's Jeremy Harrison."

The silence that hung in the room was so heavy Emma felt she could squeeze it like a sponge and expect to see drips of water rain down on the floor.

Then, "What did she say, Edna?" her father, deceptively calm, asked.

Her mother moved her head, looking in turn at Emma and her husband. "What? I don't understand. Why...?"

"Listen, I know this is difficult for both of you. I know Jeremy has caused a lot of pain for this family in the past. But he's not like that now. He's changed. He's hardworking and he regrets the mistakes he's made in the past."

She couldn't say anymore because her father began yelling, "No! No way, Emma Jean. How could you? How could you betray us like this? This will not happen. Not while I'm head of the family."

She reached over to pat his hand. "Wait, wait. I've given him a chance and he's really turned himself around. He's kind and he's sweet. And we have a good time together."

"Oh, Emma." her mother moaned. "You always do this, you want to help the underdog. The stray pet or the squirrel stuck out in the snow. Even some of your friends were the sad sacks who didn't have anyone else. That's all this is."

Emma shook her head. Would that be easier for her mom to accept or should she set her straight? "Mom, no. Jeremy's not a sad sack or a squirrel out in the snow. He's a hard-working man, on his way to success. He's a talented wood worker and he's fun to be with. I really enjoy spending time with him."

"I forbid you to spend time with him!" her father roared. "Look what he's done to me! Look at what he's made of my life."

Emma let those statements simmer for a moment, then stated calmly, "Dad, first of all, you can't forbid me to spend time with him, or anyone else. You can share your preferences with me, your advice, but I'm a grown woman. I can spend time with anyone I choose. And right now, I want to be with Jeremy. I have no idea if it'll work out or not. But I've been open to forgiving him for his past. I'd like to see you think about doing the same thing."

Her dad grunted. If he'd had something in his hand, he'd have thrown it, but fortunately, he'd left his beer can downstairs. His face was turning red and his mouth was puffing up like he was about to expel a huge breath.

"Dad, listen to me." She took both his hands and gripped them in hers, forcing him to stay where he was and look at her. "Jeremy caused you to lose your job. But Dad, you're a craftsman. You've got skills. You've been unemployed for almost twelve years now. You can't blame all that on Jeremy."

He snatched his hands from her grip and her mother's eyes popped open so wide she feared they'd burst. He stalked away from her in the small kitchen, then turned to point a finger in her direction. "Never did I think I'd see the day that my own daughter would take a Harrison's side over mine. He's brainwashing you, girl. You have no family loyalty. None. You don't have any idea what they put me through. If you did, you wouldn't look twice at that guy."

She rose and went to him. "Then tell me, Daddy. What did he do, other than the obvious? He made terrible business decisions and ran the business into the ground. The company went bankrupt and everyone lost their jobs. Are you referring to anything other than that?"

"Well, ain't that bad enough?"

"It is bad! But that was twelve years ago, Dad. What have you done lately? Why have you been unemployed ever since? Why didn't you bounce back and get another job, eventually? When was the last time you even applied for one?"

She didn't mean to yell at him but she realized when she stopped that her voice echoed off the walls. He twirled on the spot and stomped down the stairs, mumbling. Emma looked at her mother. She was frozen in place, her mouth and eyes wide open. Soon, her father's shouted words came to her, "As long as you're with him, you don't respect me. And as long as you don't respect me, you're not welcome in my house."

Mom burst into tears and ran out of the kitchen.

Emma focused on the pounding of her heart in her chest. She stood quietly for a few moments while the overwhelming beating of a bass drum passed. "That went well," she said quietly, and went to find Mom.

She was in her bedroom. Emma could hear the sobbing through the closed door. "Mom? Can I come in?" She took the non-response to be acquiescence. She pushed the door open slowly. Mom lay on the bed on her stomach, her face buried in her elbow. It killed Emma to see her mother so distraught, especially the fact that she herself had made her that way.

She rested on the bed behind her, rubbing her back. "Mom, I'm so sorry. I went too far. I shouldn't have said that stuff to him. I'm sorry."

Her mother sniffed and scrubbed her face with her palms. "You never know when to stop."

Emma shrugged. It was probably true. It was why she went into journalism. She asked the hard questions. She wanted to know the story beneath the surface. But she supposed that didn't work well with family secrets.

She rubbed her mom's back, waiting for her to calm down. After a few minutes, she did. She sat and faced Emma, wiping her tears on her sleeve since she had no tissues around.

"Mom, I don't want to upset you again. But I have to think that I didn't say anything to Dad that you haven't wondered yourself. Am I right?"

Her mother stared at her, unable or unwilling to agree with her. But she didn't disagree either, and Emma took that as encouragement to continue. "Mom, hundreds of thousands of people around the country have lost their jobs.

Sad, but true. But there are others. How hard did Dad look for a new job?"

She sighed. "You don't understand. Getting fired really ate away at his self-confidence. Your dad wasn't good at school. He never finished high school and wasn't qualified for many jobs. He'd found his niche with roofing. It's a thankless job that many men won't do. Dangerous. Up high with nothing to hold on to. Sun beating down. Sweaty work. But Dad learned the trade."

"How long did he work for the Harrisons?" Emma was relieved her mother was talking, and not as mad at her as her father was.

"Years and years for the father. But not full-time. Mr. Harrison had a small operation and only called Dad in when he needed roofing skills. It was actually the son who hired Gary on full time."

"So Dad was sort of a free-lance roofer? Went from job to job."

Edna drew in a long breath and let it out. "I guess. He would hook on with construction companies and do the roofing, move from house to house. But it was never steady. Nobody hired him on as a full-time salaried employee until Jeremy did."

Interesting.

"Until then, Dad's work was sporadic. Always looking for the next job. Sometimes off weeks between jobs. It wasn't easy. Especially since I wasn't working full-time then."

"So Jeremy helped him, you'd say."

"Yeah, for a while. Till it was all over. Then he was in worse shape than ever."

"Why? Sounds like for the several years he worked full-time, he was better off, but when he lost that gig, he was back to what he had before."

Mom placed her hands over her ears. "Oh, Emma, stop it. You're twisting my words and getting me confused."

Emma pulled her mom into an embrace. "I'm sorry, Mama. I don't mean to hurt you or Dad. I'm really just trying to get to the bottom of it." They sat quietly for a minute. Emma tried again, "So after Harrison and Son went bankrupt and everyone lost their jobs, what happened to Dad?"

Edna studied a snag in the bedspread. "He collected unemployment. For like, nine months or so. Or maybe a year? About half his previous income. But I went full-time at the agency so it about made up for the shortage."

"Okay, then what? Eventually unemployment benefits run out. Did Dad look for work?"

Her mother stood, went to her mirror and straightened her hair. She tugged on her sweatshirt and said, "I don't want to talk about that, Emma Jean. Leave it be." And she left the room.

Emma rose and followed her into the kitchen. "Come on, Mom. This has bugged me for a while. Why does Dad have to stay home all day? Why can't he work?"

Her mom slammed her hand on the counter. "Because he's an alcoholic, Emma Jean. Your father's an alcoholic."

Chapter Eight

Emma let a few days pass without getting in touch with Jeremy and coincidentally, he let the same days pass without getting in touch with her. Almost like he knew she needed some time and distance to deal with the explosion at her parents' house. The man must be psychic.

She didn't see him on Saturday because he'd signed up for another craft fair about an hour away. About eight PM, she called him.

"Hi!" His greeting sounded genuine and happy to hear from her.

"Hey, I was thinking about tomorrow morning. Mind if I go to church with you? Then maybe we can hit breakfast afterward. I've got some things to talk over with you."

He hesitated. "Okay," he said cautiously. "The first part sounds good, but the second part sounds ominous."

She chuckled. "Paranoid much?"

The next morning, Jeremy picked her up and they drove to church. It was a white wood structure with a huge white cross extending off the roof. It rested in a little valley, with hills rising up around it. It was delightful.

As they walked in, Jeremy rested his palm on the small of her back. He leaned in and whispered close to her ear, "You look beautiful, by the way."

She shivered, pleased with his praise and his proximity. She'd put on a simple cotton dress with sandals. The late November temperature was mild, and with a sweater over her sleeveless dress, she was comfortable. She beamed her smile at him and his returning grin brought warmth to her heart.

Several people waved at Jeremy as he walked into the sanctuary and selected their seats in the pew. In fact, several people raised eyebrows at him, smiling their approval that he'd brought her.

When they were settled in, she teased, "Am I the first woman you've ever brought here?"

He gave her a pointed gaze.

She opened the bulletin an usher had handed her when she walked in. She reviewed the list of activities they'd go through in the service. Lots of singing, a little bit of Bible, and a sermon. Oh, and a baptism. She hoped it was an infant. She knew some churches wanted baptisms to occur as early as possible, and others preferred people wait until they could understand what they were doing. But she loved babies and wouldn't mind oohing and aahing.

The service began and Jeremy helped her with the logistics — finding the right book, the right page, pointing out the instructions of when to stand and when to sit. There was no kneeling in this church. Jeremy seemed to know exactly what to do and he participated in all of it, but not loudly. He sang quietly. He said "Amen" at the end of prayers, but he wasn't the type to yell it or raise his hands like some members around him.

It was just like him not to want to stand out in a crowd.

She followed his lead. When the preacher finished his sermon and began a long prayer, she closed her eyes and listened. It was a long hour, probably because it had been way too long since she'd attended a church service and wasn't used to the routine. She'd definitely come again, if Jeremy would bring her. She learned a lot, and it did her heart good to hear all the positive talk. When the baptism turned out to be a baby girl wearing a gorgeous white flowing gown, she took Jeremy's arm and pointed. "Isn't she cute?"

He nodded and smiled at her, leaning his head close to hers. She wondered if he'd kiss her, but he didn't.

On the way out, they stood in line to shake hands with the preacher. Jeremy introduced her and the man said, "So nice to meet you, Emma. Glad to see you here with Jeremy."

She looked at Jeremy and his face was tinted a little pinker than normal. They walked through the lobby and a poster taped to the wall drew her attention. "Excuse me a second," she told Jeremy and stepped closer to it. He waited for her by the door. A stack of papers containing the same message as the poster sat on a table. She grabbed one and shoved it in her purse.

Later, they were settled in at an ocean-facing window at a grubby little diner. One of the best things about living coastal is that a photo-ready view of the ocean was never far away. Regardless what the diner looked like, they had the best view in the house.

After they ordered, Jeremy reached across the table and took her hands in both his. "I missed you yesterday."

"Oh yeah, how did the craft fair go?"

"It was good. Not as good as the one in Myrtle Beach, but I talked to a lot of folks and signed contracts on seven pieces. It'll keep me busy a while."

Their coffees came. They both reached for the little pitcher of creamer at the same time. Her finger jabbed into his accidentally. He grinned. "Wow, you're a little violent before your first cup of the morning."

She giggled. "I already had my first cup, before church."

They doctored their respective brews. "It was so cool that you came to church with me. What'd you think?"

"I liked it. I can see why you go every week. Like you said, it's a break from the routine. And how can you not help leaving there feeling good?"

"Yep. It's good for your soul. You're welcome anytime."

"Thank you. I'd like to sign up for next week."

His beaming smile let her know how he felt about that.

"And was I mistaken or was your pastor teasing you a little bit about having a girl with you?"

His face blushed again. Hmmm, good to know. She'd have to tuck that knowledge away for future use. "Hey, I had the prettiest girl in the place sitting next to me. He was probably just jealous."

She laughed. After a few sips, she put her cup down and looked him in the eyes. "Jeremy, I need to tell you about my visit to my parents' house last week. How it turned out. I went there to talk about, well, you."

"Me?" he said grimly.

"Well, yeah. You know they're not your biggest fans, right?"

He nodded. She told him the whole story, including the revelation at the end. Throughout the story, emotions flickered guardedly across his face. He never spoke and when she finished, he remained quiet.

Their breakfasts arrived. Neither seemed hungry for the heavy food now. Jeremy picked up his fork but pushed the eggs and hash browns around the plate. Then he put it down with a clang. "I'm sorry, Emma. This is all my fault."

She stared at him. "No! No, it isn't. You missed the whole point of the story."

"I must've. You got in a big fight with your parents because of me. Your father hates me and doesn't want you to see me. Can't say I blame him, by the way. Your mother hates to raise her voice, and she ended up yelling at you over me too."

She put her fork down too. "Jeremy, listen. My father had a reason to hate you ten years ago. He had a steady job with benefits for the first time in his life. You were generous enough to offer him that. But the reason he is unemployed today, and has been for a decade, is not because of you. Not by a long shot. It's his own fault! During the time he was collecting unemployment, he was drinking too much. By the time his benefits ran out and he should've been dragging his butt out looking for a job, he was too far gone. He was an alcoholic. He couldn't give up the beer. Not without coming to terms with what he'd done to himself. Blaming you is a cop out. It is now and it always has been."

Jeremy's eyes went wide, his mouth dropped open. He took his napkin off his lap and threw it on the table. He pushed his plate back and looked distractedly away, his mind probably racing with all she'd told him. She nibbled at her food, ate a few bites of egg and toast, but realized she was done.

"I'm sorry," he said after a few moments of silence.

She reached for his hands. "Jeremy, you don't have to apologize to me. You haven't done anything to apologize for." She squeezed his hands and then let them go. She dug in her purse. "Now, what do you think of this?"

She pulled out the flyer for Alcoholics Anonymous. A meeting was held in the church several times a week. Meeting dates and times were listed, along with a brief motto, "A New Way of Life Without Alcohol."

He blinked. "Do you think your dad would attend?"

She shrugged. "I have no idea. But we've got to ask him, don't we?"

Jeremy let out a deep breath. "We? I gotta tell you, Emma, I'm in way over my head here. I don't know how to feel, how to act. I think I need to think this through. Alone."

She nodded. "Okay. No problem."

They paid the bill and left, then drove home in a contemplative silence. When he pulled up to her apartment complex, she said, "That's okay. You stay in the truck. You don't have to walk me up."

He nodded, distracted. "Look, I hate that you got in a fight with your parents over me. I can't help but think that maybe your life would be simpler without me in it."

She turned and pulled him closer by his collar. "Who said I wanted a simple life?" Landing her mouth on his, she gave him a kiss she wanted him to remember. Whatever thinking he would embark upon over the next few days that involved her, he would think about this moment. When she broke from him, she continued, "Doing the right thing isn't easy. But it's worth it in the end."

With that, she opened the truck door and jumped to the ground.

* * *

One of the best things about working for himself was that when Jeremy wanted to be a loner and escape from people, he could. For the most part. Of course, he wasn't totally alone in the world. His dad or Leslie sometimes stopped by or called, and occasionally Marianne. After ten years of being surrounded by people he had no say in choosing, sometimes it just felt right to be by himself.

Now was one of those times. He had some thinking to do. For the first time in as long as he could remember, he had a girlfriend. Someone who made him excited, optimistic and happy. Emma knew him and accepted him, warts and all. He was a better man with her around.

But what did he provide her? He couldn't offer her anything. He certainly wasn't looking for commitment or marriage, not until he got his post-release life better underway. Not that she'd given him any inkling that she wanted that with him either. He was barely making ends meet, so he couldn't offer her anything that required funds. She deserved way better than him, but he wasn't about to be the one to convince her.

Whether she had dubious taste in men or not was debatable. But this fight with her parents over him, really rattled him. He wasn't worth losing her good standing with her parents. He didn't want the responsibility for that, not knowing what the future would hold.

For three days, he stayed home, working on his furniture jobs around the clock, not seeing or speaking a word to another soul. However, after three days of isolation, he still hadn't come any closer to an answer. When the phone rang and it was Leslie saying she had a surprise for him, she extended an invitation to come over to the Old Gray Barn.

"Yes, thank you, I'll be over," he said, ready to break his solitude.

"And of course, bring Emma along. We'd love to see her, too."

"Oh, um, you know, she's tied up all week long," he lied, although he'd never been very good at it. "But I'm sure she'd thank you for thinking of her."

Even to his own ears it sounded lame, but Leslie responded warmly, "You know she's welcome anytime. See you at five."

Late that afternoon, he got in his truck and drove the short distance to his dad and Leslie's beach house. The place was so comfortable and spacious it did his heart good just looking at it. He knocked, then walked right in. "Hello?" he called.

The house was quiet, but he walked through the length of the main floor to the screened-in porch in the back. There, sitting on wooden Adirondack rockers were his dad, Leslie and Leslie's college-aged daughter, Jasmine. He'd met her at their parents' wedding a few months ago. Jasmine was in the middle of a story which had his dad and Leslie in stitches. When he walked in, both Jasmine and her mom stood up, grinned and pulled him into a tandem hug.

He laughed, soaking it up. Family was something that confused him, attracted him. It gave him mixed feelings, due to the way his actions had messed up his own for so long. But he worked to let all that go and enjoy the simple pleasure of the hugs of these two women who loved him.

"Jasmine! Nice surprise."

She pulled away and smiled up at him. "You didn't have your heart set on a gift wrapped present, did you? I wouldn't want you to feel let down." She tapped the rocker next to her. "Come over here and sit down. Can I get you a drink? A beer? Wine? Soda?"

"A beer sounds good, but you don't have to wait on me. You sit right here and I'll be back in a second with it."

"Nope." She practically pushed him into the seat. "I've been sitting for two days in the car. Need to stretch my legs."

She popped off into the house. He rested his eyes on Leslie. "You must be happy."

"Oh yes, you better believe it. Always happy to see my girl. She's on winter break from school, and decided to spend it here at the beach. Better than coming home to the snow of Pittsburgh."

Jeremy nodded, then accepted a beer from Jasmine when she came bopping back onto the porch. He admired his new stepmother and was happy beyond words that she and his dad had found their happy ending. Leslie had sold her home in Pittsburgh to settle with Hank, and Jasmine was in college in New York somewhere, studying fashion merchandising. She completed an internship with some famous designers in Paris last summer, which, along with Leslie's pending divorce, convinced Leslie to hit the road with no destination in mind. It was a lesson in faith, following God's will in her life. What started out to be an unhappy summer with no purpose, turned out to be one of the best summers in her life, helping others and following God's path. Of course, meeting his dad and marrying him was the icing on the cake.

"So, brother," Jasmine began once she'd sank back into her rocker, "I hear you're building furniture and doing very well."

The girl was at least a decade younger than him, and their age difference showed. She was happy, carefree and unbroken. He, of course, had had a different life experience. But Jasmine was thrilled that she now had step-siblings, not to mention a step-niece in Stella. As an only child, she must've thought she'd hit the jackpot.

"I'm working hard. I don't think I'd say I'm doing very well. But I'm loving it, and building the business. Trying to make it work."

They chatted about his furniture pieces, her semester she just finished, and her final one coming up. She'd graduate in May. Hank and Leslie slipped out to finish dinner preparations. Twenty minutes later, all was ready and they moved to the long table in the house, relishing Leslie's chicken pesto and pasta, salad and Italian bread. Jasmine regaled them with stories of Paris, including the French boys she'd met and hung out with.

"You couldn't really call them dates. I was on a swamped work schedule and my designers owned me. I would work off and on all day, usually for eighty hours a week. Not only was I too exhausted to date, I never had the time. So I would chat with the male models while I was fitting them or whatever, and then we'd slip out for a baguette or a cup of coffee every now and then."

"Can you speak French?" Jeremy asked.

"*Un petit peu, mais pas beaucoup.*" She giggled. "Enough to get by. And often, they spoke English so I lucked out." She took a final bite and pushed her plate away. "One time I was running across a street, doing an errand for Pierre, one of the designers, which I was endlessly doing. I, of course, was dressed to the hilt. One of the job requirements for a fashion assistant. Anyway, it was an old cobblestone street. My stiletto got wedged in a crease, and since I was running, my shoe stayed, my body kept going. I ended up taking a fabulous spill into the curb, spraining my ankle and putting a nasty bruise on my hip. The bolt of fabric I was carrying fell and got muddied in the street. It was awful."

Leslie chimed in. "She was distraught. She called me while she lay there, unable to move. I wasn't sure what I could've done for her from the eastern US, but it was sweet of her to call. Then, I heard a male voice: *Puis-je vous aider, ne manquez?*"

"What does that mean?"

"It means, Can I help you, miss? Jasmine quickly said, 'Bye, Mom,' and broke the connection. I was worried sick. And when I tried to call her back, she didn't answer."

"He was cute!" Jasmine giggled. "He picked me up and carried me to a bench on the sidewalk, deposited me there and then went back and got my fabric bolt. He sat down with me, took my shoe off and massaged my ankle." She did an exaggerated sigh. "How romantic. Raimond," she finished dreamily.

"What happened next?" Jeremy asked.

She broke out of her concentration and looked at him. "Nothing. After all that, he had to go. Had a meeting or whatever. Never saw him again." She put on a smirk. "My missed chance at love. He was just a gentleman, I guess. A random act of kindness. I took my other shoe off and hobbled back to work."

"So an internship with Paris designers wasn't all glitz and glamour, huh?"

"Not in the least! But an experience I am very grateful for, and so glad I did."

They lingered over coffee and when Jeremy was starting to think about heading home, Jasmine said, "How about a walk on the beach? I'm only here for a few days so I want to soak in as much ocean-time as I can."

They all agreed. Even though they could get ocean-time whenever they wanted, they were generally up for a walk on the beach. They deposited their shoes on the porch and headed down the back steps. Jasmine set an ambitious pace, and the older folks soon lagged behind with a comfortable stroll. Jeremy kept up with Jasmine.

"Are you trying to raise your heart rate?"

Jasmine smiled. "Two days sitting in the car, combined with that fattening meal? I gotta burn off some calories so I can put on my bikini tomorrow!"

Jeremy raised his eyebrows at her. "I doubt you'll be donning a bikini tomorrow, sweetheart. I think temps will be in the low fifties."

"Better than where I came from! And the sun will be out, right? All I'm after is a suntan, bro. I want to go back to school with a healthy glow."

Jeremy smiled, enjoying her spontaneity. The girl was a trip; that was for sure. Was he ever that unstructured, even at her age? She was a product of her upbringing — the pampered only child of a professional couple of parents, probably received whatever she wanted. Oh, not that she was spoiled, not exactly. But he could tell she never wanted for anything. Probably never had to experience the struggle to make ends meet, as his family had in the earlier days. However, she did have to endure the breakup of her parents' marriage, which he was sure was painful for her, something he'd never talked to her about. He wasn't the type to get into deep personal conversations with anyone. His motto was to keep it safe, keep it easy.

They walked quickly, putting distance between them and their parents. Jasmine had worked up a little sweat and accelerated breathing, pumping her arms when she looked over at him and said, "So, I hear you have a girlfriend."

He'd been in the midst of taking a deep breath, and her words caused him to choke. He coughed while he walked, bending a little at the waist. She pounded him on the back.

"Wow, that's your reaction to the word, girlfriend?"

"No," he choked. "You just surprised me, that's all." They continued power-walking and he recovered. She picked up the conversation where she left it.

"So? What's her name?"

Jeremy paused. "I wouldn't necessarily call her a girlfriend…"

"Oh, come on. Mom and Hank caught you taking her out to dinner. That sounds like girlfriend material to me." She laughed. "Spill, big brother. This is what siblings do, evidently. They tell each other their deep, dark secrets."

Jeremy shook his head. "Where'd you hear that? I have two sisters and I never tell them anything."

"Well, now you got three, and this one wants to know."

Jeremy couldn't help smiling. "That does not, however, mean that I want to tell you."

"Think of it this way: I'm offering you a listening ear and a female's perspective. I'll be gone shortly so whatever you tell me will be kept private. But I can give you my opinion."

They walked another quarter mile and for some unknown reason, he decided to take her up on her offer. "Her name is Emma. Emma Jean Slotky. We have an odd sort of history, a past that could make it impossible for us to work out, but we seem to get along pretty well despite it."

"You're gonna have to give me some details on that one, bro. Sounds intriguing."

Well, he was in now. He'd have to come clean. Besides, he really could use the female perspective on his current relationship issues, and Jasmine was in a unique position to give it to him. The fact that she lived far away appealed to him. He could tell her his story, get her advice, then never have to be accountable for following it or not, because she wouldn't be around. In addition, she wasn't as vested as Marianne, who just wanted him to be happy, so her perspective was a little jaded. As much as it violated his normal code of staying quiet, Jasmine could truly do him an important service here, if he was honest with her.

"Okay, here's the deal. When I ... had my problems, back when I was working with Dad ..."

"Yeah," Jasmine said, to his relief. He wouldn't have to rehash all that mess now.

"Emma's father worked for us. But unfortunately, he was a casualty of the business when we went bankrupt. We had to lay him off."

"Okay."

"He took it really hard. In fact, he never recovered. He's never worked since."

Jasmine turned to him, her confusion showing in her lowered eyebrows. "Why?"

"Evidently, he's blamed me for the last ten years for his inability to find another job. But Emma recently found out that when he was on unemployment, he began drinking heavily and became an alcoholic."

"Oh, how awful."

"Emma wants us, her and I, to convince him to go to AA."

"Wow. Like an intervention?"

"I guess. But I don't think that's my place. I mean, the last person he would want to see is me. In fact, Emma recently confronted her parents about his unwillingness to get a job and her parents both told her they didn't want her seeing me."

Jasmine frowned. "You've become their Big Bad Wolf. All their problems, they pinpoint back to you."

He let out a huff of breath. "Yeah." They walked on. "So, as much as I like Emma and our times together, I just don't think I'm the one for her. Too much baggage. And I don't want to be the one to cause a family feud between her and her parents. If dating me makes her parents so unhappy, then maybe I should just back out of the picture."

"Take the easy way out, you mean?"

He looked at her. "No, that's not ..."

"What does Emma want?"

"She wants to convince her dad to face his alcoholism, and she wants him to get his life under control. Start working again, get up off the couch. And she wants me to help her."

"So she doesn't want you out of her life."

"No, but I don't want to be trouble for her."

Jasmine turned and gave him a dubious expression. "You sound like you're trying to be noble."

"No."

"Do you like this girl? Like, really like her?"

"Well, yeah, of course. She's beautiful and fun and talented. Of course I like her. But, let's face it, I have zero experience with relationships. I don't want to screw it up and I don't want to hurt her."

Jasmine quieted, as if knowing that his words had come at a price. He never dug that deep, and shared it verbally.

"If you think Emma could be the girl for you long-term, then you can't expect it to come easily. Love is hard, one of the hardest things in your life. But lifelong love is the reward. Can you imagine? Coming home every day to a person who is there for you, committed to building a life with you and sticking by you through thick and thin? That's what you're after. That's what everyone's after. If you have even an inkling that Emma could be that person, then I think you owe it to yourself to see it through. If you bail out now at the first sign of difficulty, wouldn't you look back and regret it?"

They stopped walking. He turned and gazed at his stepsister with new eyes. "How'd you get so smart?" he asked with wonderment.

She shrugged. "I'm a girl."

They turned and headed back slowly. Most of their steps were in silence. Then Jeremy said, "Thanks, sis. You've given me a lot to think about."

"Good. Bill's in the mail. But let me just leave you with this thought, and I firmly believe it. You deserve happiness, Jeremy. But it's not going to fall into your lap. You have to fight for it."

He was used to that concept. He'd had to fight for so many things over the last ten years. The question he had to answer was, how many fights could he take on at the same time without driving himself crazy?

Chapter Nine

A few nights later, Jeremy stood on his backyard tarp, finishing up the final layer of stain on a king-size headboard, the first of a five-piece bedroom set. When the customer contacted him, he'd specifically mentioned Emma's article in Seminal Magazine as the prompt for his call. He owed her a thank you, but it had been nearly a week now since their Sunday morning breakfast and he hadn't been in touch.

Minutes later, he realized he wouldn't have to make the call. Emma herself rounded from the side and stepped into his backyard. His heart jumped at the sight of her, and he couldn't help wondering if this was God, thumping him in the head to get his attention.

He laid his brush to rest beside the can and went to greet her. He took her hands and leaned in to kiss her on the cheek. "You look beautiful. Good to see you."

She gave him a sideways look. "Well, that's better than the greeting I feared I'd get."

He squeezed her hands, ducked his head.

"You haven't called me all week, Jeremy."

"Yeah, sorry about that. I got tied up…" Then he stopped, started again. Above all else, she deserved honesty and he would avoid lying at all costs. "I had to do some thinking."

"And did you come to a decision? About helping me with my dad?"

"No. No, I haven't. But I do know one thing. I've sure missed you this week. And I'm really happy to see you."

Emma smiled. "So, two things actually. Good job." She punched him in the arm and rolled her eyes. "I have something for you." She walked over to his makeshift workshop and placed a small paper bag on the workbench. She looked up at him.

He opened the bag and pulled out a stack of laminated cards, about twice the size of a business card, with a photo of the ocean, his name and phone number and her sentimental "Thank you" message printed on top. They really were professional and well-done. Swallowing his hesitancy, he smiled at her. "They're really nice, Emma. Thank you."

Her white smile beamed. "You like them then?"

He nodded. "I guess if I don't toot my own horn, no one else will, right?"

"That's right! It's called marketing. Put one of these in a drawer of every piece you sell. If the piece doesn't have a drawer, tape it underneath somewhere. Make it a treasure the customer finds, maybe weeks after the sale and they'll think fondly of you. Maybe bring you more business."

The fact that she took this task on herself to help him, meant more than the cards themselves. "How much do I owe you?"

"Not a thing."

"Come on, Emma. I can tell these were professionally done. I don't want you spending money on me."

"I work at a magazine, remember. I have contacts."

He studied her for a few seconds but it was clear she wasn't going to back down. "Then, thank you. You don't know how much this means to me."

"No big deal." She turned to study the headboard.

Jeremy frowned. In his heart, it was a big deal.

"This is nice," she said.

"Yeah, almost done. It's a cherry wood finish and it'll be five pieces in all. The headboard, two nightstands, a tall stand-up dresser and squat longer one. By the way, I have you to thank for the business. They mentioned the Seminal article when they hired me."

"Really?" She seemed genuinely excited. This woman had a good heart. Or maybe just the need to rescue lost souls.

"Yep. So, between the cards and the new gig, I owe you. How about dinner tonight?"

"I'd love to," she said without hesitation.

He grinned. "Let me just cover this up and go take a shower. I'll be ready in about fifteen."

* * *

He disappeared into the back of the bungalow and Emma settled into the great room at the front. When the shower turned on, she laid her head against the back of the couch and let her mind wander. Her imagination took over and presented her with a vivid image of Jeremy, standing under the warm spray of water, the wetness matting his hair down, his face upturned, washing away all the sweat and grime of the day.

She closed her eyes to encourage the vision even more. The water flowed over his lean, muscular chest. His biceps strained as he lifted his arms to rub soap all over his face, his neck, his torso and then down.

Down.

Emma jumped, jerked her eyes open, her pulse racing now. The water turned off. The man's quick, she had to give him that. Good thing, too, because without too much convincing at all, she could've found herself back in that bathroom, shedding her clothes and joining him under the water.

But what would that gain? A relationship centered around sex could rarely make the switch to lifelong commitment. She'd had a few physical relationships while she was in college. They were exhilarating, fun, and short-lived. She'd matured, and that type of relationship had no place in her life now. Besides, she really didn't want that with Jeremy.

She had no idea where she and Jeremy were headed, in fact, she didn't even know if Jeremy wanted to stick around. But she was committed to one thing: this would be a mature, adult courtship.

* * *

Jeremy went about his business, but he couldn't ignore the increasing presence of decorated trees, wreaths, red and green everything, everywhere he looked. Street lights in town wrapped with garland, wreaths in every store window. And Marianne's Inn. She'd pulled out all the stops in order to coax all her guests into the yuletide spirit. Christmas was right around the corner, which brought Jeremy a source of anxiety: gift giving. He'd gone shopping and bought items for the people in his family: his dad, Leslie, Marianne, Stella. Mostly clothes. He'd even gotten Jasmine a gift card.

But the dilemma of selecting a present for Emma stumped him. They rarely referred to themselves as boyfriend or girlfriend. They'd never verbalized the word, relationship. However, they talked almost daily and saw each other several times a week. Whether they said it or not, isn't that what they were — in a relationship? And so, it seemed that not just a gift, but a gift appropriate for the occasion, was important.

Jewelry was too much of a proclamation. It was too early for jewelry. But clothing seemed inappropriate — who was he to think he could figure out what she'd want to wear when she did such a great job of it herself?

Then he settled into an idea. He'd make her something. But what? A piece of furniture seemed wrong. She lived in a tiny rented apartment. It wasn't like she had room for a big table or rocking chair. But something smaller. A jewelry box! Yes. A wooden jewelry box, handmade, that if their relationship progressed in the future, he could fill with pieces of jewelry. Maybe. He wouldn't even think that far ahead.

So, he began brainstorming on the wooden box. Its measurements, its shape and size, the wood he'd use. After jotting down a few designs, he settled on something he was happy with. A sizable wooden box, it would turn out to be nearly a foot on each side. He'd use two unique woods that weren't often blended together in a single project — ash for the four sides, and a striking purpleheart for the legs. The corners would be rounded to provide a soft look, and he'd line the inside with velvet. After spending several days working on the design, he pondered the tools he'd need to bring his vision to life.

Definitely a band saw, a table saw, and a sander. It amazed him as he worked through the steps, just how intricate this relatively simple box was. To make it turn out right, he had to take care with a number of elements no one would ever imagine.

He lifted his head from his paper and smirked. He'd have to remember to share that with Neil, who was always looking for analogies that applied to leading a good life. He'd like that one.

* * *

Christmas Eve arrived on Pawleys Island along with an unexpected and atypical snowfall. The flakes melted as soon as they hit the ground, but still, it threw the islanders into a scurry, some worried about driving in such conditions, while the children wanted to go outside and play in the unfamiliar precipitation.

Emma studied herself in the bathroom mirror, putting the final touches on her face, a swipe of blush on each cheek, some shimmery eye shadow on her lids and a few brushes of mascara on her lashes. She stepped back and observed her black dress with random stripes of red. A red scarf and high heels, and she was ready to go to Christmas Eve church service with Jeremy.

She left the bathroom and headed toward her front room. She and her parents would not be spending Christmas Eve together, as they normally did. Ever since their argument several weeks ago, things between she and Mom were strained, to say the least. They were tiptoeing on eggshells around each other. However, as far from normal as it was, it was much better than her relationship with Dad. He had gone into hiding, not answering her calls and not emerging when she came to visit. She dreaded spending their traditional Christmas Day together tomorrow, wondering how tense it would be.

But she wouldn't worry about that now.

The doorbell rang. She ran to the door and opened it. Jeremy stood there wearing a full suit, and holding a large wrapped Christmas present. She wasn't sure which looked better.

"Come in!" she said and pulled him by the arm. She drank in the sight of him, head to toe. "I've never seen you in a suit. You look great."

"Don't look real close. It's ancient, and probably out of style by now. I wore it to my college graduation."

She patted his shoulders and lapel, then leaned in for a kiss. "I'd never know. And ...?" She looked pointedly at the present, wrapped in foil red paper, topped off with a green bow.

"Oh, this is for you." He handed it to her.

"Hold on a sec. I'll get yours." She dashed over to the kitchen counter.

"You didn't have to get me anything," he murmured but she still heard him.

"Of course I did! It's Christmas!"

He nodded, smiling. "Open yours first."

She led him to the couch and they sat. It didn't take long to rip the paper off and a beautiful wooden box emerged. "Ohhhh ..." It was a sizable box, more of a miniature chest really, made of the most gorgeous two shades of wood, one a light brown and the other a vivid red. "It's so pretty." She studied it slowly, opened the lid, closed it again. She ran her fingertips over its glossy surface. The thought that he'd worked on a handmade gift for her, a more thoughtful gift than a sweater at the mall, almost brought tears to her eyes. She fought them off. "I assume it's one of your creations?"

He nodded.

"Thank you, Jeremy. It's really a work of art."

He shrugged. "You're welcome. I enjoyed making it. Something different for me."

She set it aside, reached for her gift, and handed it to him. "Now you."

He took the big box she'd wrapped in Santa paper and carefully opened it by the tape creases. When he was done she practically could've reused the paper for another gift. He lifted the lid off the box and pulled out the black felt cowboy hat. He chuckled and put it on. "Thank you."

"For the next time we go riding together."

He didn't say anything for a moment. She watched him. Was he choked up? Then he put the hat back in the box. "That's very thoughtful, thank you."

On the drive to church, Emma asked, "So what are your plans for tomorrow?"

"Family Christmas," he said with a smile. "First one for me, in way too long. Marianne and Tom are having us all over to the Inn. My dad and Leslie, Jasmine, me. Of course, my niece Stella will be there."

Well, that settled it. If he'd had no plans, she was toying with the idea of inviting him to her family Christmas. Her dysfunctional family Christmas. But no, she wouldn't do that to him. She'd let him enjoy his day where they all loved and appreciated him. Had forgiven him for past sins.

And she'd broach the subject again of helping her father with his recovery, in the New Year.

Chapter Ten

Christmas turned out to be less dysfunctional than she feared. More like, everyone was using the avoidance technique. Avoid talking about anything that caused tension between the three of them. It wasn't quite like old times, but it allowed them to eat a nice meal cooked by Mom, without suffering indigestion.

New Years was approaching quickly and Emma wanted to get her plans in place. Her first choice was to spend it with Jeremy. But in case he wasn't game, she could accept an invitation from a group of her girlfriends to go out dancing and drinking. As each day passed, she waited for an invitation from him that didn't come. Finally, she bucked it up and called him.

"So, New Year's Eve is a few nights away."

"So it is."

"Would you like to spend it with me?" His hesitation made her breath catch, and she knew she was into this way too deep if the answer to this question would make or break her New Years.

"What did you have in mind?" his answer came cautiously.

What does it matter? Isn't just spending it with me enough? Of course, she didn't say that to him. Too assertive. Gave away too much of her inner thoughts. But in her heart, she wished he would be up for a New Year's together regardless of what they did. "Nothing, really. I thought it would be nice to ring in the New Year together and thought I'd ask."

"Can we do it without a big crowd around? Or would that put a damper on your New Year's Eve?"

"Want to just come over to my apartment? I'll get some noisemakers, streamers, champagne. We'll do the traditional stuff at midnight. Before then, we can just hang out. Watch a movie, whatever."

"That sounds great."

When she recognized the relieved tone in his voice she was glad she'd suggested it. She got the distinct impression he was glad to spend the holiday with her, as long as it was a quiet one.

She went into the office during the day and on the way home, stopped by the Dollar Store to pick up cheap decorations, then to the grocery store to pick up a bottle of champagne. At home, she taped cardboard cut-outs and sparkly garlands around the living room and smiled at her makeshift attempts at making the little place look festive.

One thing she really liked about Jeremy was she didn't have to try to impress him. He was down to earth and easy to be around.

She called a local pizza joint and asked about delivery. They were swamped with business, as she'd expected, but fortunately she'd called early enough to get into their lineup. A sausage and mushroom pizza would arrive between eight and eight thirty.

Now, it was time to relax and wait for Jeremy.

* * *

Jeremy stepped out of the shower at seven. He'd spent the day bundled in warm clothes, working on furniture in the backyard. It had been unseasonably cold this month, in the low forties. But other than a freak snowfall on Christmas Eve, there had been no precipitation so it was safe to work outside. If his business was going to continue to grow, he'd have to invest in some indoor work space. Between the tarp in his backyard, and the storage shed behind Marianne's Inn, he always worked outside.

A good problem to have and one he'd worry about later. Tonight, he had a date with Emma for New Years and he had the suspicion she'd want it to be special. After all, what woman would ask a man out for New Years, take his suggestion to stay away from the big crowds of a bar or party, and agree to entertain him at her place unless she expected that they'd create a little of their own magic? He felt a little bad for downgrading her evening to a quiet one at home, if going out and partying was what she had in mind. The last thing he'd want is the pressure of knowing that he'd ruined her holiday.

He shaved carefully, avoiding cuts. He put some gel in his hair and combed it. He'd discovered gel not because he was fussy about his hair, rather, the opposite. Swiping a palm full of gel in his wet hair, then combing it where he wanted it to go, resulted in the hair drying in place and never requiring a second thought.

A touch of apprehension made his breath hitch. He looked forward to seeing Emma, and enjoyed spending time with her, but his need to not screw up made him nervous. He still hadn't resolved his suspicions that Emma and her family were better off without him, regardless of Jasmine's advice. But the thought of cutting ties with Emma definitely wasn't setting well with him, since he found himself more and more lately thinking about her. Daydreaming, reliving conversations they'd had together. And those kisses.

He'd nearly forgotten how great intimacy with a woman felt. But he had a feeling it wouldn't be just any woman who made him feel as good.

It was Emma.

He didn't want to let her go. Was that driven by selfish, or noble motives?

So, he could decide, at least for now, that he wanted to stay with Emma. What came next? Should he push the relationship a little further, from a physical perspective? Would Emma want that? Would she be horrified?

Finished in the bathroom, he sighed and turned the light off. He was completely out of his league here. His best plan of action was to pay attention to what Emma wanted. Be sensitive to her words and actions. And honesty, that was probably a good thing too.

He drove to her apartment. She opened the door and for a moment he was speechless. She looked gorgeous. Her bounty of light brown hair hung in soft ringlets around her shoulders and she wore a midnight blue dress that reflected her eyes and clung to her curves. The sight of her caused his mouth to drop like one of those dorky cartoons. He could just picture his eyes popping in and out.

Be smooth, he begged himself.

"Can I just say, wow. You look absolutely beautiful, Emma."

She smiled, pleased. "Thank you." She did a quick little twirl in the doorway so he could see all angles of her. And he didn't miss a thing. "You look nice too."

He'd put on black dress pants and leather shoes along with a button down shirt in almost the same blue as her dress. "You'd think we'd planned this. We're color coordinated."

She giggled and stepped aside so he could enter. On his way past he lingered, placed his hand under her hair and guided her face to his. The excitement of the holiday and the moment their lips connected made his heart beat a little faster, and he came up for air once, then placed his lips back on hers. Her lips curled into a smile while he continued to kiss her. He opened his eyes and looked straight into hers. This close to her, he smelled her signature scent, coconut.

A noise in the hallway made him turn and look at a neighbor using his key to unlock his own door about three down. They nodded at each other. He realized he was mauling her lips and hadn't even made it into her place yet. Chemistry, that's what they had.

He turned back to Emma and she still had her head tilted up, her breath tripping lightly over her open mouth, her eyelids halfway closed. Her beauty reached out and grabbed him. "Happy New Year."

She opened her eyes, seemed to come back to her senses and closed the door behind him.

She took his jacket and hung it in her closet. She picked up a plastic case containing a DVD and waved it at him. "Pizza's coming in less than an hour. Want to watch this about halfway through, then take a break to eat?"

He nodded. "Sure, whatever you want."

"Have a seat." She motioned to the couch. "Don't you even want to know what movie I picked?"

He shrugged. "I'm sure I haven't seen it so it really doesn't matter."

She gave him a look, half sympathy, half acceptance. She crouched in front of the TV and before long, a movie began. She came and sat with him, so close her bare leg leaned up against his covered one.

Stop acting like a depraved teenager, he lectured himself. You're on a date with a gorgeous woman and for some reason, she likes you. Just go with it, and pretend to be a lot more smooth than you really are.

With that, he rested his right arm on her shoulder, and she nestled into him so her head rested against his chest. He said a silent prayer of thanks and tried to concentrate on the movie.

* * *

The pizza turned out to be late, but it was okay. She and Jeremy were absorbed in the movie. In fact, it was perfect timing. Not five minutes after the movie ended, the doorbell rang and the scent of delicious meat and sauce filled her place. She set out plates and Jeremy served the pieces while she poured glasses of iced water.

"So, a new year. Any resolutions?"

"Not really. Still working on my old resolutions."

"Which are?"

He looked up at her. "You know, all my assimilation stuff. All the stuff I work on with Neil. Being honest, working hard, being a good person."

"Oh, gotcha." She took a bite. Man, this stuff was good.

"How about you?"

"Well, funny you should ask. I want to help my family. Bring us to healing. We've been broken way too long."

His hand holding a slice halted on the way to his mouth. He was motionless for a moment and then placed the pizza quietly down on his plate. Great, she'd made him lose his appetite.

"That's, that's great," he said tentatively.

"Jeremy, my dad is addicted to beer. It's dominating his life. He can't go out and get a job because he can't go all day without a drink. In addition to any physical problems this might be causing, it's at the heart of all his emotional problems." She laid her slice down. "If we can get him to recognize his drinking problem, and agree to quit drinking, no matter how hard that is, he might be able to get his life back. And if he starts working, it'll help my mom. She's got no one to share the load right now. She deserves to relax a little. She works so hard."

"You said, 'we.'"

"I'll do it alone if I have to. But I'd rather have you help me." She got up and walked around to his side of the table. "What do you say?"

He stood and paced a few steps away. "Your father hates me, Emma. He has for a long time. Whether he has good reason or not, you can't take away the fact that he loathes me. Do you really think I'd help the cause? I'll just make it worse."

"Maybe he'll listen to you."

"Why would he?" He was starting to raise his voice and took care to stop, to get his temper under control.

They both sat down at the table, their interest in pizza gone now. Finally, Jeremy said, "I like you. I really do. But I don't know, this whole thing with your dad could be a show-stopper."

He'd put it out there. He was being honest with her, regardless of how much she hated the message. She guessed she could admire him for that. "I like you too." She picked up the plates and walked them into the kitchen. "Maybe I'm crazy. After everything that's happened with my dad, it would take a miracle to get him to quit drinking."

The last thing she wanted to do on New Year's Eve while spending a quiet evening with the guy who took her breath away, was to cry. She wiped tears from her eyes and turned away so he wouldn't see.

"What did you say?"

She lifted a hand. "Nothing. Let's just drop it for now. I don't know if we can come to an agreement about this and I don't want to ruin our New Year's."

"No, wait." He came to her and put his hands on her shoulders. "You said it would take a miracle to get your dad to quit drinking."

She nodded.

"So, who's the only one capable of performing miracles?"

"God," she mumbled, confused.

"Then let's ask Him. You and me, right now. We'll go straight to the source and ask Him to perform a miracle. It's our only chance, right?"

She shrugged, focused on his face. Instead of resistant and closed off, he was smiling. In fact, he was practically beaming. "How?"

He got down on one knee, then dropped his other so he was kneeling. "Come down here with me. It's worth a try, Emma. We can't do this on our own. Your dad can't either. There's too much stacked against us. But with God, all things are possible. Don't you remember the Scripture the pastor read that first morning we went to church together? Jesus was preaching and He said something like, 'With man, this would be impossible, but with God, all things are possible.' Do you believe that, Emma?"

She did. She wanted to. She wanted to believe that God could help her with her problems, she just hadn't had enough experience with Him to feel convicted about it. But evidently, Jeremy had. Jeremy went to church, Jeremy knew the Bible, Jeremy prayed. She wanted a miracle.

She knelt beside Jeremy and they grasped hands. "Do you want to ask God for a miracle?" His beautiful, earnest face made her heart race, but what he was asking her to do made it race even faster. She was out of her depth, she didn't know what to do. "No, you, please."

He nodded, bowed his head and prayed. "Father, we know You're watching over us and You want the best for us. You want us to live happy lives in the fullness of Your grace. But down here where we are, that's hard sometimes. Life gets in the way. The evils of the world tempt us. We can't do it on our own. That's why we pray to You, to ask for the help we so desperately need. Father, we have a request. Emma and I come to You with a concern in our hearts. Please help Emma's father and her mother. Please provide Your healing spirit to them both. Help Mr. Slotky give up drinking and live the life You have planned for him. Also, help him to forgive me for my past mistakes, and to accept me instead of hating me. Lord, use Emma and I as your soldiers in this war against evil. In Your name, we ask this. Amen."

His words were finished but they both stayed in position, gripping each other's hands, heads bowed. Eventually, they both looked up and into each other's eyes.

"Are you in?" she asked softly. "All the way in?"

He huffed out some air. "I'm in."

She squeezed his hands. "I mean it now, Jeremy. I need you. I have no idea what I'm doing."

"I don't either."

She shook her head. "I don't mean just about my dad's alcoholism. I mean, relying on God to get us all through this."

"He's standing at the door, knocking. We just need to invite Him in."

She smiled. They stood and made their way back to the couch. The TV started sounding the countdown to midnight. A wild party of people crowded onto the streets of Times Square in New York City were counting backward … "four, three, two, one," and before she could notice what the people on TV were doing, Jeremy pulled her to him, ran his hands under her chin and to the back of her head. The tinned noise from the box disappeared while she focused on his lips on hers, the warmth between them and the racing he caused in her heart. When he pulled away, she was breathless and a little dizzy. This man caused her pulse to race, and tingling to occur in her body. What was that plan she had for keeping the relationship respectful and wholesome, and not led by lust? The more moments she spent with Jeremy, that plan was starting to dissipate. She was drawn to him, attracted to him. He was different than anyone she'd ever dated, and her longing for him was fierce. He had the most horrible of pasts, but he was determined to make it right. She admired him to no end.

And the man was hot. What would be wrong with a little old-fashioned physical interaction between two consenting adults?

"Oh! Hold on." She raced over to her table and brought two party hats, leis and noisemakers. Slipping them on him, she made loud, annoying honking noises, and he did too.

She handed him the champagne bottle and he opened it with his thumbs, sending the big cork flying through the apartment. They shared plastic glasses full of the stuff.

What a start to a whole new year of promise.

Chapter Eleven

Jeremy was delivering a finished project to a customer about an hour inland. It was a sturdy, handcrafted oak bar for a rec room, but tailored down in size to fit the measurements of the room. It fit adequately in the bed of his pickup truck, and he'd tucked padding around it to avoid bumps or scratches.

He didn't mind delivering his furniture when it was done. He liked to see the customer's first, unfettered reaction to the piece when he pulled off the wrapping. He was getting pretty good at recognizing the true emotion at the reveal. And he was happy to report, the vast majority of reactions were positive.

He supposed that if his business continued to grow, he might have to hire someone to do his deliveries. A company with a big covered truck, so multiple pieces could be delivered simultaneously, protected from the weather. If he stuck to designing and building, and he had others to reach out to customers, make sales, take orders, do the financial transactions and deliver the finished products, he could produce a lot more and he could focus on the thing he liked the most, the creation.

Of course, he'd need money to invest if he wanted to grow and he didn't have it, and he refused to borrow it. Not that a bank would lend to him anyway. So, best not to dream about a future that had little chance of happening. He'd better just be grateful for what he had here and now. Because it was sure a lot better than he had before.

Thank you, Lord.

He continued to drive but the thought wouldn't let him go. Some of those tasks didn't require particularly exclusive skills. If he could find someone who needed a job, who could learn how to sell, how to take orders and process the payments, that would free him up a great deal. Who did he know who was looking for a job?

The realization made him snort. Emma's dad, Mr. Slotky. Although he wasn't actually looking for a job, and he'd probably rather cut his foot off than work for Jeremy again.

One of the most difficult things about trying to follow the Lord, was knowing when a thought came from Him, or when it just came from his own foolhardy brain. Had God placed a nugget of a thought about Emma's dad in his mind, when he was dreaming about expanding his business for the future? After all, he and Emma had diligently prayed on New Year's Eve, asking for God's help in rehabilitating her father, to guide them in that pursuit. Was this a message along that path?

Jeremy made a turn onto a side road where his customer lived. Well, the Big Man was going to have to be a lot clearer on the subject than that, for him to get it.

* * *

Tonight was the night.

After several idea shares about how God might be leading them to help Emma's father, they were no closer to a strategy. Emma's father needed to stop drinking. They knew it and God knew it. Now, they just had to get Emma's father to believe it.

But how? Maybe they didn't need a grand plan. Maybe they just needed to ask him the question, "Will you go to AA?" Emma couldn't recall anyone ever asking her father that question.

So, Emma had called her mom and told her she and Jeremy wanted to come over tonight to talk to them. Of course, her mom was reluctant for Emma to bring him over, and Jeremy couldn't blame her. They all knew Mr. Slotky would react strongly to his visit, probably try to throw him out. It's possible that the message would be better delivered without him there.

But Emma had gotten his commitment to help and they were in it together, so tonight was the night.

Emma drove and parked in the driveway. They walked together up to the front door, and after exchanging a glance, inside.

"Mom? Dad?"

She led him into the kitchen and found Mrs. Slotky drying a dish. Her smile at their approach was natural, but nervous. "Hello, sweetheart," she said into a hug for her daughter.

"Mom, this is Jeremy."

She looked up at him and he could read so much about her on her face. Her love for her family. Her husband and her daughter made up her small world. He had intruded into that world, and as much as she wanted to welcome him warmly, she just wasn't there yet.

"So nice to meet you, ma'am." He held out a hand and she shook it tentatively. "Thank you for welcoming me into your home."

"We're glad to have you, Jeremy," she said in an automatic response. But the tone of her voice belied her trouble believing in the advisability of having him over.

Emma took her mom's hand and led her to the table. They sat. Jeremy lingered in the doorway. "Mom, before Daddy comes up, I want to give you a preview of what we're going to talk to him about. And I'd like your support on this."

Her eyes darted between Emma and Jeremy. "Okay."

"Mom, Dad needs help. This has gone on long enough. I don't know why I never suspected he was an alcoholic. I guess I just figured he drank out of boredom, not because he was addicted to it. But it's put a dark cloud over his whole life."

Mrs. Slotky stared at her daughter, then swung her gaze slowly over to Jeremy. "No offense intended here, Jeremy, but it wasn't his drinking that brought the dark cloud. The drinking came later. Losing his job is what started his downward spiral."

Jeremy knew from the redness of her face how hard it was for her to say that. "I understand. And please, don't feel uncomfortable. I've apologized to Emma and to Mr. Slotky himself for my part in his troubles. And now I'd like to apologize to you, too. I made a lot of mistakes when I was younger, and I know they impacted a lot of people, your family included. I'll regret that for the rest of my life. I spent a decade in prison trying to pay my debt and now that I'm released, every single day I work on putting my life back together by working hard, being honest and taking responsibility for my actions."

Mrs. Slotky's face evolved during the course of his apology from uptight, uncomfortable, out of her element, to appreciation and acceptance. When he finished, she gave him a genuine smile and reached her hand out to him. He took it and squeezed it.

She looked over at Emma and nodded before releasing his hand. "He's a good guy," she said softly.

"So, are you going to support us here, Mom? You can't side with Dad if he resists our help. You know he's not living a healthy life and he needs to quit drinking."

"Yes."

The word was just out of her mouth when Mr. Slotky came into the kitchen from the basement. He came to a stop at the sight of Jeremy and glared. "You again."

Mrs. Slotky got up and shepherded him into the small room, leading him by the shoulder. "Yes, remember I told you Emma was bringing Jeremy over, Gary?"

"Yeah, I remember, Edna. That doesn't mean I'm happy about it. I don't want him in my house."

"But he and Emma are friends now. And we welcome him because of that." She became a nervous ball of energy, grabbing glasses out of the cabinet, filling them with ice and handing one to each person. "Emma Jean, please take drink orders. I've got soda cans out in the garage."

Emma nodded. "Daddy, what would you like to drink?" He shook a hand at her, declining the offer. Jeremy was glad to see he didn't have a beer can in his hand. Jeremy asked for water just to validate Mrs. Slotky's hospitality. Eventually, everyone had a refreshment except for Mr. Slotky and they moved to the living room. Everyone sat except Emma.

"Daddy, Jeremy and I have something we want to talk to you about."

It was the wrong start to the conversation.

"That monster doesn't have anything to say to me. Tolerating him here in my home is one thing. I do it under protest, but only because it's your home too, baby girl. But he doesn't have the right to tell me nothing."

Jeremy stood and took Emma's arm and pulled her aside. "He's right, Emma. Why don't I leave? I think I'm only making matters worse. This is more a family matter."

She stared at him with eyes wide. "You're bailing on me? After you promised we'd do this together?"

"No, no. I'm just thinking he'd be more receptive if it were just the three of you. He's angry at me and he's not going to listen."

Emma took a deep breath and let it out. "I need your help. I'll do the talking, but you need to stay."

He scanned her face and finally agreed. For some reason, she thought she couldn't be successful at this without him. She had way more faith in him than he did himself.

"Daddy, Jeremy's offered to leave, but I asked him to stay. Now, he's not going to do any talking, but can you at least respect the fact that I want him here?"

Mr. Slotky contorted his mouth in consideration, looked up at his daughter, then sighed. He waved a hand at her, an invitation to get on with it.

"Daddy, we're all worried about you. I'm worried about you. You have to know that for some time now, you haven't been living a healthy life. You spend most of your time in the basement, you don't have work to keep you busy, you don't even do jobs around the house. But what I'm most worried about is your drinking."

He rolled his eyes but stayed quiet.

"It's obvious to me that you have a drinking problem. You need to get help." She pulled out the flyer she'd picked up at the church and held it out to him.

"What's this?" he mumbled, peering at it.

"A flyer about Alcoholics Anonymous. I think …"

"You've got to be kidding. Did he talk you into this?" His derision caused his eyes to squint and lip to curl.

"No. This is my idea. I love you Daddy, and I don't want to see you like this anymore. I want my old dad back. My hero. The one who could tackle any problem, and accomplish anything he set his mind to." She went to him and knelt at his feet, taking his hands in hers. "I want you to be around for my wedding day, to meet your grandchildren. The way you're living, you might not make it."

"That's ridiculous," he objected, but he wasn't belligerent about it. Maybe Emma was getting through to him.

"You've been someone I've looked up to, my whole life. You've been a great dad. But you've lost your way. I want to help you find your way back. Jeremy wants to help, and Mom too. You've been mad at the Harrisons for so long, it's colored your entire outlook on life. You need to work hard to put your life back together."

"If that bum hadn't run his dad's company into the ground, I wouldn't have to put my life back together. It would still be together."

"You can't blame your joblessness and your alcoholism on Jeremy. Take responsibility. Do it for Mom, so you can start helping her. Do it for yourself so you get your pride back. Your life is worth more than it's become, Dad. But it all starts here." She waved the flyer at him. "AA says that only you can quit drinking. Mom and I can't make you quit. You have to do it."

Mr. Slotky waved his hands like he was erasing chalk from a blackboard. "Darlin', there's a difference between having a few brews every day and being an alcoholic. I'm not addicted. I just enjoy a few drinks to help ease the problems of the day. Besides, I don't think you can be an alcoholic from beer. That's hard liquor only, and I don't touch the stuff."

Mrs. Slotky sat in the corner chair, staring at her feet, her face growing redder and still as a stone. It probably took all her control not to defend her husband, but she'd promised her daughter she'd support her in this.

"That's not true, Daddy. Beer is addictive, too. Now, I want this to be a new year for our family. Let's make positive changes. We can do it together. It'll be hard, but Mom and I will help you. But you have to make up your mind to change."

Mr. Slotky wiped a tear that had fallen onto his cheek. "I want to make positive change. But AA isn't the answer. I don't belong there, honey. I'm not an alcoholic. I don't have a drinking problem. There's no need for me to quit drinking, but you're right. I need to find a job. I need to throw myself into a job search. If I were working, I wouldn't drink so much."

Emma looked over to Jeremy, her concern obvious on her face. Her dad was taking a detour and she didn't like it. "Daddy, I really think you need to go to AA first. Get your drinking under control, and then get a job."

"Baby girl, I hear what you're saying, but I'm not gonna let you push me around, you hear?" He stood and took a few steps toward her, stumbled, and she helped him stand. "You did good, honey. You came to me with your concerns, and you want to push to get me to fix some problems. I was in a rut. You saw it; I see it too. You love your daddy. But I'm not going to no Alcoholics Anonymous, I'll tell you that right now. Because it won't help me. That's not my problem. I'm not saying I can't quit drinking. I'm saying I don't need to. Don't want to. Once I get a job, it'll all fall into place, you'll see." Mr. Slotky rested a heavy arm on her shoulder. Jeremy wasn't sure if it was a gesture of affection, or he needed the support to stand without falling over.

Emma's resolve was starting to crumble. She looked over at her mom. "Mom?"

Mrs. Slotky came to her feet and joined her family, standing in a little triangle in the living room. "It's an improvement," she said tentatively. "Maybe this'll work."

Emma shook her head. "Mom, you told me he was an alcoholic. If that's true, then he needs to go to a program. He can't keep drinking, even if he plans to cut back."

Mr. Slotky stepped back and pointed a glare at his wife. "You told her I was an alcoholic?" he asked incredulously. "Why would you say that?"

Mrs. Slotky's face crumbled, tears escaping. "You drink every day, Gary. I come home every night and you haven't done a thing around the house but you manage to finish a case of beer every day! Beer I can't afford to pay for. We give up other things to pay for that, don't we?"

"Where is it?" Emma asked. "I'll take it with me and return it. I'll bring you the money back. No one needs that much beer."

"Now!" Mr. Slotky shouted. "I'm the man of this house and I have a say in this. You," he pointed at Emma, "are not taking my beer. It's staying right here. And you," he pointed at his wife, "you need to trust in your husband, Edna. I've had a rough patch. But I know how serious this is. You leave it to me. I will get a job, and I will cut back on drinking. You gonna give me a chance or what?"

Mrs. Slotky hesitated only a second, then she opened her arms to him and her husband stepped into them. "Of course I will. Oh Gary, this is such good news. I'm so glad Emma came here tonight, I was dreading it so, but this is a perfect result. Once you get a job, you'll see, you'll feel so much better about yourself, you won't want to drink so much. You won't have time. And maybe you'll even want to do some of that 'Honey Do' list that I wrote for you."

He brought his hands to her cheeks and held her face in his palms. "I love you, you know." He placed a tender kiss on her lips and they shared a moment of tears and renewal.

Emma watched her parents, then turned her head in Jeremy's direction. The question in her eyes was clear.

Ten minutes later, her parents had wiped their faces, brought their emotions under control, and Mrs. Slotky invited the two of them to dinner. Emma declined.

At the door, she said, "Okay, thank you both for listening to my concerns. I'm happy, Dad, that you're taking them seriously. But in parting I have to say I think we're going down the wrong path."

Her dad chuckled and patted her on the back. "Objection duly noted, daughter dear. But your mom has faith in me that I will make some positive changes, as you said, and I'm asking for the same faith from you."

Instead of replying, she waved and walked outside. Jeremy turned to say his good-byes to Mr. Slotky, but the man had already turned his back.

* * *

A few days passed quickly, filled with the day-to-day operation of Jeremy's furniture business. He settled into the fast-paced routine of a one-man shop. He did it all: marketing, customer relations, sales, design, building and delivering. He was living his dream. Business was good and being busy was a happy consequence of that reality.

Saturday morning, he dressed and showered early. He grabbed a banana on the way through the kitchen and poured a large glass of water on ice, then headed out to his work tarp in the backyard. He had plans to see Emma tonight but had all day to work. He had two projects planned: put the final stained color on a coffee table that he'd sanded yesterday. It was so soft it almost felt like velvet to his fingertips, and the stain would put the finishing touch on that piece. While it dried in the sun, he'd get his drafting pencil and paper out and design a bookshelf for a new customer. The shelf would be custom made to fit in a nook underneath a spiral staircase and he had a few ideas to make it an innovative piece.

Outside, he pulled his canvas covers off the coffee table. He folded them in half, then half again, turned back to the table … and froze. He stepped closer, turned his head to look up at the bright sun. Could the rays possibly be playing tricks with his eyes? He ran a hand over the surface of the table. An ugly, jagged gash marred the top.

He stood motionless, evaluating the implications. Someone had come to his house, snuck around to the back, uncovered his latest work, used a metal tool to destroy it, then covered it back up as if nothing had happened, then escaped. Completely undetected.

He burst into a fit of activity. He had at least four other pieces in various stages of construction. Had those been attacked as well?

He flipped a tarp off a dresser in its early stages. He studied every inch of it. Nothing.

He moved to a queen-sized headboard and footboard in cherry, leaning against the dresser, covered with another set of tarps. No apparent damage.

He went through the rest of his inventory and although the majority of his pieces were unharmed, the last item he uncovered was a long kitchen table with pedestal legs. A long, angry splintered ridge was gouged into the surface.

Jeremy tossed the tarps and stumbled away. A buzzing attacked his ears, increasing in sound so much that he couldn't hear anything else outside of it. An anxiety attack was coming on, but he knew how to control those now, or at least had some tips from Neil.

He bent over at the waist, forcing the blood into his head. He took long, solid breaths, evenly in and out. He straightened and stretched his arms, his legs, circled his neck. The worst of it past, he concentrated on his problem.

Vandalism. It wasn't a good problem to have, but he certainly wasn't the first business owner to deal with it. Pesky, that's all it was. He could deal with it. He walked over to the two affected pieces. He studied them, ran his fingers into the gouges.

No, there was no way he could salvage these. He'd have to cut his losses on the inventory, materials and his time, and move on. He'd be behind schedule now, having to re-do two nearly completed pieces. He would make calls to his customers and explain. And hope they'd understand.

But a more troubling implication popped into his mind. He couldn't work here in his backyard anymore. It wasn't secure. He needed four walls and a door, and a place to lock up his inventory and materials at night. Someplace he needn't worry about vandals.

What about his finished stock? The vandal evidently knew he did his work here at home — did he also know he stored inventory at Marianne's Inn? One way to find out.

He circled the house to the pickup truck, then drove it around to the backyard. He hoisted each of the pieces into the bed of the pickup and jumped into the cab.

A few minutes later, he pulled into the Seaside Inn, and drove around the side to his shed under the Inn on stilts. He left the truck there, then walked around the back, up the wooden stairs on to the sundeck, and entered the Inn through the sun porch.

January wasn't a hopping month for guests, but Marianne attracted a modest "snowbird" crowd; retired couples who lived in the Midwest or northeast, and escaped the snow and cold of their region to stay at the Inn for a month at a time. Marianne loved her senior guests, and they tended to come back year after year.

The last thing he'd meant to do by entering unannounced through the back door was to alarm anyone, but that's exactly what he'd done. A gray-haired woman sat on the sun porch, facing the beach, enjoying a home baked muffin and a cup of coffee. She looked at him, shrieked and jumped in her seat. Her muffin took a dive to the floor.

"I'm sorry, I'm sorry, ma'am!" He went to her side, knelt and scooped up the muffin and tossed it in a trash bin. "Let me get you another." He spied the basket full on a side table and selected one that looked identical to the other, wrapped it in a napkin and handed it to her.

"My word, son, you startled me."

"Yes, I'm sorry, I didn't mean to. Very careless of me. I should've announced myself."

"Are you a guest here?" The old lady now peered at him over the tops of her glasses, clutching the muffin.

"No, ma'am, I'm family. I'm Marianne's brother, Jeremy." He held his hand out.

She fluttered a hand in front of her face. "Mercy me."

Marianne entered the porch holding a coffee pot. She noticed him and he was relieved to see her face light up with joy. Maybe the lady would believe him now, and calm down. "Jeremy! What a nice surprise!" She pulled him into a hug and squeezed him, patting him on the back.

"I startled your guest by coming in through the back."

Marianne let him go and smiled at the old woman. "Oh, Mrs. Robins, I'm so sorry he startled you. But he's welcome anytime. He's my big brother. I'm so glad you had a chance to meet him. Jeremy, Mr. and Mrs. Robins have stayed with us three winters in a row now. They love Pawleys and getting away from upstate New York winters."

Mrs. Robins rose and waved her departure, taking her coffee and muffin into the great room. Jeremy watched her leave, then turned to his sister. "I didn't mean to scare her."

"Of course you didn't. Don't worry about it."

"Did you tell her about my, uh, background?"

Marianne frowned at him. "Why would I do that?"

Jeremy shrugged. "I just wondered if part of her reaction had to do with being startled by an ex-con."

Marianne punched him on the arm, dismissing his concerns. "Want some breakfast?"

"No. Do you have a minute to come see something?"

She followed him outside and around to the truck. He jumped up into the bed and held a hand out, helping her climb up. She spotted the vandalized piece right away and gasped, "Oh Jeremy! What happened?" She rubbed her fingers in the damaged wedges in the wood.

"Vandal. Woke up this morning and found two pieces like this, attacked by a tool, I'm guessing a chisel of some sort. Gouged enough of a wedge in the wood that I can't possibly repair them. I'm going to have to start over on this coffee table, and this kitchen table here." He pointed to it.

"Oh, my gosh. How much in damages?"

He did a quick calculation in his head. "About eight hundred for both these pieces together. And probably … five days wasted."

Marianne shook her head, her face scrunched as she tried to hold in tears. "Who would've done something like this?"

He laid a hand on her shoulder. Leave it to his sis to feel his pain nearly deeper than he did. "I don't know. I'll have to give it some thought. I mean, I guess it could be old enemies, people who haven't forgiven or forgotten. It's the price I pay for my past."

"That's not fair," she said with a vengeance.

He smiled sadly and gave her a look that said what words didn't have to. "I love having your support, but honestly, this is not a disaster. I'll just have to be more careful in the future. First, let's look at my stock here. If someone broke in here and damaged furniture, it gets way more personal. The thought of someone with a chisel this close to you and Stella …" He dropped off the thought, and jumped off the truck bed, turning and helping her down.

Fifteen minutes later, they'd uncovered all the furniture pieces he was storing in the shed and both were relieved to discover that not one had been touched. Reassuring, but not enough. He needed to make some changes.

"First thing I need to do is look around for a building, or at least a part of one. I could use it for a workshop, but also a storefront to draw customers in. Then I gotta transport all these inventory pieces over there, and stop luring danger to your door."

She waved a hand in dismissal.

"No, sis. You've got Stella here. No way would I want any danger getting near her, or you."

"We've got Tom to protect us too, you know."

"I know, but you're both busy with the Inn. I don't want to take advantage of your generosity. As soon as I can, I'll move this stuff out."

She came in close and gave him a peck on his cheek. They unloaded the pieces from the truck into the storage shed and Jeremy carefully locked everything up.

* * *

That night, Emma was putting the finishing touches on her eyelashes and lips when she heard a tap. She took one last glance in the mirror and rushed to the door. Jeremy stood there in jeans and a form fitting thermal shirt in a light blue. The color made his gorgeous blue eyes pop. His dark hair looked recently ruffled by fingers, and the stubble on his chin was in the "just right" category.

"Hi," she said probably a little too breathlessly, and moved in close. She sank her lips into his and he immediately reciprocated with a warm welcoming response. As they parted, she couldn't help running her fingers across his abdomen, glorying in the tight muscles underneath the fabric. Suddenly, she found herself yearning for summer when she could invite him to the beach and admire his swimwear.

That thought made her smile and he noticed as she stepped back and let him in.

"What's the smile for?" he asked.

She giggled, just feeling happy that things were so right in her life. Dating Jeremy, both their jobs going well, her father committed to cutting back on drinking and looking for a job. "Just glad to see you."

He nodded. "Me too. Did you have any plans for us tonight?"

She shrugged. "Had thought of a few options but we can come up with something fun."

They headed down to his truck and decided on a local favorite, The Crab Trap, very casual décor and some of the best shellfish not only on the island, but in the whole area. Due to the season, there wasn't a long wait, and within twenty minutes they were digging into their selections of shrimp, mussels, crab legs and lobster.

"I had some bad news today," Jeremy said.

"Oh no. What?"

"A vandal came to my backyard and destroyed two of my works in progress. Chucked away at them with a chisel. Big gouges in the wood surface. I won't be able to repair them. I'll have to ditch them and start over."

She dropped a fork and reached for his hand. "Jeremy. That's terrible. What are you going to do?"

He knitted his brow in frustration. "Maybe an enemy has figured out where I live and where I do my work. The fact that they were behind my house, destroying my livelihood while I was potentially right inside, puts it a little too close to home. I moved all my pieces."

"To where?"

"To Marianne's. But I can't leave everything there for long. If, whoever it is, figures out what I've done, I'd put Marianne and her family in danger. I refuse to put them at risk because of me."

"Do you think this person is dangerous?"

He shrugged. "I have no idea. But I have to plan for the worst. If anything happened to someone I care about because of me, I'd never forgive myself."

She rubbed her hand absentmindedly over his.

"I'm going to have to find a permanent location for my business. I've grown enough now that I can't just work out of my yard or Marianne's. I wasn't quite ready yet to rent a building, but maybe this is God pushing me to make that step."

She lit up. "That's exciting! How about we go out together with a realtor and we'll look at the options?"

"Sure, thank you."

They sat in silence for a few moments. "Do you have any clue who would do this?"

"No one in particular. But it could be any number of people. Someone who did time with me, who is now released. You don't exactly build friendships in there. Maybe someone who resented me, or didn't like me is now on a vendetta. Or, more likely, someone from the Harrison and Son days. Someone I wronged. Instead of confronting me and letting me apologize, they've held a grudge and now that I'm released, they want to make me pay."

"How would they know where you live? How would they know you're building furniture?"

"Pawleys Island is a small town. If you wanted information about anyone or anything, all you need to do is ask enough questions."

They devoured their seafood and let their stomachs settle over cups of coffee. Jeremy sat so quietly she could almost hear his thoughts churning in his head. Something was bothering him. Eventually he let her I on it.

"Listen, I don't want to alarm you but a few months back, I heard about a big-time convict that I did time with who is now released. He's settled in Myrtle Beach."

"Oh, my gosh!"

"Yeah. He's no one you want to mess with. He's a mean one, and he's not afraid to use his strength to go after what he wants. Sources say he's getting bored with the clean life. He's not getting any jobs, he's finding it difficult to fit in, and it would be just his MO to try to stir up a little trouble, especially for people he previously served time with."

Emma frowned. "Does he know about you being here in Pawleys?"

Jeremy shrugged. "I don't know. I can't think of any particular reason he'd come after me, unless he's just, like I said, bored, and looking for fun. He and I tolerated each other in prison, but we weren't friends, not by a long shot. If someone told him I was trying to start my own business, keeping my nose clean, making a little money, I could see him trying to mess that up for me, out of spite or jealousy. Or just because he could get me in trouble."

"That wouldn't be fair at all," she said with vehemence, then her anger died at the look Jeremy gave her. Of course it wasn't fair, but it was life and life was never fair, especially for someone in Jeremy's position.

"Could you talk to the local police and have them keep an eye out for this guy, what's his name?"

"Leroy White. And no, I wouldn't do that necessarily, but I did mention it to Neil the last time I met with him. Leroy isn't one of Neil's flock but he said he'd contact Leroy's probation officer and give him a heads up. Hopefully this is all speculation, and Leroy is actually doing the right things."

"What was Leroy in for?"

Jeremy shrugged. "A variety of crimes, burglary, theft, violence of whatever sort." He brought his eyes up to look into hers.

She shivered. "Vandalism?"

"I wouldn't rule it out."

"Seriously?" she went on, her anger rising. "So he could've gotten out of jail, figured out where you were, located your inventory and come after them with a chisel in your backyard. All under the radar."

"I guess it's possible, but that's a major jump to conclusions. I haven't even seen the guy. He'd have to be pretty sneaky and savvy to have done all this without me knowing anything about it."

Despite the scary news Jeremy had just shared, a shiver of optimism flitted through Emma. Her dad was on the right track, her mom was happy, and this Leroy character could be a suspect in the vandalism. Now that Neil was aware of him, the authorities could keep an eye on him and hold him accountable for any wrongdoing. And she could focus on her future with Jeremy.

He smiled. "I'm sorry to worry you. Maybe the incident was random and isolated. Meanwhile, we've got a plan. I'll call a commercial realtor I know and we'll go out and look. This will force me to make this a real business and not something I just do as a hobby. With your help, I'll make this thing work."

Before leaving, they took a moonlit walk on the beach. The January breeze made it a little chilly, which gave her a good excuse to snuggle against Jeremy when he wrapped his arm around her. She leaned against his chest as they walked, breathing in his scent of soap and wood chips. They talked about other things than the vandalism, but it never left her mind, and she was sure, his as well.

When did growing up get so hard?

* * *

A few nights later, Emma's mom invited her over for dinner. As soon as she arrived, she could tell the tension had been lifted from the house. The living room was tidy and picked up, free from loads of unfolded laundry. Her dad greeted her at the door instead of hiding out in the basement. He gave her a kiss and she couldn't help taking a sniff to see if she smelled beer on his breath. She didn't. Mom was finishing a salad in the kitchen while the lasagna cooled on the stovetop, so Dad took her drink order. He prepared a tall glass of Diet Coke on ice and handed it to her. The two were working as a team and it was so nice to see.

When the three sat down at the table it brought back pleasant memories from her childhood. Mom talked about a customer at work today who had some crazy demand that the office declined. Mom always had crazy customer service stories and they all shared a laugh.

"What about you, Emma Jean? Anything happening at work these days?" Dad asked.

"Yeah, I'm working on a story about an Army vet who came home with one leg. Instead of being destroyed by such a horrible injury at such a young age, he's spending lots of time with his sons. Through that, he's started a local Paralympics chapter and is teaching other amputees how to be more active. I hope to make it very inspirational. He deserves some great press."

Over dessert of ice cream and chocolate syrup, Emma brought up the subject that had been weighing on her all night. "So Dad, how's it going with your drinking and your job hunt?"

He gave her a surprised look. "Get right to it, huh? Okay. I have reduced my drinking to two a day."

"He's been doing really well, Emma," her mom said.

"Two a day?"

"Yep. When I'm done with two, usually in the afternoon, I get up and find something else to do. I find that if I just sit and watch TV, I crave beer. It's become a habit. So I get up and do something else, get my mind off it."

"He's already done some home improvement jobs. Painted the laundry room, working on scraping the exterior so he can repaint the house."

Oh, how Emma hoped that this newfound good behavior was a permanent change. For her mother's sake, who was so, so hopeful. And for her father's sake. He needed to turn his life around.

"That's great, Dad. I'm proud of you." She smiled at him. "Keep it up."

He nodded. After dessert, they took cups of hot tea to the living room.

"How's Jeremy doing?" her mom asked.

She gazed over at her. The subject of Jeremy hadn't come up all evening. She wondered if it would. "He's doing great. But he had a little bit of a setback. Two of his furniture pieces that were stored in his backyard were vandalized."

"Oh no!" her mother said. Her father looked into his tea cup. "What happened?"

"Evidently while he was home one night, someone came into his backyard where he keeps his work in progress and gouged trenches into the surface of two tables. Completely irreparable. Such a shame. He has no insurance so it's a complete loss."

Dad looked up. "Why doesn't he have insurance?"

Emma shrugged. "He hasn't been at the business that long. He's trying to stay within his means without going into debt. If the money doesn't come in, he doesn't send it out."

He scoffed. "Learned his lesson, I guess." His resentment was obvious in his tone. And so was his criticism.

"Yes, Dad. He's learned his lessons and he's doing things differently this time around. He's starting small and growing. But the problem is, he doesn't really have a workplace other than his yard, and obviously his yard isn't secure, so we're going to look for a place he can afford on his earnings."

Her dad put his cup on the table with a thump. "You really are in deep with him, aren't you? You refuse to see it, but you're much better off forgetting about him, and finding someone else."

"Dad, you're not going to like this, but I really like Jeremy and I don't want to find someone else."

He sat motionless, without a word for a moment, then got up and stomped back to his bedroom.

Chapter Twelve

"I've got several properties to show you today. Hopefully one of them will meet your needs."

Jeremy looked at Emma as they followed his realtor friend, Cam, and climbed into the back seat of her swanky sedan. He squeezed Emma's hand, holding on tight even after helping her in. She gave him an excited grin.

"The budget's low, Cam," he warned again. He'd already told her twice.

The realtor waved her hand from the front seat. "I know, I know. But it's an investment, remember. You get more space, you'll build more inventory to fill it."

His heart brimmed with mixed emotions. Nervous about the limb he was crawling out on. Fear that he'd go into debt again by committing beyond his means. A trickle of déjà vu tickled his spine.

But it was different this time. He had Emma by his side and that was a little miracle all its own. He had no idea how he'd ever deserve her admiration, but he'd spend the rest of his days trying to earn it, if that was God's will. When she looked at him, he caught a glimpse of the man she evidently thought he was. And although he wasn't worthy, she made him determined to live up to her vision.

"You'll do fine," she said softly. "This is the right time, the right thing to do for you and your future."

He took a deep breath and it caught in his chest. Maybe he should've asked his dad to join them. His dad had run a successful business for years before Jeremy had …

No. He was an adult, a professional. As much as he respected Hank, he needed to prove to his dad that he could do it on his own. That he was on the right path this time, the straight and narrow. He had a need, deep in his soul, to redeem himself to his father.

"Okay Cam, show us whatcha got."

Two hours later, they had toured three locations. One, Jeremy ruled out entirely. His hope was to use this rental space as a multi-purpose location: workshop, showroom and retail storefront, and the first place didn't meet that need. But the other two did. And although the sticker price on both of them made his head spin, he'd just have to get over that, he guessed. One was a better location with other businesses nearby, but smaller floor space. The larger one had more room than he could ever imagine needing, but he'd have to ask his customers to drive off the beaten path to come find him. There were pro's and con's to each. He needed to think on it a while.

"Cam, you're pretty sure there's nothing else out there to look at?" He squinted at her in the afternoon sun when she returned them to her realtor office.

"Not if you want to stay on Pawleys. There are additional locales in Myrtle."

He immediately shook his head. Pawleys was home. Pawleys was where he needed to make up for past mistakes. Pawleys is where he would stay. "We'll stay on the island. So, can I take a few days to think about it?"

"Sure thing. I'll let the owners know you're considering and ask them if they have any other bites on the line."

He thanked her for her help. He and Emma got in his truck and drove toward Marianne's inn. On the way, they discussed options.

"I like the smaller place," Emma said.

"I do too. But it'll end up costing me more than the bigger place. That seems kind of crazy."

"The basis of real estate: location, location, location."

"Yeah."

"The neighboring businesses will help draw customers in. And that place has a big display window. Put your most enticing pieces there to help draw interest. Change them frequently so it brings people back."

He looked over at her while he was driving. She was full of good ideas.

"Offer an internship to a college student to be the window dresser," she went on. "You'd get someone to do the work for free, while offering them something unique for their resume."

He checked his rearview mirror, then pulled the truck to a stop on the side of the road. Emma, startled, stopped talking, looked around. He reached for her, pulled her into his arms and landed his lips on hers. She made a sound in the back of her throat, sort of an "mmmmm" like she was settling into a comfortable bed. He didn't have the words to tell her how much she meant to him, so he hoped he could somehow convey it with his kiss. He focused on telling her, with his lips, with his embrace, with his fingers in her hair, and his tongue circling her mouth what he failed to say verbally.

He pulled back, his breath coming faster, his hands still buried in that gorgeous mountain of hair, and gazed at her. He was tempted to try to explain, but he knew he'd screw it up. He was never good at that stuff. He was his father's son, after all.

So he settled for, "It means a lot to me that you're here helping me, supporting me, getting excited about my business. Thank you."

He rested his eyes on her for another few seconds and chuckled at her reaction. He'd caught her by surprise. She was speechless, and that hardly ever happened. He rested back in his seat, put the truck in gear and pulled out onto the road again.

Beside him, he heard a breathless word escape her lips, "Wow."

Jeremy pulled onto the road leading to the Inn, dead-on to a most fearful sight. "Oh no," Emma murmured beside him. He parked on the road and ran. A fire engine, lights flashing, sat in front of the Inn, taking up the entire yard. Sea oat grasses crushed underneath its tires and Jeremy's heart pounded. A firefighter in full gear came his way, hoisting a hose behind him toward the truck. Jeremy raced up to him.

"What's going on, man? Is the Inn on fire?"

The man raised a hand. "Done. The fire's out. Go talk to the captain if you want more."

Jeremy didn't see anyone meeting the description of a fire captain, so he raced around to the back of the Inn, where there was more commotion. Marianne, Tom and Stella huddled together, Stella bawling, Marianne with tears settling in her eyes. Several snowbird guests stood on the sand, looking up at the inn.

"Sis, what's going on?" He ran a hand behind her back, pulling her and Stella in close to him. He nodded at his brother-in-law. "Hey Tom, is everyone okay?"

Marianne shuddered, gripping her crying daughter tighter. "Oh Jeremy, it was just awful. Although could've been worse. Thank God it's out."

"What happened?" he asked, rubbing a hand across his mouth. The remaining firefighters were emerging from the sandy storage shed underneath the Inn. The same location where he stored his ... "Is that where my inventory is?"

Of course it was. He took off at a dash, ignoring Marianne's shout. A firefighter holding a clipboard grabbed his arm just as he ducked his head into the storage shed. "You can't come here. Need to ask you to step back."

His voice was no-nonsense. Jeremy looked over the man's shoulder at his inventory of finished pieces. One completely charred chest, multiple surrounding wooden pieces dripping with water. His heart jumped as the scenario became clear. "This is where the fire started? With that chest right there?"

The captain eyed him curiously. "Are you associated with the Seaside Inn?"

"The owner is my sister and those are my wooden pieces there. I built them, and she let me store them here."

He released Jeremy's arm and looked back at the damage behind him. "Yeah, that oak chest was the originator. We're not sure why yet, but it started the burn and was starting to spread when fortunately we got the 9-1-1 call and came out immediately. We got it before it spread."

Jeremy swung his head. "Is anyone in danger? Did anyone get hurt?"

The captain shook his head. "We were lucky. Could've been a disaster. This whole Inn is wood, not to mention the decks surrounding it. Could've gone up like a pile of matchsticks." He looked around at the scene of the fire.

"You really shouldn't do finishing here. Most finishes are combustible. Need a lot of ventilation till they're dry."

"No, sir. I apply the finishes somewhere else – usually in my backyard at home. I only bring them here when they're fully dry."

"Well, we're going to investigate this fire, see if we can figure out what started it. We'll keep the Innkeepers and the insurance company informed."

Jeremy nodded his thanks, and after the captain moved on, he eased into his impromptu furniture storage area, compiling a mental list of the damages. The chest, obviously. Charred to a crisp. The water from the powerful hoses, soaking everything around the chest, removing any possibility of a fire surviving. Five, six, seven. By the time Marianne, Tom and Emma came looking for him, he'd counted close to a dozen water logged pieces.

He turned away from the detritus and faced them. Marianne reached out and put a hand on his shoulder. He put his hand on top of hers and squeezed. "I'm so sorry, Marianne." He looked to his brother-in-law. "Tom. I can't believe it was my furniture that put you guys in danger. It's out of here tonight."

His throat choked, overwhelming him and he stopped short. Marianne protested. "Jeremy, you didn't do anything. It wasn't your ..."

He gave his head a brisk shake. "Marianne, my furniture caught fire. It could've spread. It could've damaged your inn, heck, it could've brought the whole thing down in flames. Thank God someone called 9-1-1. Who was it? Who discovered the fire?"

Marianne looked away. He darted a look at Tom. "Who, Tom?"

"It was Stella. She was on the beach, digging as usual. She said she smelled something weird and looked up and saw smoke billowing out of the Inn. She was scared to death. She started screaming and crying and ran in to find one of us. Once we figured out what she was going on about, we called 9-1-1. Thank God they came fast."

"Where is she now?"

"Up in her room." Tom pointed.

"I'll be right back." Jeremy took off for the back door of the Inn. He climbed the stairs to Stella's room. The little girl laid in her bed, sobbing quietly into her pillow.

"Stella," he said, settling himself gently beside her on the bed, rubbing her little back. "Shhhh, sweetheart, shhh. It's okay."

"Uncle Jeremy?" The scared little voice about ripped his heart out of his chest.

"Yes, darlin', it's me."

She maneuvered in her bed, flipped to her back. "Your furniture burned."

"I know, sweet pea. I'm so sorry about that."

She frowned at him. "Why are you sorry?"

He heaved out a breath. "Because the fire is all my fault. If I weren't storing my furniture here, it wouldn't've caught on fire, and you wouldn't be crying right now."

She sniffed. "You didn't do it. It was an accident."

"But you're crying because of the fire. Are you scared, baby?"

She nodded, her lower lip starting to wobble again. "I smelled the smoke and it made me cough. I was coughing and I looked up and saw it pouring out from under the Inn. I didn't know what it was but I knew it was dangerous."

"You were the hero of the whole day, you know. It's because of you that no one got hurt. You're brave and fast and smart. You know that?"

A little glimmer of a smile lit her lips. "Really?"

"Yes, really. Your mom and dad are so proud of you, and so am I."

Her shoulders relaxed slightly. "I don't want to sleep here tonight. I don't want to fall asleep."

He wrapped his arms around her and pulled her into his lap. "Because you're afraid of a fire starting again, and you won't be awake to find it?"

She nodded a little tiny nod. "And I'm afraid I'll have nightmares."

"I won't let any of that happen, sweet pea. I'm moving all that furniture out. It'll all be gone by tonight. Nothing for you to worry about. No danger at all. Okay?"

She took in a deep breath and let it out. "Do you think Mommy and Daddy will let me sleep with them tonight?"

He had to laugh. His Stella, working an angle. "To make sure you don't have nightmares about the fire?"

"Yep."

"I'll help you ask them." He got to his feet and pulled her up, flipping her leg around his neck so she sat on his shoulders. Emma stood in the doorway, listening to their exchange. He winked at her. "Emma will ask them too."

Stella waved a few fingers at Emma as they passed.

Later, when they had done a good job of convincing Stella's parents to let her sleep with them tonight, and Stella acted like she'd had a load removed from her shoulders, she went back to the beach to dig. Jeremy turned to his sister and her husband. "I'm loading all this stuff up and getting it out of here."

Marianne started to protest, but Tom said, "That's the right thing to do."

Marianne turned to her husband. "He doesn't have anywhere to put it yet, Tom."

Tom shrugged. "He'll have to figure it out, won't he? Marianne, we had a fire at our inn. Do you understand how serious this could've been? With fire damage comes renovations and loss of business. And injury! With all these guests here? They could've been injured, or worse yet, killed." He gave a firm shake of his head. "No. It just makes sense to remove the items that were the originator of the fire. It's too dangerous."

Jeremy said, "He's 100% right, sis. I wouldn't be able to live with myself if there'd been damage because of me. I'm taking it out, right now. Tom, can you help me load it?"

They worked together, pulling out the damaged furniture first. At least half of them were unsalvageable. Jeremy calculated in his head the dollar loss, then told himself it wasn't important. The fact that the Inn was unharmed, other than a little smoke in the rooms, which the ocean breezes were working to clear out through open windows. They'd dodged a bullet and he was thankful.

The other half of the damaged pieces, he may be able to restore. Water marks could be removed, the wood could dry out, and he could re-apply the finish. He was hopeful that he could salvage them and sell them at a reduced price.

A firefighter approached and tapped on the charred chest. "We're taking this one to study for arson."

Jeremy and Tom eyed each other. Jeremy knew exactly what he was thinking. First, vandalism and now, arson. Bad news was following Jeremy, and Tom couldn't wait to get him as far away from his business and his family as possible. And he didn't blame him in the least.

"Do you use lacquer-based wood finishes like shellac?"

"Yes."

The firefighter nodded. "Sometimes they spontaneously combust when they're applied, not fully dried and not enough ventilation."

Jeremy ran his hand along the surface of the chest. "But this one didn't have shellac. It was for a baby's nursery. I used a glossy paint on this one, non-flammable."

"Non-flammable?"

"Yes. I'd never use anything remotely flammable on a nursery set."

The firefighter nodded, made a note on a notepad.

They were cleared to remove all the furniture except the chest. Jeremy made a trip to the dump and unloaded all the furniture that was a total loss. He came back for a second load, the pieces he hoped to restore. He had nowhere to take them, so he took a gamble and returned to his house with them. If a vandal and an arsonist wanted to hit him on the same day, he had little control over it.

Later, he and Emma sat in his living room, ruminating over the events of the day. "I can't afford to rent the warehouse, especially after losing six more pieces."

Emma shrugged. "But you can't afford not to rent the warehouse. You have nowhere safe to store your stuff without it."

Jeremy let that one settle in. She was right. He couldn't afford to do it, but worse, he couldn't afford not to. This would require a leap of faith.

"Will you pray with me?"

She nodded and he turned to face her on the couch, gripping her hands. "Our dear Father. Tough day today, but nowhere near as tough as You faced on Your crucifixion day. You tasted all the pain and suffering of human life and rose above it all. You set the example for weak men like me. Help me keep my eyes on You, follow Your will and do the right thing. Guide me through this difficult time and let me know the right thing to do. Amen."

They spent a few moments in silence, gazes connected. Then he reached for the phone.

"Cam? I'll go ahead and take the smaller spot. Yeah, the one in the strip mall with the big display window. Okay, thanks."

Emma jumped on him, her weight sinking him deeper into the couch cushions. "Nice job." She leaned in close, brushed her lips against his and he forgot all his troubles.

For a moment.

* * *

Emma drove in the direction of her parents'. Her mother had invited her and Jeremy over for dinner and normally she would've loved to have him there. But this time, she didn't bring him. Although he was putting on a brave front, trying to be thankful that no one had been injured in the fire, and the Inn hadn't been damaged, she knew he was distressed. He'd written off six exquisite creations as a total loss, and six more, he was now spending his time trying to renovate what he could to earn a little bit of money from them. Time was money. Time he'd originally spent on the items, bringing them to their previous state of grandeur. And now time again to try to restore them. And knowing Jeremy, if the pieces weren't up to his impeccable standards even after spending the time on renovations, he wouldn't sell them, not even at a discount.

So of course, money was an issue, a big one.

But the investigation was bugging him too. If someone had set the fire, targeting his furniture, what message were they trying to send? And did they have no regard for the safety and well-being of everyone in the Inn? Who could hate him that much? And why?

Dinner was lovely at her parents' house. The house was clean and tidy and her parents were calm and easy with each other. Her dad was attentive and cooperative when her mother spoke or asked something of him. In fact, she couldn't remember a more pleasant evening with her parents. Ever. They laughed, they joked, they were happy.

And her father was sober.

Maybe he was right in resisting her attempts to send him to Alcoholics Anonymous. If he was able, this easily, to control his drinking, then he most likely was not an alcoholic. Life seemed to be so good for them.

Might as well go for broke, she thought. This next question had the potential of turning this whole perfect evening into disaster.

"So how's the job hunting going, Dad?"

He paused, took her question in for a moment, and looked down at the table. "Well, baby girl, I've been looking, I really have. But there's not much out there. And my skills aren't current. They wonder why I haven't been working for so long, and that right there is enough to knock me out of the running. There's so many people looking for work, it's easy to eliminate someone. Not to mention my age. Why would a boss hire an old guy like me when he's got someone in their twenties or thirties also applying?"

Her mother put a hand over his on the table and patted it. "Dad's thinking about going to the community college and taking some classes. Maybe getting a certification, a new trade. There are several options that he's considering."

She smiled. "Awesome, Dad. That sounds good. I'm proud of you. Learning something new is good."

They moved on to other topics and Emma embarked on an internal argument. She had another question for her father but was it really her business? Was she pushing her luck? Did she want to risk his anger? Finally, when momentary silence hit the room, she ventured, "So Dad, how's it going with the drinking?"

He blinked slowly at her. "How does it look like it's going?"

"You're sober tonight."

"Yes, I am." He winked at her mother, who gave him an adoring glance like he was the most perfect man in the world.

"How about other days? Are you cutting down? I believe you wanted to limit your drinking to two beers a day."

He nodded, lips pursed. She knew that look. He was starting to lose patience with her because she continued to push when he was trying to dismiss. "I'm doing fine, darlin'. I thank you for caring, but really this is between your mom and I, ain't it? And she's very happy, can't you tell?"

She looked over at her mom. Sweet, loving, conflict-hating Mom. She did look happy. In fact, she looked thrilled. Emma smiled at her, and her mom responded with a full-out grin. "I'm glad. I'm so happy things are going so well. I love you both."

Fifteen minutes later, they all kissed and hugged, said their good-byes and Emma drove away, hopeful that things were beginning to look good, for the first time in a decade.

Chapter Thirteen

Emma took extra care in the mirror with her hair. Curl, twist with her fingers, spray. Now, her eyelashes. Coat them just enough, not too much. Her summer beach tan had long since faded, making foundation and powder necessary on her face. She didn't do it much, one of the advantages of only being in her late twenties, her complexion was in good shape. Past the acne, hadn't encountered wrinkles yet. But a light coating helped her feel more attractive.

And tonight, she wanted to feel attractive.

She drove over to Jeremy's house, her pulse pounding more than usual. *Calm*, she thought. *No reason to be nervous. He's going to want this as much as I do. He's a guy, for God's sake.*

She parked in Jeremy's driveway and walked up to his door, holding a bottle of chilled pinot grigio. He probably wasn't a wine drinker as a first choice, but she needed it tonight to bolster her courage. It was time for her to let him know exactly how she felt about him. And hope that he felt the same way.

She knocked out of habit, then went ahead and opened the door. A waft of deep fried awesomeness met her nostrils just a few steps in. "Hello?" she said.

"I'm in the kitchen," his voice came.

She walked through the tiny house, turning into the kitchen in the back. He stood at the stove, a fork in hand. Sizzling drips of oil jumped from the cast iron skillet. Strips of fish lined the counter, lying on dishtowels. She leaned in and gave him a quick smooch on the cheek, then backed away.

"I went fishing this morning, caught six groupers. I figured, what would be better than frying them up for us tonight?"

She smiled. "You fish?"

He laughed. "Not often, but sure, I grew up on the beach. I can fish and crab with the best of 'em."

Shredded cabbage and carrots sat in a bowl. "You making cole slaw?"

"Yeah. I had to abandon it when the oil was ready."

She opened the refrigerator and pulled out the slaw dressing. "I'll take care of it." She set to work. "Good dinner." Good thing she was hungry.

"And I made some hushpuppies too. They're in that basket over there."

When all was prepared, she poured them each a glass of wine and slid his glass to his spot at the table. He glanced at it and gave her a look. "Wine? Are we celebrating a special occasion?"

Hope so. "Sure. Your lease signing. You're moving into your warehouse in a few days. That's a huge milestone for your new business."

His gaze rested on hers, his movements from dinner quieted. "You've supported me from the very beginning. It's nice to know you believe in me. Even when there are pit stops."

"There will always be pit stops, Jeremy. Just because the journey isn't perfect, doesn't mean it's not worth traveling."

They dug into the fresh fried fish and the flavor exploded on her tongue. The slaw and hushpuppies were just right as well. When the meal was done, Emma gathered the plates, and despite Jeremy's protests, she took them to his kitchen and loaded them into the dishwasher. He joined her.

"I saw my dad recently. He was sober as a stone."

Jeremy looked at her. "That's great. Has he stopped drinking, do you think?"

She shrugged. "At least for that day, or that evening that I was over, he didn't drink. I guess that's a start. Not nearly enough, I'm afraid, for the long term." She sniffed. "My mom's ecstatic, but of course, that poor woman is just happy there's been an improvement. She's not going to push it. She likes what she sees, so she's happy. Period."

"But you're suspicious."

She nodded. "Too easy. I just think there's more to it than that. A man drinks almost a case of beer every day for ten years, his daughter finally says something to him about it and he suddenly stops drinking?"

"Yeah. But like you said, it's a start. And it wouldn't have happened without you being brave enough to bring it up. Because I know that wasn't easy."

She paused, trying to formulate words that she couldn't quite get straight in her mind. "He seems to have turned a corner, Jeremy. Controlling his drinking, looking for a job, even talking about taking some classes to qualify him for more work. He's pulling his life together."

"That's the best news I've heard all day." He blessed her with a smile that made her heart race.

"He's not there yet, but I see steps to improvement." She finished her kitchen chore, and his proximity gave her the jitters. She wanted to take a step forward in their relationship tonight, but first, she needed to validate her true feelings for him. And in light of what she had on her mind, she was done talking about her father.

She turned and gripped his cotton shirt, and went motionless, simply looking into his eyes. He seemed to sense the importance of the moment because he stared back at her, his eyes darkening and his expression going soft. Concentrating on the face of this man in the quiet, she knew it. She was falling in love with Jeremy. She hadn't professed it to him, or even admitted it to herself prior to this moment. But it was true.

She released her hold on him, but as she lowered her hands, he noticed and grabbed them. "Your hands are shaking. Are you okay?"

She grinned and nodded. "Yes, in fact," she said and pulled him back to the table. She lifted her glass. "Time for a toast. Here's to a night to celebrate finding each other and building a future."

He blinked as she took a generous swallow, then he followed suit. She gripped her near empty wine glass and strode intentionally to the couch. She looked over her shoulder and caught his eye before she sat, leaning slowly against the back. A second's hesitation, then he joined her. He sat, and she scooted, closing up the short distance between them. She let her head drop back, swallowing the remainder of the wine, then rested the empty glass on the table.

"Is there something on television you'd like to see?" he asked, picking up the remote and fumbling with it.

"No." She pressed her thigh against his, and with her palm, caressed his denim-coated leg. He shuddered and let the remote fall.

She turned into him and kissed him, first on the skin visible between the top two undone buttons of his work shirt, then up, covering his Adam's Apple with her lips. It jumped as he swallowed and his breathing came heavier, gasping softly. She brought both hands to his face, cupping his cheeks while her mouth journeyed, resting now on his jawbone under his right ear. She sucked on his earlobe until she heard a moan in the back of his throat. As she moved her lips onto his cheek, his hands got into the dance. They roved over her back, up and down, pressure, pulling her closer to him, till finally she shifted and straddled him, facing him on his lap.

Her hands left his face and settled on his arms, massaging his biceps and glorying in the firm masculine form hidden beneath his clothes. Her lips moved to his, and his enthusiasm thrilled her as he pulled her closer, her hands exploring his lines and angles.

He moaned, a tormented sound that validated her desires. She had to touch his skin. She wanted to touch every inch of him, and she wanted it now.

They'd moved so slow, this relationship, and she liked the pace. Jeremy wasn't your typical guy, after only one thing. They'd gotten to know each other, but tonight, she was taking charge. Barely a minute went by that she didn't think of him, yearn for him. She was falling for him, deep. She could be in love with this man.

It was time.

Joined by their mouths, she tugged at his buttons, unfastening each one till his shirt hung loose around his chest. She pushed it off his shoulders, and tossed it to the floor.

"Jeremy," she breathed, and her hands took over, running her palms over him, every inch of exposed skin, exploring him, his firm abs, his chest, then around to his back. Her heart raced and her breath was coming in gasps.

He pulled back from her. Uncertainty shone in his eyes, and his hesitation told her she would have to set the pace. He respected her; he wouldn't put her in a position she might be uncomfortable with, even if he wanted it. Even if it took superhuman strength to resist in the heat of passion.

"It's okay," she whispered, nodding her encouragement. She wanted them to be in sync. Yes, she wanted him, she craved intimacy with him. But he needed to want it just as much as she did.

And still he waited. Physically, he was still sitting on the couch, her facing him, perched on his lap. But emotionally, a distance was forming.

"Emma," he murmured.

"Jeremy," she said in a low moan and returned to kissing him. She ran her hands up his chest, over his arms, reveling in the feel of an unencumbered caress.

Propped in his lap, a breeze of cold air caught her skin and made her shiver. She took his hand and slowly, intentionally, placed it on her belly, covered by the fabric of her dress. An invitation, a clear message of what she wanted from him.

His eyes widened as he stared into hers, his torment playing across his face. She released his hand and he kept it in place. His fingers splayed across her abdomen, his hand so large that outstretched, his fingers brushed the underside of her breasts. She gasped and his eyes came to hers immediately.

"Yes, please," she whispered.

"Emma, I don't …," his low voice broke off.

"What?" she urged. "You don't want me?" As much as it pained her to say it, she had to know. As much as her feelings for him were growing and her dreams of a future with him were taking shape in her mind, she needed to know if he wasn't attracted to her. Painful, but vital.

"No!" he said, voice raised. "No, baby, that's not it at all. Emma, you're so beautiful." Leave it to him to compliment her. He constantly did. It was one of the things she loved most about him, always recognizing things about her to comment on.

Fortified, she whispered close to his ear, "I want you, Jeremy."

He shuddered. "Baby, I can't tell you the last time I was with a woman. I don't want to hurt you, or … us."

Love for him flooded her heart. "I know you've been away for a long time. But you and I, I don't know, it just seems right, doesn't it?"

He took a long moment to study her eyes. She wished she could read exactly what was going through his mind as he stared. She wished she could let him know just how ready she was to take the next step in their relationship. Did he understand what she was offering? Because he obviously wasn't taking her up on the invitation.

He went motionless. His hands and his mouth stilled, his shoulders quieted. And in the silence of the moment, a cooler head prevailed. And it was his.

"I think we're starting to stray off-track here, baby." He wrapped his arms around her back and in one strong swoop, he lifted her off his lap and placed her on the couch beside him. Then, he stood and walked to the other side of the room, his back to her. His deep breaths were visible to her from behind. He was the picture of a man struggling to gain control.

He turned then, and despite herself, she nearly gasped at the beauty of him. His chest glistened with health and fitness, not an ounce of fat evident on his slim frame. His dark hair, unruly now from her hands running through it, just a tad too long. He'd missed a haircut, probably too busy with the craziness that his life had become lately.

And his eyes. She was drawn to them. Crisp blue like an ocean sky. Almost too blue for the light complexion and coal black hair, an unexpected but irresistible combination of colors that formed the face of her true love.

He came to her, kneeling in front of her on the floor. He captured both her hands in his and stared into her eyes. "Emma, you are gorgeous, inside and out. I'm so lucky to be with you." He dropped one of her hands to trace his fingers against her cheek.

Tears stabbed at her eyes. She'd put herself out there, and he'd rejected her. She'd never been rejected in a sexual scenario and had no idea what was going on. "Jeremy, I'm so confused. You say you're attracted to me."

"Yes, of course I am."

"Are you going to make me say it? Are you that bad at reading clues?" That clueless, she meant, but even in this devastating situation, she didn't want her harsh words to hurt him.

I want to love you — I want you to love me — I want us to make love.

Her thoughts were racing, but she was smart enough to stifle them before they came out in words. Jeremy obviously didn't want to take their relationship into a sexual realm. So how much more would he object to her profession of love for him?

Embarrassed, humiliated, she ripped her hands from his gentle grasp, grabbed her purse and headed for the door.

"Emma, no, no, please." He came to his feet. Was she so wrong about this man? About her feelings?

She had almost reached the door when he slid his body between them, blocking her from leaving. "Don't go. Not now. I want to tell, I *need* to tell you. Please, Emma."

She blinked tears back, determined to gain control. She looked into his face, his earnest eyes, then dropped her head. "I'm so embarrassed," she said softly.

"No, don't be. Please, just let me explain."

It was his earnestness that made her turn around and head back into the room. But not to the couch, no, it would be painful to ever sit on that couch with him again, memories of his rejection swirling around her head. So she went to the table and sat primly on the edge of one of the seats.

He joined her, pulled his own chair out so he could face her, and took her hands. "Emma, I can't really explain my actions tonight. I do want you, I'm very attracted to you. I've dreamed about seeing you, touching you. Seriously."

She kept her eyes locked on her knees. She didn't want the sight of his handsome face to get in the way of his message.

"But you're clean and pure and beautiful. You're on the ball, and smart and successful. I can't live up to the standard you set. I'm …." He exhaled a sharp breath and tried again. "I'm an ex-con. I made bad decisions and landed in jail. I did that to myself. I was sentenced to a decade away from good people to try to turn myself around, to get back on the right track."

"And you paid your price. You earned your release." Her whispered words were so soft she wondered if he heard them.

"Yes, I did. I worked hard, I got with the program. But you don't know what I had to do in prison, just to survive. I was surrounded by rough, tough men who would as soon cut you as look at you. You couldn't be seen as weak; that was a mistake you only made once. You had to fight for yourself. And I did. I may not have always won, but I competed with my fists. And I gained their respect. I wasn't a violent man when I went in. But I learned to be while I was there."

She brought her eyes up to meet his. He was studying her, looking for a response. "But what does that have to do with us? With this, tonight? You're not violent now. You can't think that you'd hurt me."

"Oh, no, no. Not a chance. That's not what I'm saying." He stopped speaking, ran his fingers through his hair, struggling to find the words. His eyes swung away from her, searched around for inspiration, then returned, locked in with hers. "I need to prove myself. I need to cleanse myself from my past. You deserve so much more than a sullied ex-con. You deserve the best man life has to offer you. The best man God has to offer you."

She shook her head. "I want you. You are my choice, Jeremy."

A glimmer of a smile emerged on his lips. "And I want to be deserving of you, Emma. I want to be the man who gets you, a full partner. I just haven't gotten there yet. But give me time. I'll prove myself to you, you'll see. Once I am a success and my past is truly behind me, then I will be a good man for you."

Emma stared at him. Who was this guy? A true man of honor? She'd never run into one before. Was that a pedestal he had her up on? And to think he'd started out as the man who'd ruined her father's career, her family's life. God sure planted some interesting barriers in life's path.

Her head was spinning. Her emotions, confusing her. She needed to get out of here to think. "I'm going to go."

He gave a brisk nod and followed her to the door. "Emma?" And he took her chin gently into his hand and kissed her. A sweet, chaste kiss, one that showed her exactly what boundaries he was putting around their physical connections.

For now.

"Good night, Jeremy."

Chapter Fourteen

Jeremy unloaded the last of his slightly damaged inventory into the new space. If he had more pieces, he would divide the open space into workshop and salesroom. But because of his current situation, he had nothing sale-worthy at the moment.

But that didn't mean he wouldn't have pieces again eventually. He'd built up inventory before, and he'd do it again. He was used to working hard. This wasn't an insurmountable problem. He'd just put his nose to the grindstone and dive into the task.

He did love building furniture, after all.

He scooted the meager pieces throughout the space and so he could get to work stripping each one. If he could strip the water-damaged finish off, sand the wood down and let them dry thoroughly, it's possible he could stain them again, salvaged.

It was mindless work, and he regretted that, because while he was working his mind had plenty of time to focus on the one person it couldn't seem to forget: Emma.

She'd completely floored him the other night when she came on to him. The thought of what might've happened, what probably *would've* happened if he hadn't put an end to it, was mind-boggling.

She'd wanted him — all of him. And turning her down had taken all the self-control he could dig up. Because of course, he'd love to have had sex with her too. But in his mind, it was clear. Lust was taking over in the situation, lust was leading the way. And Emma wasn't a woman who merited his lust. She was classy, smart, successful. She was the kind of woman he could fall for, hard. She was the type of woman any guy would be happy to spend his future with.

Any guy ... but not him. Not yet. If and when he ever professed his love for Emma, and maybe way in the future, proposed to her and asked her to be his wife ... his transformation from ex-con who'd done a lot he was ashamed of, to a new creation in God, a man she could be proud of, a man who was worthy of her, would be complete.

And not until then would he ever allow himself to sample her body in the way she was offering.

Yes, it was clear in his mind. But he'd completely blown it with her because of the way he handled it. His words had failed him and he feared that Emma had left that night feeling rejected and unwanted. When that was the furthest from the truth.

He had no idea how to move forward, and evidently, neither did she. He hadn't heard from her, and he hadn't contacted her. Sure, it had only been a few days, but was the silence intentional? On his end it was. He didn't know what to say. Bring it up again? Make sure she understood his motivations, had no questions? Or just let it slip into their past, never to be spoken of again.

He turned off his power sander and placed it at his feet. He grabbed his white cloth and ran it over the sandy finish on the top of the damaged dresser. It looked okay. He could probably salvage this one. Once it was done he could decide if he would discount it, or if it was good enough to sell at full price.

He smirked. If only he could come to such quick, sure decisions about his relationship as about his furniture.

The cell phone in his pocket buzzed. Pulling it out, he didn't recognize the caller. He answered.

"Yeah, I'd like to order some furniture for a new house I'm buying." The male voice was somewhat hard to understand but Jeremy was unsure why. Strange accent? Muffled?

"Yes, sir. Thank you for calling. I have an inventory catalogue of pieces I've made before, or I can meet with you and get your requirements and design you something new."

"I've already seen your catalogue. I know what I want." The voice started rattling off products: the Shaker dining room set, the Beach Cottage coffee table and end table set, the Farmhouse bedroom set. Jeremy scrambled to find a pencil to write them all down. When the order finished, the price tallied into the five-digit range, and his time estimate was several months.

"You've got a big house to fill. All new furniture?"

"It's a second house. I'll rent it out when it's ready but I gotta fill her up."

"Well sir, I appreciate your business. I'm a new business owner just starting out and I appreciate the support of the community. Now, I'd like to take a day to write everything up with an accurate price and time estimate, then meet with you to show the specs and get your agreement before I start working."

"No need. I'm out of the state. I won't be back for a while and I don't want to hold up progress. You know what I want. Just get started."

Jeremy pulled the phone away from his ear and glanced at it. It was a local number. Maybe the man was local, but was traveling out of state. "Could I at least call you when I've got the paperwork done? I don't want to get started building till I've covered this with you, and we have an agreement on the price, the timeline, the types of woods, the stains. All the details. Prevent costly mistakes later."

"Okay, call me when you got it ready and we'll talk."

"And we'll work out the deposit. I'll require a 50% down payment on each item as I start them."

"I'll have to mail you a check and I don't want the USPS to slow you down."

Jeremy copied down the man's name, local address, and the cell phone he was calling from, and hung up.

The big order would take him a long way toward profitability, but it would eliminate time available to restore this damaged furniture. Time for another business decision: spend time on the projects that will make you the most money. So, for the rest of the day, he worked on the spec for the new customer, Joe Martin. He took his time to suggest creative extras on the furniture pieces from his catalogue. He wanted to give his customers customization, a little bit of uniqueness for each creation. Unique wood combinations, unusual color pairings, stains or finishes. He took pride in making sure each finished piece caused admiration from its new owner.

Darkness had fallen outside the store when he finalized the proposal. He was happy with it. He hoped Joe Martin, whoever he was, and however he'd become aware of Jeremy's work, would be happy with it too. If not, Jeremy would alter it till he was. The customer deserved his best effort.

Rolling out his tight shoulders, he stood and took a glance at the other projects. He checked his phone. Eight thirty. Sure, he could still put in a couple hours on the damaged furniture. Hopefully tomorrow, he'd have the okay from Joe Martin to start the new work.

A sharp rap sounded. Startled, Jeremy's eyes darted to the door. A figure stood outside in the darkness. Jeremy made his way over and unlocked the glass door. Must be a customer checking things out.

"Sorry, I'm not open yet. Just moved in today and won't have my grand opening for a few weeks yet."

He was a large man, with massive thighs covered in jeans and a sweatshirt covering his chest, the hood pulled up, obscuring his face.

"Thanks for your interest though. I'd appreciate you coming back after I open." Jeremy started to close the door when the man reached an arm in, blocking him.

"Harrison."

Jeremy peered closer at the man's face still in shadow. "Yes. Who …?"

The man pushed past him and into the store. With the bright showcase lights, even with the hoodie still on, Jeremy recognized him. "White."

Leroy White, terrifying leader of the prison gang, stood here in his store in Pawleys Island. His past was quite literally catching up with him.

Leroy pushed his hood off, exposing his face. A bruise rounded his right eye and a busted lip was healing. Jeremy wasn't about to inquire.

"So, you've been released," Jeremy said.

"Obviously," the big man replied. "Did you think I'd escaped?"

"No."

"What you got going on here?" Leroy glanced around the empty space, then settled his gaze on the wood pieces clustered on the far side of the room.

"I'm starting my own furniture building business."

"Business must be good if you're able to rent this big space."

"It's more of a leap of faith, actually. Not making much yet but I figure I'll invest in my future."

Leroy studied Jeremy's face, his expression a mix of irritation and sarcasm. "Investing in your future, huh? You think you have a future? You think you can fit back into a normal life after everything we went through inside? What makes you think you won't screw up again?"

"I'm determined, Leroy. I'm going to make it work."

"Well, aren't you a precious little girl?" His lip curled up, his eyes narrowed and Jeremy had a rush of memory from this same man, years younger, in a different place, saying some similarly infuriating remark, with the very same meaning: menacing, intimidating words, his intent to humiliate him for following the rules, for doing as he was told.

Jeremy sized up the big man and gathered his wits about him, readying himself for a fight. With Leroy, it was the only way. He clenched his fists and squared his shoulders. "Come on, Leroy. You don't scare me," he snarled. "Give me all you got, man. Looks like you got a head start on me, anyway." He motioned to Leroy's beat up face with his head.

Leroy considered, but the surprise in his eyes gave him away. He looked around and back at Jeremy. "I ain't here to fight you, man. What's wrong with you?"

Jeremy lowered his fists, still cautious.

"I don't need another fight on my record. They're keeping a close eye on me."

"Why? You been getting into trouble again?"

"Nah, man. But I'm not sure I like it out here. Can't find a job. Everyone waiting for me to screw up so they can haul me back in."

Jeremy shook out his tense arms. "So what brings you by, Leroy? Why are you on Pawleys Island, and especially my store?"

Leroy shrugged. "There's a gas station down the way there. I interviewed at one of their stations in Myrtle and it seemed to go okay. But they said the opening was actually out here and I'd have to go meet the station manager. So I drove all the way out here and he wasn't even here. Isn't that a bite on the ass?"

Jeremy ran his gaze over Leroy's clothes. Not exactly interview wardrobe. On the other hand, maybe for a gas station, it was fine.

"So that explains why you were at the gas station. How did you know I was here, in this storefront?"

"I didn't. What, you think I came looking for you? Tracking you down like I have a crush on you? Don't flatter yourself." He erupted into low chuckles, probably pleased he'd used the phrase correctly. "I stopped down at the convenience store at the end of this strip mall. Got me some M&M's." He pulled the empty wrapper out of his pocket to prove it. "Walking back to my car, I saw this store with the lights on, came down to see what was going on. I looked in the big plate window and thought I recognized you, sitting there at the desk. So I knocked."

The story sounded feasible. He could be telling the truth, or he could be lying through his teeth. With Leroy, either one was entirely possible. And, Jeremy realized, he didn't really care if Leroy was behind the vandalism or the fire. He just wanted to eliminate the chance of him returning for another visit.

"Well, you need to get going, I'm sure. Best of luck, Leroy. Keep your nose clean and I'll do the same."

The big man gave him a sneer. He didn't like being bossed around, never had. He liked to move at his own pace, in his own direction. But they'd already established the fact that Leroy didn't want to fight Jeremy tonight, so Jeremy felt safe pushing his luck.

Leroy ambled toward the front door. Jeremy opened it for him and he slid out. "Good seeing you, Harrison. Happy for you, I really am."

He walked into the darkness, and Jeremy let out a big breath.

* * *

It had been a week since the "Jeremy Rejection," as Emma was coming to think of that humiliating evening. And she hadn't talked to him since. She couldn't face him – her embarrassment was too deep. She'd made a total fool of herself, throwing herself at the man, and he didn't want an intimate relationship. If she could get up the nerve to ask her girlfriends about it, she was quite sure she'd learn that she was the only young woman in America with a steady boyfriend who refused to make love to her.

She took a deep breath and let it out. So, although she didn't consider herself and Jeremy officially broken up, she could say they had hit a major bump in the road. The fact that he hadn't called her either, spoke volumes in her mind.

She left her apartment and headed for her car. She drove to her mom and dad's. Her mom had invited her to do some clothes shopping and Emma had offered to pick her up. Not only was it easier on her mom, it also gave her a chance to do a visual check on her father.

According to Mom, he wasn't drinking excessively, and hadn't since their intervention. Some days, he had a beer or two, but had not lost control and had not gotten drunk. She wished she had full confidence that Mom was telling the truth. Not that she would lie, exactly. But she wouldn't put it past Mom to sugarcoat the truth so that Emma wouldn't be worried or upset.

She pulled into the driveway of the little red ranch, knocked and let herself in. Dad was sitting in the living room, watching TV.

"Hey, sugarplum. How's it going?" he asked with a calm smile. She leaned in to his cheek and he passed the sniff test.

"Good, Dad. Really good. How about you?"

"Can't complain."

"Any luck on the job front?"

He reached for the remote on the chair-side table and muted the sound. "Put a couple applications in earlier this week so I'm hoping for an interview or two. Nothing came from the last batch of applications though. Nobody called me back."

She gave him another kiss, this one on the top of his head, and gave him a sad smile. "The important thing is, you're trying, Dad. Good job. I'm proud of you."

Mom walked into the room and greeted her with a happy hug. "I'm proud of him too, Emma. He's working hard."

Dad's cell phone rang. He pulled it out of his front shirt pocket and peered at the screen.

"Is that an employer maybe?" Emma asked.

He shook his head and silenced the phone, returned it to his pocket. "No. I know who that was, and it's not anyone I want to talk to."

"Are you sure? Do you think that's a good idea, Dad, when you have so many resumes out?"

"You don't worry about your old man, baby girl." He stood and practically shooed them out the door. "You go on, now. Buy yourself a pretty outfit and I want to see it when you get home."

They said their good-byes and went out to Emma's car. On the way to the outlet mall, Mom asked, "So, how's that young man of yours? You haven't brought him around lately."

Emma sighed. Leave it to Mom to get right to the heart of what was bothering her. "I don't know, Mom. We're sort of taking a break from each other, I guess you could say."

Edna frowned. "How come?"

One thing was certain. She wouldn't tell Mom the truth about their last encounter. So, what?

"You know, Mom, relationships are hard. And I know they're never perfect. A perfect person doesn't exist. But when you look at Jeremy, there are just so many red flags. His history, for one. He's an ex-con. He broke the law and spent a decade in prison. And his history with Dad. Those two things might be a little too hard to get over. I'd probably be better off dating someone else. Someone without all that baggage."

Her mom had been silent throughout her diatribe. Emma looked over at her and gave her the eyebrows-up question look. "Is he a good man, Emma?"

"Yes. Yes, he is."

"And do you love him?"

Tears erupted from her eyes and in place of words, she nodded her head, hard.

"Then I'd say you two can get over just about anything."

* * *

Jeremy was at his store, working on the big order. He'd kicked butt over the last ten days and finished the coffee table and two end tables. Amazing how much time he had to apply to work when he no longer had a girlfriend to spend time with. Evidently. From the fact that neither one of them was reaching out to the other. Maybe he should just call her and face his lumps.

Or maybe not.

He turned back to the furniture. He'd like to start one of the bigger items, but he hadn't received the deposit check yet. He'd come to the end of his own funds to finance the order. He had to get some compensation or he wouldn't be able to continue. However, if he didn't continue, he'd never meet the aggressive deadline requested by his client. Unfortunately, Joe Martin wasn't answering his phone. Jeremy had called at least three times over the last few days and the phone rang and rang before going to voicemail. He was starting to feel like a pest.

On the other hand, he was also starting to feel duped. Sure, if this client turned out to be nothing and he never saw payment, he'd just put the three tables in the front window and offer them as a set or separates. But it sure would be better to be paid in advance for the work.

His cell phone rang and he glanced at the screen. The police? He answered it immediately.

"Mr. Harrison, could you come over to the Seaside Inn? We have some information to share about our investigation of the fire and since it was your property that was damaged, we'd like to tell you and the owners."

"Yes, sir. I'll be right over."

He practically dove out the front door of the shop, turning to make sure he locked it, then ran to his truck. He made it to Marianne's in record time, and pulled into the front drive, parking behind the unmarked police car. He walked around to the back of the Inn, where the fire had originated. Marianne, Tom and three other men stood talking when he interrupted. His sister introduced him, and also the fire chief, the police detective and the insurance investigator.

The detective cleared his throat. "We've conducted a joint investigation and we have determined the fire was not an accident. It was intentionally set. It was arson."

Marianne gasped and Tom pulled her closer. "What brings you to that conclusion?" he asked.

The fire chief answered. "Mr. Harrison used a non-flammable finish on the chest and he dried it in a spot with plenty of ventilation. Upon investigation, we traced a puddle of lacquer shellac in the center of the surface. Lacquer shellac is extremely flammable. We feel it was most likely ignited with a match."

Jeremy walked over to his sister and her husband and put an arm on each of their shoulders. "Do you have any suspects?"

"No, we don't. We'll continue to work on that. In fact, we'd like to isolate each of you and ask you a series of questions."

Tom said, alarmed, "You can't suspect any of us, now, do you?"

The police chief responded, "It's all routine. We have no suspects now, so we need to start with you all."

Marianne said, "We'll cooperate, of course, to help move the investigation along. Tom, do you want to take them to one of the tables in the dining room, the far corner?"

Tom nodded and escorted the three officials into the Inn. Marianne collapsed onto a beach chair.

"I'm so sorry, sis. This is all my fault. If my furniture hadn't been stored under there, the Inn never would've been in danger."

"Jeremy, don't be silly. You're my brother and I love you. You needed help and I wanted to help you. None of us knew a crazy person would track down your furniture and set it on fire. Or, did it have anything to do with you? Maybe your furniture was just the start. Maybe it was a disgruntled previous guest of the Inn who thought they received bad service and wanted retribution."

Marianne looked at him, eyebrows up, like she'd just uncovered a potential answer. Then they both broke into laughter at the same time.

"Yeah," Jeremy chuckled, "one of those shifty snowbirds wanted to teach you a lesson. You know how nasty vacationers can get. Really, sis."

"It sure will be nice to get some answers."

Yes, an answer is what they needed. Not the endless supposition his mind was taking him through lately. One suspect that had been plaguing his mind was Leroy. Was White one step ahead of Jeremy? Had White known Jeremy was here, trying to go clean and make an honest business? Was White holding a grudge, or was he simply, as Eddie said, bored and looking for some fun? How fun would it be to locate and destroy several thousand dollars' worth of product built by a fellow ex-con? One who was trying to go clean?

That could be right up Leroy's alley.

On the other hand, when he saw Leroy the other night, he'd seemed honestly surprised to run into Jeremy at the store, and even wished him well when he left. Could Leroy have figured out not only where Jeremy lived, but where he was storing his excess furniture, without Jeremy catching any wind of it at all?

Supposition and guesses frustrated him. He'd best leave the investigation work to the professionals. Jeremy turned his attention back to his sister. "Meanwhile, my stuff is out of here and you're no longer in danger, if it was me they were targeting. I moved into my new storefront space. Tons of room. So nice to be able to spread out. I'm looking forward to a grand opening when I have enough inventory built up."

Marianne shifted in her chair. "Oh gosh, I totally forgot. Good for you, Jeremy! Were you able to repair any of the water-damaged furniture from the fire?"

"I started to. Finished a couple, then I got a call from a really big client. He wanted a ton of new furniture built. He knew exactly what he wanted and I started work on it."

"Fantastic! I'm so happy for you. Word about your work is getting out. See? I told you it would."

"Yeah," Jeremy mused. "But the question is, how? When he called me, he said he'd seen my catalogue. He requested a bunch of pieces by name. I really didn't think my work was that well known yet."

"The power of the internet."

"Yeah, I guess."

Marianne thought for a moment, tapping her finger on her chin. "Remember the photo album I made for you to display at the holiday craft fair at the high school? In fact, I still have it. I put it on my book shelf in the great room for customers to see." She hoisted out of the low-sitting chair and headed for the Inn through the back porch door. Jeremy followed her. "Eight by ten photos of each of your pieces that I made into that photo album. I guess it could be called a catalogue." She dug around in the book shelf. "Hmmm, I wonder if someone took it to their room to peruse and never brought it back." She ended up taking everything off the shelf, sorting through, and returning them. "It's gone."

They blinked at each other. "So, what does that mean?" he asked.

"Well, like I said, we may find it in a guest's room when they check out. Or it could mean that the man who placed your big order had been a guest at the Inn, took the album and never brought it back."

"Well, I hope he was better with compensating you than me. I've completed three pieces for him and he's never paid his deposits. I'm basically building this stuff on my own dime and hoping beyond hope that he comes through soon with the check he promised me. He did say he was out of town, which would explain why he was a guest here. Maybe a snowbird from the Midwest. On the other hand, he had a local cell phone number."

Tom came out from his interview session with the officials, and told them they were ready for the next. Jeremy went in next and answered a series of questions about what he remembered seeing, hearing and smelling that night. He answered to the best of his ability, but he really had nothing useful to share.

When he returned to the great room, Stella had joined her mother and Marianne was telling the little girl that she'd have to wait, that they couldn't go digging in the sand until her meeting with the nice men in the dining room was over.

"Marianne, you go in with them. I'll take Stella outside."

Marianne gave him a grateful glance. He took Stella's hand and walked with her through the sun porch, across the wooden deck outside, down the stairs, and onto the sand. When she got to her favorite spot on the sand, she dropped to her knees and started digging with her plastic shovel.

"How you been, pretty girl?"

She shrugged and kept digging, dumping sand into the bucket, digging some more.

"You feeling any better after the fire? I know it was so scary to be the first one to see the smoke."

She nodded. "I guess so."

He watched her, his heart breaking just a little at her lack of responsiveness. His little Stella was a spitfire, a ball of energy who entertained everyone and made all the adults want to hug her.

A little charm hung from a chain around her neck. It glittered on the outside of her tee shirt, reflecting what was left of the day's sun.

"That's a nice necklace, sweetheart. Is that new?"

"Yep."

"Was it a gift?" He reached for it, caught it in his palm and studied it. It was a simple pink rhinestone with fake sparkly stones mounted on each of its four corners. Exactly the type of cheap ornament a little girl her age would adore.

"Yep." Stella brought a hand up from her work and pushed a lock of hair off her forehead.

"Your mama get you that?" It would be just like Marianne to take Stella shopping for a little trinket to get her mind off the fire and the smoke.

"Nope. Grandpa Joe gave it to me." She kept digging, then, her bucket full, she stood and made her way to the water's edge and added a little moisture into the sand. He watched her on her way there and on her way back, but for the life of him, he couldn't come up with a Grandpa Joe in their family or Tom's. When she returned, she dumped the bucket upside down and it emerged as a full, firm bucket-shaped mold of sand, the beginning of one of her castles, famous among anyone who stayed at the Inn.

"Good job, sweetie. So, who is Grandpa Joe?"

She shrugged. "He's a grandpa. He talks to me sometimes and he digs with me. He gave me this present."

Jeremy nodded. One of the guests who stayed here for the winter maybe? Stella must be a favorite among the old folks, she was so sweet and personable. But with all the weirdness going on, Jeremy made a mental note to ask Marianne if she was acquainted with one named Joe.

* * *

A few days later, Jeremy was finishing up the re-staining of one of the water-damaged pieces. He applied the last of the finish on a shaker design bedroom set. He had selected northern maple, and using tips he'd learned from research on the internet, he used a 12-step finish process to bring out just the right color combinations. He'd built this piece as one of a set – the customer could select between a bed with headboard and footboard, this tall, stand-up dresser, a matching armoire and a nightstand or two. It was modern with a touch of old-style traditional.

At first glance, he wasn't sure he could restore this bureau to its original beauty after the fire hoses sprayed water so close to it. When he started, the entire top surface was a soggy mess. But after the extensive rehaul, it was looking good. He'd start next on the armoire. If he could rescue these two pieces, it would be well worth his time.

The cell phone rang, sitting on the counter. He grabbed a cloth and wiped the wet stain from his hands and answered it.

"This is Joe Martin here. I'm ready to meet with you and get some of my furniture."

His pulse rate took a little jump on its own. "Mr. Martin, so good to hear from you. Have you gotten my messages? I've left you several."

"I got one, I think. I've been traveling and cell phone coverage is sketchy. But I told you to get started on the pieces and I'm now ready for some delivery."

"Great, that's great, sir. I've got several of your pieces ready."

"How many?"

"Three."

"Is that all? All right, then. I'll see you about two thirty today."

The man didn't ask if he was available, he assumed he would be. But he would let it pass.

Mr. Martin gave him an address which, even after spending his entire life on the island, Jeremy was unfamiliar with. "I'll need some directions. I don't know where that is."

Jeremy grabbed a pen and jotted directions as the man gave them. Seemed out in the middle of nowhere, but he'd find it. "What is this, a cabin in the woods?" Sounded homey, a nice little getaway.

"Yeah, that's about right."

"Okay then, I'll see you at 2:30 with your three tables. And you'll bring me either cash or a check in payment." He pulled his paperwork closer and did some calculations. He gave Mr. Martin a final price for the three items, as well as the deposit on the remaining pieces.

"Whoa, that's getting mighty pricey there, ain't it?"

"Well, normally you would've paid me half as a deposit to cover my expenses before I started building. I never received your deposit check so I floated the cost myself for the smaller pieces. Now I'm finished so you need to pay me the full price."

The man cleared his throat. "You must think you're pretty good to be charging those high prices."

Jeremy hesitated, a little feeling of dread attacking his throat. "Mr. Martin, you and I did agree on the price list, remember?"

"Yeah."

"Are you having second thoughts?"

"No, no. I'm fine. I'll see you at 2:30." And he broke off the call.

For the next few hours, Jeremy kept busy restoring the shaker set, doing his best not to think about the odd conversation with Joe Martin. However, his best wasn't enough to keep the exchange out of his mind. He kept coming back to it. This Martin was an odd duck, for sure. Calling out of the blue, knowing exactly what he wanted, being in such a rush for him to start, being out of touch for weeks, then finally calling and disputing the agreed upon price. Jeremy applied the tenth coat on the armoire. He was new to this business, still learning. But in retrospect, he definitely could've handled this transaction better.

Should he have raced to meet Mr. Martin's deadlines? Should he have started the work without a deposit? Probably not, however, he'd pray for a positive outcome and he'd learn for the next time. Once he was recovered from the damaged furniture incidents, and he'd built a full inventory again, he could establish some business processes and not deviate from them. Meanwhile, he desperately needed the money, and he would do his best to satisfy this Martin character.

Soon it was time to go. He loaded the finished pieces into the back of his truck, strapping the pieces down as tight as he could so they wouldn't get damaged in the transport. He started up the truck, leaving early to allow himself time to find this place. Out in the woods somewhere. He was sure he'd find it, but it wasn't like a GPS would take him right to it.

After fifteen minutes or so, he arrived in the general location of the woods. Now he just had to find the cabin. As he drove over a gravel road, he looked around. Very isolated. Very remote. In fact, he couldn't imagine that mail service delivered out here. There were no housing developments that he was aware of. This cabin of Joe Martin's must be a rustic getaway for hunting and fishing. Why, then, would the man pay good money to furnish the place with all brand-new, custom-made furniture?

He ran into a few dead ends, turned around, tried again. He pulled out the note paper he'd jotted directions on and tried to get back on track. Once he even called Mr. Martin's cell number, but not to his surprise, there was no answer.

Finally, he came across a run-down dump of a cabin. Considering it was the only construction he'd encountered in his exploration, it had to be the place. On the other hand, it couldn't possibly be the place. It was a heap of a building, roof sagging, weeds overgrown all around it. No one could live here in its condition. Nature was taking it over, in its neglect.

He jumped out of the truck and walked toward the structure. He tried the front door, but curiously, it was locked. He walked to the side and looked through a broken windowpane. A raccoon startled, and he caught the reflection of two eyes shining in the sheltered darkness. There were no signs of human life – no furniture, no blankets, not even a refrigerator in the tiny corner of the place designated as a kitchen.

* * *

Emma sat at her desk at work, staring at her computer screen. The cursor blinked at her, a mockery of her writer's block. *Go ahead, type something. You'll just have to back up and delete it anyway. You suck.*

She smirked. Her vivid imagination was her best feature as a writer, but also her worst. She could easily outsmart herself and destroy her own confidence in her writing.

She was working on the closing paragraph of her injured warrior assignment, a wonderful topic, one she felt extremely passionate about. Why did the beginning of this story literally flow off her fingertips onto the white screen, and yet the end was like slogging through the muck?

Because she wanted to do justice to bringing this important story to an inspiring conclusion.

She leaned back in her chair. Who was she kidding? She was blocked because of her relationship with Jeremy.

She'd spent nearly every waking moment reliving in her mind that humiliating encounter with him. Was she wrong to show him how much she wanted him? Had he ever given her signs that he didn't want a sexual relationship with her? Despite his heroic speech, could they ever recover from this and move on? Did she even want to date him knowing that she was crazed to throw him into bed at any opportunity, while he had some standard or timetable in his head that only he knew about?

She didn't like the sounds of that. On the other hand, the thought of walking away from him didn't appeal to her either.

Her endless mental rambles were interrupted when the cell phone in her desk drawer sounded. She pulled it open and glanced at the phone. "Hey, Mom."

Her voice was frantic, her tone wild. "He's gone, Emma!"

"Mom, what's going on?"

"Your father. I got home a little early from work and there's empty beer cans everywhere. He must've drank a least a dozen, maybe more."

"Oh my gosh, Mom. Where is he?" Adrenaline pounded through Emma's veins, leaving her a little lightheaded.

"He's on a bender, I have no idea what caused it. But Emma, the car's gone. He's driving! It's not safe."

Emma stood, grabbed her purse. "I'll come get you, Mom. We'll look for him together."

* * *

Jeremy sat in his truck in the woods, waiting and waiting. Silence draped over the whole place, no human intervention, no traffic noise. But the longer he sat, through the open window, nature's loud soundtrack emerged: birds chattering, insects chirping, long grass rustling.

His phone rang. "Hello?"

His dad's voice filled his ear. "Jeremy, you free?"

He looked around. *Yes and no.* "I'm waiting for a client so I can deliver an order." In the background Jeremy heard raised voices, commotion, chaos. "What's going on, Dad?"

"Marianne's really worried. She's misplaced Stella."

"*What?*"

"Stella is missing. At least, we don't know where she is. She's not in her normal spots around the Inn and she doesn't come when she's called."

Jeremy pulled the phone away from his ear to check the time. Two twenty. "Dad, I'll be right there. Maybe I can help find her."

"Thanks, son." The fact that his dad didn't protest was not lost on Jeremy. Hank was all about work – servicing the customer, being productive. But when Jeremy offered to leave a client in the lurch to help look for Stella, he didn't even blink.

This must be serious.

Jeremy started the truck and shifted to reverse. But before he took off, he really should call Joe Martin. If he was a legit customer, despite all the red flags, he at least deserved a call. Jeremy shifted back to park and placed the call.

Two sounds had him moving his head to the right: a distant tinkle of a ring tone, and the arrival of a car pulling up right beside him. Mr. Martin. Good. He'd explain the family emergency and set up a new time for delivery of the furniture order.

He cut the engine and jumped out of the truck, cell phone still in his hand. He circled the front of his truck and approached the car. "Mr. Martin. Glad to see you. I …"

The man stumbled out of the front seat of the car, falling into the deep grass, then laughing – *laughing* – as he righted himself. Confused, Jeremy jogged over to help. When the man lifted his head, Jeremy gasped and froze in his tracks.

The man's phone, still in his hand, stopped ringing, most likely moving to voicemail. But this man, laboring on the ground to get to his feet, was not a new client, Joe Martin.

This man was Emma's father, Gary Slotky.

Jeremy stared, motionless, his mind whirling to put together the pieces, and coming up empty. Mr. Slotky finally clambered to his feet, still chuckling, and Jeremy gave him a hand to steady him. A gust of breath shot into Jeremy's face and Jeremy recoiled.

Mr. Slotky was drunk. Stinkin', falling down, no brain capacity, drunk.

Jeremy took a tight grip on Slotky's arm and pulled him out of the deep grass. "Mr. Slotky, why don't you get into my truck and I'll drive you home? You're in no condition to drive."

The man roared in the false bravado of the enraged intoxicated. "Don't you touch me, you horse's ass. You ruined my whole life. You're the root of all my problems. I'll never forgive you. How dare you think you can help me now? I'm goin' to ruin you like you ruined me."

Apprehension trickled down Jeremy's chest. He was starting to understand. Slotky showing up here at this moment was not a coincidence. Jeremy was here waiting, because Slotky had put him here. "What do you mean, you're going to ruin me?"

The older man snatched his arm from Jeremy's now sagging grasp. He stepped over to the bed of Jeremy's truck, perusing the furniture. "That the order you made, huh?"

Jeremy narrowed his eyes as realization hit him. Joe Martin, his huge customer who'd called out of nowhere. There was no Joe Martin. "You placed the order, didn't you?"

"I sure did. And you fell for it, hook, line and sinker. Didn't take much to fool you. You're not the sharpest tool in the shed, are ya, boy?"

At this moment, Jeremy had to agree he wasn't.

"All I had to do was give you a big order and you were salivating, thinking about collecting all that money from some poor sap. Your overpriced goods. You have no training, no education in furniture building. Yet you charge huge prices. Just like a Harrison to rip off the little people, take advantage of them, for their own gain."

It wasn't even necessary to say it, but the words came out anyway, "You never had any intention of paying me for this work." In his head he started calculating how much more this ruse had cost him. How much more behind he was in his inventory, in addition to the vandalism at his house, and the fire at the Inn.

Jeremy jerked his head up at the man. He had to know. Was it all him? Had Emma's father been tracking him for weeks now, looking for opportunities to sabotage him?

Mr. Slotky was fiddling in his pocket and now pulled out a weapon. He brandished it, then put a foot up on Jeremy's bumper, preparing to hoist himself onto the bed. Jeremy sprang into action. He covered the distance between them in a few steps, grabbed the man, pulled him away from the truck and threw him on the ground. While the man rolled around, Jeremy grabbed the tool in his hand and held it up for a closer inspection.

It was a chisel – he had at least a dozen in his own collection – purchased at a hardware store for twenty bucks or less. Curved wooden handle, solid metal blade, a woodworker's tool to mold a piece into the shape he wanted.

"Did you use this when you came over to my house and vandalized my furniture in the backyard?"

"You bet I did. And I'd've done every single one, too, if I hadn't heard you coming out the back door when I was there. I got away without you seeing me." Slotky had come to a sit, and now was struggling to stand as he continued. "That was just two little pieces, though, works in progress. That wasn't enough of an impact on your business. If I wanted to bring the whole thing down, I needed to go where you stored all your finished stuff." He came to his feet, tilting and wobbling.

"How'd you figure out where I stored my finished stuff?"

The question brought another angry roar from the drunk man. "You Harrisons, you're all alike! You don't think I have a brain in my head, do you? You think I'm ignorant just because I haven't worked in a while. Well, no. It wasn't too hard, actually. Everyone in Pawleys knows it's your sister who owns the Seaside Inn. So I moseyed over there to see what's what."

Slotky stumbled back in the direction of his car and Jeremy followed close behind, keeping a close eye on the lunatic. He'd already disarmed him of the chisel. What else did he have in his bag of tricks that could be dangerous?

"I went into the Inn and what do I see, a display in the corner about your furniture business. I took a closer look, and there on the bookshelf was a photo catalogue. That's how I knew exactly what to ask for when I placed my order. As Joe Martin." He let loose a huge chortle, so pleased with himself. Half a minute in, he started hacking and coughing, then bent in two at the waist, resting his hands on his knees.

Jeremy turned away, disgusted. The man had bested him. He'd destroyed his furniture, he'd placed a huge fake order that he never intended to pay for, he'd put his whole family in danger. Although the man was in no condition to drive, Jeremy decided then and there, it wasn't his problem. Let the man drive drunk and take the consequences, as long as he was done with Jeremy and his family.

And as for Emma … as much as it pained him, in light of their recent non-contact, maybe God was telling him to move on without her.

He wasn't prepared for the stab of pain in his heart at that revelation. But how else could it be? Emma's father hated him so much, he'd go to this extreme level to ruin him? Of course, Slotky thought that Jeremy had ruined him, years ago, and this was payback. Although Jeremy could point at a number of actions in this revenge plot that were illegal, he wouldn't call the police and report him. He'd try to reason with the man. Convince him it was over now. He got his revenge. If he left Jeremy and Jeremy's family alone, Jeremy would leave the Slotkys alone. Period.

His mind made up, Jeremy turned back to Mr. Slotky. Out of the corner of his eye, he caught a flash of movement in the man's backseat. What was back there? It had moved of its own accord, so it was alive. Had he brought a pet along with him? Had a wild animal settled back there?

His investigation stopped short, though, with Slotky's next words. "And the Inn is where I met your little niece."

Jeremy froze, a buzzing taking up residence in his ears. Stella. He gave his head a shake, stalked to Slotky, grabbed hold of his shirt and jerked him so mightily, he practically lifted him off his feet. "Stella? You met Stella?" A terrible dawning settled over Jeremy. What had this jerk done? How far had he gone? Just how crazy was he?

He shook, the older man's head rattling back and forth on his spine. "What have you done with Stella?"

The crazy man didn't answer, he just laughed, that drunken, crazy sound, now maniacal. Then it hit Jeremy: Grandpa Joe. "You gave Stella that necklace, didn't you? The necklace with the pink sparkly stone. You gave it to her so she'd befriend you."

He dropped the man in a heap. He raced back to Slotky's car, searching in the windows for any sign. Movement, something she'd left behind. The crazy son of a bitch – had he kidnapped Stella?

"You stole my little girl, took her away from me. She loves you; God knows why. I can't seem to do anything about that, but I can steal the little girl close to your heart. I sure can do that."

Jeremy searched the car. Within seconds, he frantically scoured the driver's seat and the driver's side back seat and found nothing. He raced around the vehicle and peered into the back seat. Then a door slammed and the car rolled away. The drunk had gotten back in the car and started the engine. As it passed, he pounded on the car and caught a glimpse of pink in the front passenger seat.

Pink, pink. Stella's favorite Myrtle Beach Pelicans baseball cap?

He raced for his truck, jumped in and shoved it into gear. Slotky was right in front of him and he had no trouble catching up to him. They had gone off the gravel path now, and they jumped and bounced in their vehicles across the uneven terrain.

That lunatic had Stella in that car! Driving under the influence! It wasn't enough to chase him, he had to apprehend him, force him to come to a stop.

Jeremy floored the accelerator and the powerful truck roared. He steered to the left, planning to pass him, then come to a fast stop in front, forcing Slotky to stop. But he drove into a trench and his truck momentarily grinded to a stop, spinning its tires as Slotky raced away.

Jeremy rocked the truck out of the decline, reversing inches, forward inches, back and forth until he freed it from the ditch's confines. He sped off.

He drove down the gravel road he'd come in on. Hopefully he could catch Slotky before he turned on the highway, so he could follow close behind him. Then, once he hit the open road, he'd pull him over.

Minutes passed with Jeremy's heart in his throat. An unconscious prayer passed through his mind, "Help us, God, be with us, keep us safe. Let us get Stella back," a string of thoughts on repeat through his head over and over.

As he hoped, he caught up with Slotky's car just as he was turning left on the highway. Jeremy turned and accelerated to pass him. But as he was beginning to apprehend the car, the back driver's side door of the car flew open and flapped in the wind. Stella! Was she back there? Would she fall out? Was he pushing her out?

Jeremy floored his gas pedal, passed the car easily and swerved in front. He squealed to a stop and braced himself. Slotky's car slammed into his truck, broadside. The screeching sound of metal hitting metal filled the air, and the collision jolted the truck. Jeremy held on tight. Then, silence.

He flung his door open and jumped down from the cab. He ran as fast as he could towards the car. In passing he saw that the wooden furniture had taken a major hit in the crash, random pieces of finished wood splintered everywhere. He reached the car. Slotky slumped unconscious in the driver's seat, head on the wheel, blood flowing from a gash in his forehead. He ran right by him. He went first to the open back door and looked inside.

No Stella. He raced around to the passenger side. He flung open the front door and in slow motion, he reached in and picked up the little girl's baseball cap.

* * *

Within an hour, a small army had gathered to search for Stella. Marianne and Tom, Hank and Leslie, a bunch of the Seaside Inn guests who adored Stella. Jeremy called the police and they immediately came out, taking over the search and organizing the volunteers. Total strangers, trained in Search and Rescue, flocked around them, ready to lend a hand. From surrounding towns, as well as local Pawleys Island searchers, everyone wanted to find the precious little girl.

The search area spanned from the broken down cabin where Jeremy first saw the flash of movement in the back seat of the car, all the way out to the crash site. Although Jeremy hadn't seen her roll out of the car in motion, they weren't going to rule it out. They would find her.

Jeremy was assigned to the original site outside the cabin. He'd broken in through the cracked window, climbed in and unlocked the front door. He and his dad searched every inch of the place, small as it was, and didn't find a trace of her.

But that's okay. He and Hank worked well as a team, always had. As long as they were working, sweating, doing the absolute best they could, they didn't dwell on the reality.

Stella was missing. She was alone. Kidnapped from the safety of her own home by a crazy man.

Finished with the cabin, they circled around the back, planning to walk in circumference, widening their diameter as they went. Jeremy heard his dad say, "Jeremy."

Jeremy's head went up and he joined Hank. He was studying the rusty metal door of a storm cellar in the overgrown backyard of the cabin. They glanced at each other for a second, then went to work on the door. After some pounding, hoisting and pulling, the door sprung open with a groan.

"Hold on," Hank said, and he went to his truck, returning with two flashlights. He tossed one to Jeremy. They ventured down the short stairwell to the concrete floor, sweeping the lights back and forth at their feet. Once down in the cellar, they had to bend at the waist and walk leaning over. They took time to inspect every centimeter of the place.

Nothing here. Certainly not Stella.

Relief flooded Jeremy that they hadn't found her here in this dark, moldy place. Then reality. If she wasn't here, then where?

He followed his dad back up the cement steps and heard his voice say, "Oh, hello there." Jeremy emerged a second later and saw Emma.

He had no idea what to do or say, no idea at all what she was thinking, or where they were at in their so-called relationship. He was clueless, but fortunately, she knew exactly what to do. She stepped right up to him and wrapped him in her strong arms. She patted her hands on his back and his shoulders and she whispered into his chest. He couldn't detect what she was saying, or maybe she was just shushing, a comforting sound, to calm him like a mother would to her child. All he knew was, she was here, she was holding him and she knew exactly what he needed.

Eventually, she pulled back and placed her hands on his cheeks. He said, "Your father ..."

She said in an urgent tone, "I know. I know everything. My father went crazy and caused all this chaos. My mom and I met his ambulance at the hospital. He was driving drunk, totally fell off the wagon. I'm so sorry, Jeremy. So, so sorry for what he did to you and your family."

Her eyes filled with tears and her voice choked. All he could think to say was, "Stella ..."

Another surge of anger strengthened Emma. "He kidnapped your precious little niece. He put her in the car and put her in danger. I will *never* forgive him for this. Neither will my mom. Let's search together. I want to help you find her."

He pulled her into his chest again, holding her warmth against himself. It helped. He cleared his head, squared his shoulders, and together, he and Emma went to work.

* * *

By nightfall, with the help of all the volunteers, they'd covered the entire search zone. Still, no Stella. The Search and Rescue professionals consulted with Tom and Marianne about expanding the zone. Would they also discuss the possibility of stopping for the night, Jeremy wondered. It really didn't matter to him if the professionals stopped or not. He wouldn't. He'd search until he found her. Period.

Jeremy and Emma were about a mile and a half out from the Last Known Point – the cabin's front yard. Sweeping back and forth over the terrain had proved monotonous and tiring but entirely necessary. Stella could be injured, unconscious, asleep, or hiding due to fear. She may not do what you'd expect her to do. They couldn't rely on her finding them, they had to locate her.

"Are you hungry?" Jeremy called over to Emma, a few yards away.

"No, I'm ...," she took her eyes off the ground to look at him and stumbled. She fell, and he rushed to her side. He put his arms underneath her shoulders and lifted her up, her head falling back as he did. He gazed down into her face and couldn't help his next action even if he'd wanted to.

Which he didn't.

He covered her mouth with his own and ran his tongue over her lips, tasting the salty sweat and dirt from her hours of searching. She moaned and he pulled her closer, running his fingers through her long hair. His heart pounded and he ran his fingers over her neck. His Emma. Here with him during the worst time of his life. Supporting him.

He pulled back and looked deep into her eyes. "I missed you."

Her face crumpled. "I'm sorry. I kind of freaked out when you rejected me."

He interrupted, "It wasn't a rejection. It was sort of, I don't know, delayed gratification. I really wanted to wait until I deserved you. Till the time was right."

She rolled her eyes and said sarcastically, "I'm sure you don't think I'm much of a catch now, do you?"

He frowned, not catching her meaning. Then, "What, because of this? Because of your dad?"

She nodded, suddenly serious, moisture appearing in her eyes. "Yes. This never would've happened if I weren't dating you. This is all my fault."

"No," he said firmly. "That's not true. I mean, your dad's whacked, sure. But it was me he wanted to sabotage. Because of *my* past. Because of what I did to him."

She heaved a big sigh. She looked at her feet and then got distracted. She kneeled to the ground, down on her knees and reached for something. "Jeremy. Take a look at this." She lifted a pink, fuzzy circle. "It's a scrunchie!"

He gave her a confused look.

"A ponytail holder! Like little girls wear. It's pink, to match the hat. It's been sitting here in the woods and it's not that dirty. Maybe it just recently fell here."

She stood up and the excitement in her voice and her face made his adrenaline pump. "Stella!" he called. And so did Emma, "Stella! Are you here? It's Uncle Jeremy! Stella!"

They bounded about the area with newfound enthusiasm, calling loudly. Then Emma did a "shhhh!" shushing sound and Jeremy shut up. "I think I hear something. Stella?"

Jeremy strained his ears. Then, he and Emma gasped and quieted, staring at each other as they dared to hope. Together, they heard it, a tiny voice saying, "Uncle Jeremy."

They searched frantically. The woods and undergrowth were heavy and unchecked in this area. If she were lying down on the ground, she'd be completely covered. She could be hunched behind a log, under a bush, up in a tree.

"Stella! Sweetie! Lift your hand! Can you do that, lift your hand and wave for me. I'll come get you."

Jeremy and Emma stood with their backs to each other, each scanning half the perimeter of a circle. Then Jeremy caught a motion. He pointed, "There!"

They dashed over just as Stella was trying to sit. He pulled her up and into his arms, and with Emma wrapping her arms around both of them, they all embraced. Stella was crying,

Emma was crying, and soon Jeremy let loose with tears of relief as well.

"Oh baby, what happened to you?" He held her so tight he had half a fear he was squeezing the breath out of her, but she needed to know she was safe, she was in his arms and he'd never let anything happen to her again.

"Grandpa Joe said he would take me for a ride. He said Mama was at the store and called and told him to bring me there. I couldn't open the door. It wouldn't open." Her story took too much of a toll on her self-control and she sobbed wildly. Both Jeremy and Emma did their best to comfort her, rubbing her head, her back, covering her cheeks with kisses and telling her how much they loved her.

"When he got out of the car, I kept trying to open the door, but it wouldn't open, so I climbed into the back seat and got it open. I was going to jump out, but Grandpa Joe started the car. So I had to roll out while the car was moving." She sobbed again. "I hurt myself." She lifted her ankle and pointed at it. Her left ankle was swollen and bruised.

He placed his lips against her forehead. "You are the bravest little girl I know. I'm so proud of you." They stood there, the three of them, all connected, praying silent prayers of thanks.

"Uncle Jeremy?" Stella's tiny voice whimpered.

"Yes?"

"I'm thirsty. And I want my mommy."

Jeremy and Emma smiled at each other. Jeremy pulled his cellphone out of his pocket and called his sister. She answered on the first ring. He didn't even say hello. "We've got her." His sister's shouts were so loud he pulled the phone away from his ear and held it out for Emma and Stella to hear. Bringing it close to his mouth again, he interrupted her, "Here she is," and handed the phone to Stella to chat with her mama as they started the long hike back.

Chapter Fifteen

Jeremy arrived at the furniture store at the crack of dawn, and still, it was obvious that Emma had beaten him to it. Or, maybe she'd stayed late last night when he'd wimped out and went home. Either way, the huge "GRAND OPENING" banner draped across the show window was a dead giveaway, as was the "SALE!! IN CELEBRATION OF HARRISON DESIGNS GRAND OPENING" posters she'd hung in the windows of every last business in the strip mall.

The girl was a marketing genius. It was her brainstorm to get all his new neighbors to offer special sales today to entice traffic, and also the 20% off coupons for his custom designs that she placed in stacks at each neighboring business's check out area. "Neighbors help each other," she said. And she was right about that.

However, he really wasn't up to a big hullaballoo. He just figured he'd quietly open his doors, advertise occasionally and see if he could make this work.

Huh uh.

He unlocked the front door and let himself in. He'd produced enough inventory over the last three months to cover every foot of floor space with custom-made, hand-crafted fine wood furniture. Emma was organizing displays of cut fruit, vegetables, cookies, little cakes and sandwiches on the linen tablecloths hanging over three of his dining room tables.

Yeah, he wouldn't have thought of that either.

"I figure if they shop till they drop, they'll be hungry," she said with a grin, met him halfway as he walked to her and pulled him into her arms. He breathed in her scent, wrapped his arms around her and squeezed tight. Their kiss was soft, warm and heart-stopping. It also threw his attention way off his store's grand opening, onto the enticement of another activity all together.

Over those same three months, much had changed in the Slotky family. Emma's father was arrested for multiple counts of vandalism, arson, kidnapping and driving under the influence. He was held at the county jail, eligible for release on bail, but Emma talked her mother out of bailing him out. He needed to cool his heels in there and learn a lesson. Besides, a jail sentence pretty much forced him to quit drinking for good. His trial was still three months away, so he'd have time to make some positive changes in his life if he chose to.

Jeremy pulled back from Emma to look around the showroom, attempting to regulate his heart rate as he did. "Looks pretty good around here."

Emma laughed. "King of the understatement. You've really kicked butt and made some gorgeous furniture. This grand opening is going to attract a lot of people. You'll sell a lot of floor models, but you'll also get tons of custom orders. I predict, you're going to have to hire support staff soon."

"One day at a time. Let's not get ahead of ourselves."

"Good thing I believe in you. Enough for the both of us." She went back to organizing sales tickets behind the counter. Next, she swept the floor before going out to the parking lot to make sure all looked welcoming from the outside. Jeremy watched her, and said his millionth prayer of thanks to God for putting her in his life.

She came back in and called to him, "Did I tell you I have the TV station coming with cameras at one o'clock? They agreed to do a feature for the 5:00 news."

He shook his head, speechless. He glanced at the clock on the wall and saw he had forty minutes till opening time. He'd better get busy, and right now. "Emma, could you come over here, please?"

She looked up from whatever it was she was looking at, and walked over. He stood facing her, took both her hands in his and drew a deep breath. She quieted and studied his face, curious.

"We've been through a lot together, especially in the last three, four months."

She chuckled and rolled her eyes comically at him. Another understatement.

He bolstered his courage and went on. "You are the finest woman to ever come into my life. I thank God every day for you. I want you to know…" he cleared his throat, which suddenly had cramped up, his voice giving out on him. "I love you very much, Emma."

He had planned to say more. In fact, he'd practiced it several times over the last week while the little velvet box occupied his pocket. But he didn't have a chance.

"I love you too! I've known it for a while, but I haven't said it."

Jeremy felt the stupidest, happiest grin cover his face. "You have? You do? You love me too?"

Emma's smile beamed. "I do, I do, I do."

Their lips met and his heart was beating so fast, he could barely breathe. He concentrated all his energy on where their lips connected, and how much love he felt for this woman. When they parted, he pulled the box out of his pocket, squeezing it in his hand. "Emma, I have a present for you. It's not *the* present. It's a preliminary present. Someday, it'll be bigger and better, but for now, I just wanted you to know how I feel about you. It's a symbol of my love ..."

She'd had enough of his explanation. She reached out and grabbed his hand, prying it open. When she saw the little black box, she squealed. "Remember, it's just ...," he stammered.

"Beautiful," she gasped. She was staring at the red ruby ring on the gold band as if it were the big solitaire diamond that he'd wanted to give her ... that he would give her eventually. But, first things first. He had to profess his love to her, and he had to hear if she felt the same way. He had to know if they had a future.

And it sure sounded like they did.

"It's just beautiful." She tugged it out of its slot and handed it to him, outstretching her left hand, palm down.

He took the ring, then with a grin, got down on one knee. She gulped but stayed quiet, wiping a tear from her eye. "Emma, I love you. Will you stay with me, help me and hold me and promise yourself to me forever?"

"I will."

He slid the ring on her finger, a perfect fit. She admired it, letting the showroom lights catch it and it sparkled. He started to stand up, but she put her hands on his shoulders and held him down. "Hold on a minute. Jeremy, I love you, too. Will you stay with me, work with me, build our lives together, so that when the time's right for both of us, we honor our union before God?"

He was so happy he thought he'd explode. "I will."

He came to his feet and lifted her off of hers, twirling her around in a circle as he kissed her. So much to celebrate, so much to be thankful for. God had blessed him with abundance beyond his imagination and he'd live the rest of his life trying to be worthy of it.

"Oh my gosh, look!" she said.

He turned to the door and at least a dozen people lined up, wanting to come in. He gave her a squeeze and said, "I guess we've got some furniture to sell."

THE END

About the Author

Laurie Larsen is a multi-published author of inspirational and contemporary romance. 2015 will mark her 15th anniversary as a published author. Her first book, *Whispers of the Heart* finaled in the 2001 Golden Quill Contest in the Best First Book category. Since then, she's written and published eleven books for women, ranging from women's fiction, contemporary romance, Young Adult romance, and now, she's focusing on inspirational romance — love stories with a Christian theme. As a special project for next year (2015), Laurie plans to pull out *Whispers* and see if she can whip it into shape to re-release to modern readers.

Laurie celebrated 25 years married to her husband Norm, and they have two adult sons together. They live near the cornfields of central Illinois and she spends her days working for a Fortune 50 financial services company. In her spare time, she writes wonderful stories that make you laugh, cry and savor the happy ending.

The picture was taken the night Laurie earned a career milestone, winning the prestigious EPIC Award for Best Spiritual Romance of 2010 for her book, *Preacher Man.*

For more information on her other books, as well as a blog, photo album and a chance to sign up for her newsletter, visit Laurie online at her website, www.authorlaurielarsen.com.

Excerpt: Book 3, Pawleys Island Paradise series

Chapter One

The cell phone went dead, crushing with it the fragile connection she had with her five-year-old daughter.

"Stella? Stella?" Marianne Mueller gasped, knowing the frantic tone in her voice would accomplish exactly nothing. She inspected the face of the phone and it verified that the line was, indeed, lost. Suppressing the urge to throw the silly thing, or stomp her foot on it into the grassy ground, she lifted her head and scanned the heavy foliage all around her.

It was a miracle they'd gotten Jeremy's call in the first place. Cell towers were sketchy in these parts, in the best of times.

Her husband Tom pulled her close and guided her head into his chest, his warmth and scent drawing her home. She gulped cleansing air, trying to hold off the tears threatening to make a fresh appearance. She'd cried all day. Well, of course she had. Her daughter was missing.

Kidnapped by a crazy man who was driving drunk in the car he hadn't even belted her into when he enticed her to take a ride with him.

The same crazy man who'd set their Seaside Inn on fire.

"It's over now," Tom said. "We'll see her soon." She concentrated on drawing in air, slowly. Yes. How would she have ever gotten through the last few months without his strength and level-headedness?

A smile emerged through her tears. "Yes. She'll be in my arms and I'll never let her out of my sight again."

Tom pressed his lips against her forehead and hugged her tighter. "She's safe now. How'd she sound?"

She glanced at the phone again, and thought of the short but life-changing phone conversation she'd shared with Stella. Somewhere on Pawleys Island, Marianne's brother Jeremy had found her baby. Safe and sound, just tired, hungry, dirty and scared, hiding in the woods, trying to stay safe and escape the crazy man.

She could only imagine the joyous celebration between Jeremy, his girlfriend Emma and Stella. Fortunately, Jeremy had called her and shared the jubilant news, "We've got her," and handed the phone right over. They'd talked just long enough for Marianne to agree that indeed, it was Stella. To ask her if she was okay, and to let her know that Daddy and Mommy loved her, oh so very much.

Stella had started a story about a little pink elastic scrunchy that had been in her hair, but had come loose when she'd pulled her pink Pawleys Island Pelicans baseball hat off and left it in the crazy man's car.

A sign? An assist to the dozens of volunteer searchers, friends and family members who were combing every inch of this island for some sign of precious little Stella? The story continued so Marianne didn't have time to ask.

The scrunchy held on through the adversity of hiking several miles alone through the woods, while Stella made sure she put distance between herself and the dangerous man. But it eventually fell loose and landed on the forest floor. And that — that one random hair accessory was what led Emma, then Jeremy to find her.

Thank the Lord. Thank God for small miracles like pink scrunchies.

"She sounded wonderful. I mean, she's exhausted, she's starving, she's scared. But she's so happy to be safe, her ordeal over. You know her Uncle Jeremy is her hero, now more than ever."

Tom didn't respond but he didn't let up his strong hold on her shoulders.

"Want to try calling her back?"

It was worth a try. She pulled back from him, tried a redial and waited with the phone on speaker. Silence, then one ring tone, then straight to some recorded message from the phone company. She sighed and disconnected.

"It's okay. I got to hear her. We'll just have to wait. Even if it kills us."

His lips gave a little grimace that she was sure was intended as a smile. "I assume he'll take her back to the Inn. He has no idea where our part of the search party is and we have no idea where to meet him."

She nodded. "True."

They turned to make the trek back to their car. They ran into one of the rescuers in charge. "My brother found her. She's safe. He's bringing her home. Thank you for everything."

A grin lit his face. She was sure he had some mountain of announcements, process and paperwork to follow now that the search was over. But she had a daughter to wait for.

* * *

At least forty minutes had passed from the time they got the call, till they now sat waiting at the Seaside Inn, their home and place of business. Sharing their home with up to a dozen vacationing families was both a blessing, and an inconvenience, depending on the situation. Tonight, word had evidently spread among the vacationers, mostly retired snowbirds. Six or eight of them waited anxiously in the great room. Stella was a favorite among all guests, with her easy socialness, her happy smiles and her expert sand castles out back on the beach.

"They found her," Tom announced immediately, and a rush of relief filled the room, murmurs of thanks to God for many answered prayers. "She's on her way now."

After hugs and pats on the back by loving well-wishers, the room cleared, leaving Tom and Marianne. She checked her watch. "Do I have time for a shower, you think?"

"Sure. Make it quick."

She nodded and headed to their family's wing of the inn, separate from the guest rooms. She dug in her purse for her key, then pushed through the door, pulling clothes off on the way to the bathroom. She couldn't bear it if Stella's arrival occurred while she wasn't there to greet her. Her baby — her only child. A shudder wracked her shoulders. She couldn't protect Stella from the evils of the world — *obviously* — but she sure could show her with her words and actions how much she loved her.

She stepped into the hot spray and lifted her face. Jets pinged off her forehead and eyelids as she started a silent prayer. *Thank You, God. Thank You for bringing Stella safely home. She's my life. My child that You have entrusted in me.*

She turned, her back now to the firm fingers of water. *I didn't do a good job of keeping her safe, did I? I failed her, and You.*

The evils of the world grabbed her from me. I was no match but I will be. I will be, God. Stella is my top priority, and I will keep her safe, no matter what. With Your help. I'm sorry. I'm sorry, God. Help me do better.

The tears hit with a vengeance then, and she couldn't even keep up with the silent prayer. Sobs wracked her middle and her legs gave out, no longer able to hold her. She bent her knees and slid down the wall of the shower till she hunched in the corner, weeping.

Other Books by Laurie Larsen

(Books available in all e-book formats and paperback. Click on link for excerpt and more details)

Roadtrip to Redemption, Book 1 of the Pawleys Island Paradise series (inspirational romance) It started as a trip to lose old memories. It became a journey to find her heart. Leslie's whole life is falling apart when she decides to ditch her routine and hit the road, following God's will. When she meets hard-working Hank, she realizes that the worst summer of her life could turn out to be the best.

Preacher Man (inspirational romance) *EPIC Award winner!* When Regan moves to Chicago, she's determined to raise her teenage son and adjust to the single life after an ugly divorce. Falling in love with a pastor? Not even on her radar. Yet, as she and Josh grow closer, she knows the secret she's hiding about her past could destroy him.

Hidden Agenda (contemporary romance): A millionaire businessman romances an ambitious advertising executive to get closer to the long-kept secret she holds in her care. When his desire for her trumps his original motives, can love survive her discovery of his hidden agenda?

Break a Leg *FREE!* Sequel to *Hidden Agenda.* (contemporary romance) The holidays can be stressful, especially for New York advertising exec Tony White, who just got dumped. Will his Christmas be as dismal as he expects, or will wannabe Rockette Joss McGee dance her way into his heart?

Keeper by Surprise: (contemporary romance/New Adult) College student Keith Hanson cares about grades and girls, not necessarily in that order. But when his parents are killed in a tragic accident, and he becomes guardian to his siblings, life changes drastically.

Inner Diva (contemporary romance) Monica is a modern-day Cinderella who longs to get out from under the expectations of her family and into the spotlight. Carlos is from the wrong side of the tracks with a violent past. Opposites attract, but these two are about as opposite as you can get. And yet, maybe they're just what the other needs to make their dreams come true.

Made in the USA
Columbia, SC
20 March 2018